"This novel sneaks up on you the way life does—full of chance and yearning. It's a precise, subtle, sad, and graceful story about how we care for each other, and how we try to, and how we fail."
—Jia Tolentino, author of *Trick Mirror*

"There's so much life in this novel! Alix Ohlin is such an effortless, absorbing stylist."—Owen King, author of *Double Feature*

"A spellbinding fever dream of a tale that will leave you forever changed, and will surely earn Ohlin a place among the greatest writers of our generation. I loved it."—Joanna Rakoff, author of *My Salinger Year*

"Ohlin is a thrilling and singular writer who intimately captures and celebrates a lifetime of desires, disappointments, and everyday triumphs in these two sisters' lives...*Dual Citizens* will take up residency in your mind and heart for quite some time."—Jennifer Gilmore, author of *The Mothers*

"Alix Ohlin's novel, true to its title, quietly refutes monolithic tenets that regard identity as something fixed and singular. Dividing its narrative between Canada and the U.S., the urban and the wild, solitude and solidarity, creativity and caregiving, *Dual Citizens* is a long-term sororal love story and affecting double portrait of female self-actualization untethered from established paradigms of ambition."
—Scotiabank Giller Prize Jury Citation

"With supreme confidence, Ohlin's quicksilver prose and brilliant characterization at once seize and pull the reader into the wide-ranging and complex world...*Dual Citizens* is a compulsively readable novel about family, sisterhood, and those uncontrollable forces that drive and haunt us."—Rogers Writers' Trust Fiction Prize Jury Citation

Also by Alix Ohlin

Dual Citizens

The Missing Person

Babylon and Other Stories

Inside

Signs and Wonders

We Want
What We Want

We Want
What We Want

STORIES

Alix Ohlin

Published in Canada in 2021 by House of Anansi Press Inc.
www.houseofanansi.com

House of Anansi Press is committed to protecting our natural environment. This book is made of material from well-managed FSC®-certified forests, recycled materials, and other controlled sources.

House of Anansi Press is a Global Certified Accessible™ (GCA by Benetech) publisher. The ebook version of this book meets stringent accessibility standards and is available to students and readers with print disabilities.

25 24 23 22 21   1 2 3 4 5

Library and Archives Canada Cataloguing in Publication

Title: We want what we want / Alix Ohlin.
Names: Ohlin, Alix, author.
Description: Short stories.
Identifiers: Canadiana (print) 20200393073 | Canadiana (ebook) 20200393081 | ISBN 9781487004897 (softcover) | ISBN 9781487004903 (EPUB)
Classification: LCC PS8629.H54 W4 2021 | DDC C813/.6—dc23

Cover design: Janet Hansen
Text design: Betty Lew
Typesetting: Scribe, Philadelphia, Pennsylvania

House of Anansi Press respectfully acknowledges that the land on which we operate is the Traditional Territory of many Nations, including the Anishinabeg, the Wendat, and the Haudenosaunee. It is also the Treaty Lands of the Mississaugas of the Credit.

 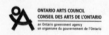

Canada Council   Conseil des Arts
for the Arts   du Canada

ONTARIO ARTS COUNCIL
CONSEIL DES ARTS DE L'ONTARIO
an Ontario government agency
un organisme du gouvernement de l'Ontario

With the participation of the Government of Canada
Avec la participation du gouvernement du Canada | Canadä

We acknowledge for their financial support of our publishing program the Canada Council for the Arts, the Ontario Arts Council, and the Government of Canada.

Printed and bound in Canada

MIX
Paper from
responsible sources
FSC   FSC® C103567
www.fsc.org

Child. We are done for
in the most remarkable ways.

—BRIGIT PEGEEN KELLY

Contents

We Want
What We Want

The Point of No Return

BRIDGET LIVED IN BARCELONA FOR A YEAR. FIRST SHE STAYED with her college friends Maya and Andrew, who were trying to be poets, and then she sublet from a man named Marco, whom she'd met at a grocery store. She had a fling with a woman named Bernadette, who was from New Zealand and shared a flat with a Scot named Laurie, whom Bridget also slept with, and that was the end of things with Bernadette. She smoked Fortuna cigarettes and wrote furiously in her journal about people she'd known and slept with, or wanted to sleep with, or slept with and then been rejected by. She was twenty-three years old.

One night at Marco's apartment, she was awakened by loud knocking. Still semi-drunk from an evening with Maya and Andrew, she stumbled to the door and opened it to find three junkies standing there, asking for Marco. She knew they were junkies because Marco was a junkie—he'd told her this—and all his friends were junkies, too. They needed Marco's furniture, for reasons that were unclear, and they shoved her aside and began moving the kitchen table, the futon. For junkies, they were robust and rosy cheeked, and she didn't put up much defense. Somehow this incident was all her fault. Marco kicked her out and she went to live in a cheap hotel, drinking anise in bed and staring at the peeling wallpaper. Later, Marco made her file a false police report saying that his laptop had been stolen. He said that it was the only way she could make up for her transgressions.

The person who rescued her from the cheap hotel was Angela, whom she'd met at the restaurant where they both waitressed. Angela was from Vancouver, and some dewy freshness that Bridget associated with the West Coast seemed to cling to her always, even when she was sleep deprived or drunk. Angela had a German boyfriend with a face so feminine that he looked exquisite, like a porcelain doll. His name was Hans, or maybe Anders. He was always nice to Bridget, and when Angela brought her home he made up a little bed for her in the corner of their tiny living room, a pile of blankets and pillows, as if she were a stray dog. Once, in the middle of the night, she woke up to see him crouching in front of her, staring.

"What are you doing?"

"I wanted to make sure you were comfortable."

"I'm comfortable," she said, and he went back to bed with Angela.

ANGELA AND HER GERMAN BOYFRIEND WERE LITTLE PARENTS. They liked to make a fuss over people and put on elaborate dinner parties, and then they'd get drunk and spend the night bickering. It was tedious, and yet you had to indulge them, because you could see how much they enjoyed it, this performance of adulthood. Bridget stayed with them for two months, and would have felt guilty about mooching, except that they so clearly wanted to gather around themselves a collection of misfits to take care of. In addition to Bridget, they often hosted an assortment of hard-drinking Germans from Hans/Anders's work, whatever it was, and Mei Ling, a Chinese Canadian woman who had a little cluster of grey whiskers on her otherwise smooth cheek, like a tuft of crabgrass thriving on a lawn. Mei Ling's reasons for being in Barcelona were unclear; whenever Bridget talked to her, she scowled and left the room. Angela said that she was very depressed.

Bridget would have stayed there indefinitely, but one morning Hans/Anders brought her coffee in her dog bed and said that they had to talk. "We're leaving," he said.

"For work?" As usual, she was hungover.

He shook his head and patted her shoulder. "Angela and I are getting married and moving to Canada. You can come visit us anytime."

"Does Angela know this?"

He laughed. "It was her idea," he said tenderly. "Everything is always her idea."

Bridget was stunned and a little irritated. She was used to a constant exchange of friends and lovers, and the idea that one of these relationships should be considered permanent struck her as inconsiderate. It went against the way they were all trying to live: stepping lightly on this earth, skirting the folly of human certainty. That night, she and Angela went out for drinks. They sat in an outdoor courtyard eating tiny meatballs and cockles in tomato sauce. Angela's blond braid nestled against her neck. She and Bridget had once showered together, had swum naked together at a beach in Sitges. Angela had the kind of flesh so pale that if you pressed a finger to her thigh the skin blushed dark pink, as if embarrassed by the touch. Now she was drinking cheap rioja, her teeth turning purple. "I'm going to enroll in an education program and get certified to teach kindergarten," she was saying. "Hans will work with my father once his paperwork is settled. The business is very secure. Like my father always says, empires may rise and fall but people still need lightbulbs."

In Bridget's stomach, the cockles swam restlessly in a river of wine. "You seem young to get married," she said.

Angela shook her head, and her braid flapped against her shoulder. "Oh, we won't get married for at least a year. We have to plan. Not to mention book the church. The flowers alone! You have no idea."

She was right about that. Bridget let her go—from the conversation, their passing friendship, the country of Spain. She found another place to stay and, when Angela hosted a last dinner party to say goodbye, Bridget said that she was sick and didn't go.

TO HER SURPRISE, SHE HERSELF WAS BACK IN CANADA WITHIN six months. Marco stopped by the restaurant one day to tell her that her mother had been calling, and, when she called back, her mother didn't even scold her for being hard to reach. "I have some news," she said tightly. "Your father isn't feeling well."

Bridget held the receiver in her hot palm. She was on break, a stained white apron around her hips, her armpits still dripping from the evening rush, and a table of three men eyed her with the impersonal but aggressive sexual hostility she'd grown used to. She burst into tears, and the men rolled their eyes and turned to a better target. As if in one movement, she hung up the phone, untied the apron, collected her passport from Maya and Andrew's apartment, and went home.

Her father lived for a year so dreary and relentlessly full of pain that she was forced to wish him dead. He had been a jokester, her father, spilling over with inappropriate remarks. Since she once wore a bikini at age ten, he had called her Bardot, after Brigitte, whom she did not resemble in the slightest. He gave whoopee cushions as gifts. He did impressions so terrible that no one ever guessed who he was supposed to be. In the hospital, tethered to a bouquet of chemotherapy drugs, he gritted his teeth and attempted to make light of the situation, but there was no light to be made. His body shrank; he was smaller every morning, as if repeatedly robbed in the night. Bridget wanted only for his suffering to end, and, when it finally did, she sobbed so hard she felt as if her lungs were liquefying. Her mother was a husk, dried out by grief. She didn't want to stay in the house alone, so she sold it, bought a condo downtown, and took up choral singing. One day, she pressed her cool palm to Bridget's forehead and said gently, "What will you do now, dear?"

Bridget hadn't thought that far; she had conceived of herself as a source of support and nothing else. Now she saw that her mother needed her to go, and she felt abandoned. In the year of tending to her father she hadn't worked and had lost touch with most of her friends. Sitting in a café downtown, she wrote a letter to Angela, the kind of letter you write only to someone you haven't seen in a long time and perhaps never knew well, the kind of letter you probably shouldn't send at all. Angela replied within a week. "My heart is with you," she wrote, and Bridget's eyes swelled with tears.

Angela and her German had not gotten married after all; he had met a girl named Mavis and moved to Edmonton and "You know what? Good riddance!" Angela no longer wanted to be a teacher; she was training to be a masseuse instead. She invited Bridget to visit anytime. "We'll cook and have long talks just like we used to," she wrote, a revision of their history that Bridget found sweet.

• • •

SHE DIDN'T VISIT. SHE WENT TO LAW SCHOOL AND MADE NEW friends and when she graduated she got a job in labor relations for a midsize corporation. She wore suits to work, with kitten heels, and saw her mother every other weekend, whether her mother wanted her to or not. In the evenings, she still sometimes wrote in her journal, but the entries tended to turn into grocery lists, so she stopped. She was not unhappy. She liked being an adult, being good at her job, owning a car, painting the walls of her apartment on a Saturday afternoon. She didn't know why she'd ever resisted it.

When the invitation to Angela's wedding came, Bridget stared at the envelope for a few minutes before she remembered who Angela was. She sent her regrets and forgot about it until the phone rang at eleven o'clock one night and on the other end was Angela, weeping.

"I *knew* I must have offended you," she said. "I have to explain. We both know you should have been a bridesmaid, but Charles's family is enormous—I swear he has ten thousand cousins—and, you see, in their culture things are quite different. I wish I could explain—"

This went on for some time. Finally, Bridget said, "Angela, it's fine. I wasn't offended."

A pause, a sniffle. "So you'll come, then?" Angela said. Her voice was tinny, a child's, with a child's manipulation edging around the distress.

Bridget felt trapped. "Of course," she said.

She and Sam, her fiancé—he was also a lawyer—decided to treat it as a vacation. They hiked and swam and went zip-lining at Whistler before ending their trip in Vancouver. "How do you know her again?" Sam asked in the hotel, where she was steaming her dress, feeling nervous for reasons she couldn't define.

Bridget smoothed the dress with her palm, as if stroking her own lap. "I barely do," she said. "It'll probably be dull. Forgive me for what we're about to experience."

"Oh, I'll make you pay," Sam said, smiling, and kissed her.

The wedding, though, was not dull. Angela's husband turned out to be a Nigerian cardiac surgeon and his large family was raucous and witty. Everybody had to meet everybody. Nobody was allowed to skip the dancing. At one point Bridget found herself sitting with an elderly uncle, telling him a long story about her father, as he nodded and listened gravely, his wife meanwhile instructing Sam in a dance. Angela came up behind Bridget and put her hands on her shoulders, her cheek against Bridget's cheek. She was still blond and fresh faced but skinnier now, her dress a severe column of white, no frills or lace. Her hair was pulled back in a chignon. Grown up, she was all geometry.

"Thanks for being here, Bardot," she whispered in Bridget's ear. "It wouldn't have been the same without you." Bridget squeezed her hand, touched that she'd remembered this old nickname. And then Angela was swept away by a crowd that lifted her to the dance floor and demanded she perform. She danced gamely, but her hair was coming loose; she kept lifting a hand to poke at the strands, and her smile tightened each time she felt the disarray.

BRIDGET AND SAM MOVED TO OTTAWA AND HAD TWO CHILdren, Robert and Melinda—Bobby and Mellie. Their kids were joiners; they hated to be alone, and every weekend they wanted to see their friends at soccer, birthday parties, figure skating, hockey, dance recitals, sleepovers. This took up much of life. Bridget began to dream of travel: spas in Costa Rica, yoga retreats in Scandinavia.

"I think I'm burning out," she said to Sam, and he thought she meant on work, but she meant on everything. Sam was stable and good for her, absorbing whatever she threw at him, the tofu of husbands, but it didn't help. She considered an affair, but it seemed like too much work. Anyway, her days were full of meetings and carpools; there was no time for malfeasance. Instead, she spent more hours than she should have online, seeing whose life had turned out to be more dramatic than her own. That was how she found Angela, who maintained active accounts on Facebook, Pinterest, and Instagram. Angela was still in Vancouver and, judging by her pictures, she had one child, an astonishingly beautiful boy who was a perfect combination of her and Charles—her eyes, his nose—as if they'd divided up the genes by legal agreement. Angela photographed him playing soccer and baking muffins; she pinned recipes for organic pancakes with hidden spinach and discussed the importance of fish-oil supplements. She redid her living room and posted the swatches; everything was off-white. She said that her favorite color was bone. Bridget clicked "Like." Within a day, a message from Angela popped up in her in-box, frothing with six years' worth of news. Much of it was already known to Bridget, from the internet, but she pretended it wasn't. As it happened, Angela was coming to Ottawa for a conference, and they made plans to get together. Bridget asked what kind of conference it was. "Medical," Angela wrote.

On the day they were to meet, Bridget went straight from the office, in her pencil skirt and heels, to the bar at Angela's hotel downtown. It was a modest hotel that catered to visiting bureaucrats. Angela was sitting in a booth, wearing jeans and a light cardigan. A bone-colored cardigan. Her hair was cut in a pleasant bob, and she was still blond. When she saw Bridget, she stood up and flung her arms around her, pressing herself against Bridget's chest. It was the way Bridget's children had hugged her when they were little, holding nothing back, and Angela's body felt like a child's, thin and pliant and eager.

Bridget asked what kind of work she was doing at the conference, and Angela waved her hand shyly. "I'm not working these days," she said. "The conference is for people who have my illness." The illness was one that Bridget had never heard of. Angela described a set of diffuse symptoms—fatigue, muscle aches, cognitive impairment—that defied diagnosis. Doctors were perplexed. Much research still had to be done.

"What kind of cognitive impairment?" Bridget said.

"Oh," Angela said, smiling. "I'm in a fog most of the time."

She didn't seem in a fog to Bridget. They sat drinking wine and discussing the annoying habits of their husbands and children, the dirty socks left on couches, dishes unscraped in the sink. Angela's son had bought a frog at a pet store and tried to sleep with it in his bed. Her husband was always at the hospital. He'd suggested that her symptoms were psychosomatic.

"Men always say that women are crazy," Angela said vehemently, "but men have been in charge for most of history and look how that's turned out!"

Bridget laughed.

"Bitches be crazy," Angela went on, shaking her head and making air quotes with her fingers. Bridget didn't know what, or whom, she was quoting.

Angela sighed. "I shouldn't complain, though," she said. "He keeps us in frogs and fresh sheets."

Bridget laughed again. She was enjoying herself more than she'd expected to. They ordered another bottle of wine, which Angela chose because it was organic and sulfate-free. "I can't taste the difference," Bridget said.

"You'll thank me tomorrow," Angela said.

Around them, the hotel swelled with people sitting alone, stroking their phones with one hand while eating or drinking with the other. Even when it was full, the place was quiet. By ten o'clock, the bar was empty again and the street outside was dark. It was a government city, sedate in its schedules.

"I'm not sure I can drive," Bridget said to Angela.

"Why don't you come upstairs for a while first?"

She nodded. The room was decorated in surprisingly offensive shades of mauve and green. Angela's things were flung everywhere, her suitcase open on the closet floor, handouts from the day's seminars scattered on the desk, wet towels dampening the carpet. Bridget lay down on the bed, and Angela sat next to her. It seemed lovely to be there, with her head on Angela's lap.

"I'm sorry you're sick," she said, and Angela nodded, stroking her hair. Bridget turned then, and wrapped her arms around Angela's waist. The two of them fell asleep that way, body to body, flushed cheek against warm leg, an embrace that was not about sex but not not about it either, a hunger for touch somehow satisfied by this middle distance, this mutual understanding. Later, when Bridget thought about the night in the hotel, she would remember how Angela, down at the bar, had said with sudden sobriety, "Nobody takes care of me," and then laughed, dismissing her self-pity with a toss of her pale hair.

THEY SWORE TO KEEP IN BETTER TOUCH, BUT DIDN'T. ONCE Angela was back in Vancouver, her social media accounts took a turn from organic cooking and home decorating to alternative health and New Age spirituality. She was doing chelation and oxygen therapy. She smudged her home with sage. Her thinking seemed dire. She was preoccupied with the tensions in the Middle East and believed that global conflict was imminent. She adopted two cats because she wanted her son to experience as much joy as possible before the world came to an end. But she and her son both turned out to be allergic, and #catproblems accompanied most of her posts.

Then came a year when Sam—always the steady one, the implacable base—almost died of heart trouble. For months, Bridget took care of him and their family, and, when he was better, their marriage was better, too; it had solidified under the stress, like a building settling on its foundation. During this time Bridget rarely went online. She found it hurtful to see other people's smiling, healthy families or, even worse, to hear about lives that seemed as fragile as her own; she didn't need to be reminded that everyone's happiness was in jeopardy.

When she checked back in, Angela was gone. All her accounts had disappeared. An email sent to her in-box went unanswered. Bridget didn't have her phone number and couldn't find one listed. One evening, while the kids were in the basement watching a movie with their friends, she sat down and wrote a letter by hand, mailing it to the last address she could find for Angela. "We're all fine now. Just wondering what's new. How are those pesky cats?"

As she had so many years earlier, Angela wrote back quickly. She no longer had the cats, she wrote, with a lack of explanation that was slightly ominous. She and Charles had gotten divorced, "on good terms more or less," and she now lived in a little cottage outside the city. "A little cottage" sounded to Bridget like a euphemism for something, though she wasn't sure what. Angela had decided that her symptoms were caused by an allergy to electricity, so she lived without it. She had a woodstove and candles. She didn't use computers and was reading a lot. "I feel a bit better every day," she wrote, a statement that seemed to herald its own contradiction. Of her son she said little.

Bridget wrote back, wishing her well, and the correspondence seemed to die a natural death; there was no habitual rhythm in Bridget's life for such letters. When, a year later, her cell phone lit up with a Vancouver area code, she assumed that it was Angela, but the voice that greeted her was low and commanding and male.

"This is Dr. Charles Adebayo. We met at my wedding," he said.

"Yes, I remember," Bridget said, confused. She was sitting in her car, listening to music, while Mellie fought her way through a soccer game in terrible blustery weather.

"My former wife is ill," Charles said. There was a solemnity to his voice that was hard to reconcile with the laughing man of years ago. It was the voice of a man who'd had practice speaking about difficult topics and knew to provide them careful containment. "She would like for you to visit, and I would like so as well."

"Is this the electricity thing?" Bridget asked. She looked out over the dismal soccer field, more mud than grass, where teenage girls were flinging themselves around with abandon. Mellie was her aggressive child, a lover of tackles and hits; Bobby always played defense. They were both more wholesome, her children, than she'd had any right to expect.

On the phone, Charles sighed, a long, soft note. "We are not sure," he said. "Angela continues to believe that she suffers from electromagnetic hypersensitivity. I believe she may have other significant health problems, but she refuses to see a doctor or be tested. We hope that you can persuade her to do so."

"Me? Why?" Bridget said. She felt capable only of single syllables, beyond which tens, hundreds of lengthier questions loomed.

"Because you are her best friend."

On the field, Mellie went down hard, and Bridget involuntarily straightened in her seat, but a few seconds later her daughter bounced up again, laughing. She shook her ankle and high-stepped in a circle, as if she were doing the hokeypokey. And then everyone was running again. Bridget caught her breath, sometimes, when she saw how athletic her daughter was, how reckless her grace, how fully she possessed her youth.

The other thing happening in the car—the phone call, the man's voice, his bewildering request—did not seem real compared to Mellie's loping stride as she deftly stole the ball and toyed with it, her skittering feet driving it toward the net and then past the goalie. Mellie clasped her hands over her head and glanced over at the car. Bridget honked the horn. *I saw*.

"Are you there?" Charles said. "The situation may be critical. We request that you come as soon as you are able."

Bridget didn't say, "I haven't talked to Angela in years." She didn't say, "I would have thought she had closer friends." She simply agreed to answer the summons.

SHE LANDED IN A DRIZZLE OF RAIN THAT CONTINUED ALL THE way from the airport to the hospital where Charles worked, obscuring the city behind a swish of windshield wipers. Traffic moved slowly and she saw nothing but other cars and a horizonless sky.

Angela's son was waiting at the hospital, too. He was all gangly legs in skinny jeans, his eyes half-hidden beneath his hair. Charles wore a purple shirt and yellow tie, strangely buoyant colors that contrasted sharply with the gravity of his expression. Over the shirt he wore a white coat. He gripped his son's thin shoulder with a strength that was clearly both dominant and reassuring.

They drank coffee and talked about Angela. Charles mentioned Angela's weight loss and her "ideation." The son's eyes were partly closed, as if he were trying to fall asleep. At last Charles wrote down directions to the cottage—"you won't find it with a GPS"—and suggested that she arrive in the early morning, when Angela was most hospitable. He didn't explain what he meant by "hospitable." Then he asked his son whether he had any messages for his mother. The boy shook his head.

THE DRIVE TO ANGELA'S COTTAGE TOOK HER THROUGH EMERald hills made brilliant by the previous day's rain. The city fell away, then the suburbs, and then she passed through small towns with no posted names. The road Charles had instructed her to take dwindled from asphalt to gravel to mud, and Bridget began to worry that her economy rental car wasn't up to the task. Her phone reception shrank to a single bar. Then the road ended. Charles had said, "You will have to park and walk." She stepped out into woods that smelled like fir and mushrooms, earthy and chilled, and hoped that the tiny clearing between two trees was the start of a trail. She crashed through it, the loudest thing around. Everything else was still, as if some kind of bad magic had blanketed the place. But, before she could get too worried, she saw Angela's cottage, a normal and well-maintained post-and-beam with geraniums in planters out front.

"It is best if you approach her gently," Charles had said.

Bridget didn't knock on the door. She stood in front of the house, allowing herself to be seen. How she knew to do this she couldn't have said. It was a calculation made on instinct. There was a flicker of movement at a window, and Bridget turned in a full circle, taking in the dense and quiet woods, the pine branches dripping, the surprisingly rapidly drifting clouds. Sam and the kids were visiting his parents this weekend; they had planned a cookout and a horror-movie marathon with the cousins. They would hardly think of her.

Behind her, the reluctant opening of a wooden door.

Angela stood silhouetted like a girl in a fairy tale. She was wearing jeans and a T-shirt and her blond hair was in a long braid, the way she used to wear it. She was very thin. One hand rested on some kind of machine from which tubing ran up her arms, under her nose, and around the top of her head. Her whole face twitched, either with tremors or an attempt to smile; Bridget wasn't sure. "Do you know me?" she said.

Angela nodded. Her eyes were cloudy, marbled. "I shouldn't let you in," she said. "For your own good."

"What do you mean?"

"I'm in self-isolation. What I have may be contagious."

Bridget didn't ask what she had. "I don't care," she said. "I want to see you."

Angela turned and disappeared into the house. The open door was not an invitation. Bridget spent some moments staring at the darkness where her friend had been. After a while, a window above her opened and a sealed plastic package was thrown down to the ground. It was a medical kit, which, when she tore it open, turned out to contain a surgical mask, plastic gloves, and shoe covers. She put it all on obediently and waited until Angela came back to the door and nodded, satisfied.

Bridget followed Angela through a foyer and into a dim room; the far wall held large windows but they were crowded with greenery that let in almost no light. As her eyes adjusted, she saw that the room was comfortable, with couches and armchairs and a woodstove in the corner. Angela settled into one of the chairs with the machine at her feet like a pet.

"Charles must have called you," she said. Her voice was raspy, asthmatic, and it made her tone hard to interpret.

"He did," Bridget said. She didn't want to talk about Charles, didn't want the freight of marital disagreement in the room. She leaned forward, putting her hands on her knees, and saw her friend recoil. "Tell me how you are," she said.

Angela stared past her. "There's a light," she said. "When I close my eyes at night, I see it and think it's waiting for me. Sometimes I think it's my father. You know he died."

"I didn't know that."

"I remember when your father died," Angela said. Her eyes grew sharper. "You changed so much. I didn't understand at the time, but I do now."

Even years later, the mention of her father shifted a weight in Bridget's stomach, tilted her center of gravity. The sadness of his death was still a sinkhole that she could fall into and be swallowed by.

"My mother got married again," she told Angela. "To a dentist named Dennis. Dennis the dentist. She has these beautiful movie-star teeth now. Veneers, I guess they are? She seems happy. They have a time-share in Florida. So."

Angela bared her own teeth, which were not beautiful, small

and brown, little emblems of decay. "Would you like some tea?" she said.

"Yes," Bridget said. "Let's have tea. You rest. I'll make it."

She had anticipated putting together a tray of biscuits or bread and jam, brewing a pot, and serving it with sugar and milk. But there was no food in Angela's cottage. The cupboards held only bottles: capsules of bee pollen, vitamins, apple-cider vinegar. Next to a teapot on the counter was a bowl holding what looked like loose tea leaves; they smelled like mushrooms, like the forest outside. She boiled water on the woodstove, brought a tray into the living room with two cups. Angela's legs were now tucked beneath her. Her head lolled to the side at a violent angle, as if her neck could no longer support its weight. She was asleep.

Bridget left the tea. She took off the surgical mask, hiked to the car, and drove to the nearest store, where she bought some root vegetables and rice and fruit. Back at the cottage, Angela was still asleep in the chair, and Bridget arranged a blanket over her lap, tucking it in at the sides. Then she cooked the vegetables and strained them into a broth. She cooked the rice to a bland pudding. She mashed sweet potatoes into a puree. When Angela woke up, Bridget spooned the broth into her mouth, wiping away dribbles with a tea towel. Angela did not object; she parted her lips like a baby. Later, Bridget moved her to the couch. Bridget herself slept in Angela's bed upstairs, which was narrow and hard. The next day, more broth, a little rice. She read aloud to Angela from the only material on hand, old copies of *Chatelaine* and *Reader's Digest* that must have been left behind by some previous occupant; she couldn't imagine Angela buying them. She read recipes, "Laughter, the Best Medicine" columns, stories about brave pets and remarkable women. It was hard to tell whether Angela was listening; she mostly lay back with her eyes closed, her fingers playing idly with the tubing of her machine.

Once evening fell, Bridget lit a fire in the stove and fed Angela again. When she was about to go upstairs, Angela grabbed her hand and said, "Please, no." So she took some pillows and cushions from the armchairs and made a bed for herself on the floor.

In the morning, Angela's eyes looked brighter. She disconnected herself from the machine long enough to take a short walk around the house. Afterward, they sat outside and drank Angela's terrible tea, which tasted like moss and feet. Angela had allowed Bridget to dispense with the mask, saying only, "I suppose you've been exposed. I just hope your immune system is stronger than mine."

"Does your son come here to visit you?" Bridget asked her. She didn't mention that she had seen him in the city. Angela's eyes brimmed with tears, and she shook her head.

"I lost him," she said.

"But why?" Bridget said. After two nights at the cottage, her eyes and skin ached. She couldn't stop thinking about hamburgers and red wine. She wondered what Sam and the kids were eating, watching, what jokes they'd be making later that she wouldn't understand.

"Bridge," Angela said. It was a sunny, windy day and her fine hair was lifted in the breeze, floating up and away as if it wanted to escape her. "You must understand," she said. Her voice was patronizing, kind, and sad, as if she were a parent explaining death to a child. "With what I have," she said, "I'm past the point of no return."

"Come home with me," Bridget said impulsively. "Stay at my house. We'll watch movies on the couch and eat junk food." She could feel Angela recoil but kept going, unable to stop. "We'll drink wine and stay up too late. You can meet my kids. You'll like them, Angela. They'll make you laugh."

They were holding hands now. Some geese flew overhead in a V formation, and the trees swayed back and forth, as if they, too, were seeking touch. In one of Angela's magazines, Bridget had read an article about a scientist who had proven that trees could form a kind of friendship, twining their roots together. Sometimes one tree would curve its branches away from the other's, so that its friend got enough sun to survive. Angela said nothing, and the trees fell silent, too, as if to make sure that Bridget heard her refusal.

SHE DIDN'T SEE ANGELA AGAIN. SHE FLEW HOME TO HER FAM-ily, leaving the cottage stocked with soups and stews, and fell gladly back into the mad routine of extracurricular activities and conference calls and neighborhood dinner parties. For a while she tried to stay in touch with Charles, but he never sounded pleased to hear from her; she understood that she had failed him. He finally removed Angela from the cottage by force, and she spent time in and out of hospitals. She didn't respond to Bridget's letters, and Charles said she refused to use a phone.

"How long do you think she can go on like this?" Bridget asked him the last time they spoke.

"I cannot hazard a guess," he said, and hung up.

Bridget stood in her kitchen, watching the wind twist maple leaves off a tree in the yard. The kids were upstairs in their rooms. Bobby was going away to college next year; Mellie the year after that. Sam was traveling more for work these days. Bridget would soon be stripped back to herself. Sometimes she thought of this aloneness as a luxury. Sometimes she was afraid of it. Sometimes she saw her life as a tender thing that was separate from herself, a tiny animal she had happened upon by chance one day and decided to raise. It was terrifying to think how small it was, how wild, how easily she could fit it in the palm of her hand.

Casino

WHEN TRISHA COMES TO TOWN WE HAVE TO GO OUT. SHE'S the bitterest soccer mom of all time and as part of her escape from home she wants to get drunk and complain about her workaholic husband and overscheduled, ungrateful children. No one appreciates how much she does for them. All she does is give, give, give, without getting anything back, et cetera. I don't really mind—I enjoy a good martini, and while Trisha rants I don't have to worry about getting sloppy, given that she's always sloppier—except that even her complaints are part boast. She has to mention her busy husband and the two hundred thousand he rakes in a year. Her children's after-school activities *for the gifted* are just so freaking expensive and time-consuming. There's a needle in every one of these remarks, pricking at my skin, saying, *See, Sherri? See?*

I do see. I see it perfectly clearly.

This year she shows up with new hair. Her old hair was nicer—she inherited our mother's dark, shiny waves instead of the thin, blond frizz I got from our dad's side—but now she's highlighted it two or maybe three different shades, I can't really tell. There are some blond stripes in there, some red, something she calls "caramel." Her head looks like candy corn. "You like?"

she asks as soon as she gets inside my house, setting her luggage down. It's a rhetorical question, so I don't answer. She's wearing pink Juicy Couture sweatpants and a French manicure and looks like she could be on one of those reality shows, a housewife from somewhere, mascara'd and miserable. I give her a hug and tell her I'm glad she came, which is mostly true. She is my competition, my Irish twin, the thorn in my side. Also: she is my best and oldest friend.

She takes a deep breath and looks around my house, stretching out her hands like she's feeling the air inside it. "I'm so glad to be home," she says, by which she means Easton. Because she lives off in Silver Spring, Maryland, she can afford—in addition to a five-bedroom McMansion and a Lincoln Navigator—to be sentimental about the Lehigh Valley. She's always inviting me to visit her place but I don't feel comfortable. It's not her husband's fault. He's actually nice, Mike, but I sit around the table with him quizzing the kids on homework and current events and I keep a vacant smile going while I think, *I'm not smart enough for this.*

One time he asked me a question about rhesus monkeys. Now, I have thoughts on many aspects of the world, but on the subject of rhesus monkeys, I will leave opinions to the experts. I just looked at him, desperately I guess, and he dropped the subject, the kids smirking down at their plates of seared tuna and organic salad. Ever since then, I can't sit in their house without a rising panic in my mouth that I might be asked to weigh in on rhesus monkeys. So now Trisha comes to me, usually in January after she's suffered through another Christmas that failed to live up to her Martha Stewart–generated expectations and needs to blow off some steam.

I fix her a drink.

We sit in my kitchen, sipping screwdrivers for the vitamin C. It's snowing outside, light and dry, the kind of flakes that don't so much fall as hang in the air like dust. She asks me if I've heard from Rose.

"No," I say.

She puts her hand on mine. Her nails are so pretty. "Just had to ask," she says, and we move on.

The first night we stay up too late watching movies and drinking vodka. I wake with a headache, which I seek to repair with eggs and bacon. The house seems smaller with Trisha in it, in a good way. When Rose was little I used to make Sunday breakfasts like this, and Sid would come downstairs with his hair all mussed, what was left of it anyway, and he'd go straight from sleeping to eating. He was a man who liked his food. I'd make a face for Rose out of a pancake and two strips of bacon. Even when she was a teenager, even during that gruesome year before she left, she'd still come out of her room for Sunday breakfast.

Trisha comes in and tells me I'm cooking the eggs too long. "You're drying them out."

"I don't like them gushy."

"Not gushy. Soft. It keeps them flavorful."

"*Flavorful?*" I ask. I don't know where she gets these words, probably the Food Network. "Full of salmonella is more like it."

She sighs and waves her hand dismissively. Trisha has this gourmet side. I blame it on Silver Spring. When I serve the eggs she pokes at them, frowning sadly, like they're some poor animal that died without dignity. She also remakes the coffee, saying mine's not strong enough. I tell her she's being obnoxious and she says I'm oversensitive; by the time the meal is over we're barely speaking. To make peace, I let her dictate the plans for the day: tonight she wants to go to the casino. And before we can do that she wants to get dolled up—a massage, a pedicure.

When she sees the look on my face, she adds, "I'll pay for it."

I both hate and am grateful to her for this. So I say, "You mean Mike will pay for it."

Instead of getting mad she raises an eyebrow and says, "Honey, I pay for it *all the time,* " and we both laugh.

So we doll. We sit side by side in lounge chairs at the mall while Vietnamese girls pumice our feet. It makes me feel funny, the way they're down there working on us, but Trisha kicks back, closes her eyes, and moans with enjoyment. She likes to be treated like a queen. In between the pumicing and the polish she keeps up a stream of commentary about her life. She wants to redo the kitchen but Mike says the current kitchen works just fine. "The current kitchen is crap," she says. "The fridge leaks and there's mold behind it that five different cleaning ladies haven't been able to get out. Meanwhile the countertop, which was supposed to be scratchproof, is totally scratched. That granite cost a fortune and it looks like a bathroom stall in a bus station. I'm telling you, my life is a *nightmare.*"

I glance at the Vietnamese girl below me, but she's half watching music videos on a karaoke TV on the wall and doesn't seem to be paying attention.

"And then there's Kyle," my sister says. Kyle's her youngest. "Sherri, he picks his nose and wipes it on the walls of my house. He can't use a tissue why? Every time I round the corner there's another booger on the freaking wall."

I'm on her side with this one. "That's disgusting."

"Obviously," she says. "Every time I talk to him about it he just denies it. Like there are any other possible suspects. Like maybe there's some stranger that breaks into our house at night and doesn't steal anything, just leaves his boogers."

"What does Mike say?"

"What he always says. That he'll grow out of it. That I'm too negative."

We exchange a meaningful glance. Mike's always saying that Trisha's too negative. Our parents raised us to say the truth about the world, same as they did. I remember the day Trisha brought home her first boyfriend, Nick Perreira. He was no prize; he just had a car and a fake ID. "You're an idiot," our mother said. "He'll treat you like shit and you'll wind up crying on the phone to your friends on a Friday night." Six months later Trisha flung herself onto my bed sobbing because he'd gotten her pregnant and wouldn't have anything to do with her. We grew to appreciate our mother's blunt honesty. Our children don't seem to feel the same way about us. But maybe we just have to give it time.

Trisha and I agree on this much: people who look on the bright side all the time are hypocrites at least some of the time. To say that shitty things are shitty is to speak honest truth about the world.

We tip the girls and leave the salon with painted toes.

THE CASINO OPENED SINCE THE LAST TIME TRISHA WAS HOME and to hear her talk about it, the Lehigh Valley was a desert that just got its first oasis. Which is kind of a joke I'm making because the casino is called Sands. We go to dinner first, wearing dresses and heels, and I look okay but Trisha looks better. The older you get, the more money helps you out. When we were younger, we were both pretty, but now people's eyes skate over me and settle on her. Although this could also be because she talks real loud and keeps telling our waiter, "You're a cutie, James!" She's already a bit drunk. She gets out of James that he goes to Penn State Berks and majors in biology.

"I bet you're really smart," she says to him.

"Ask him what he thinks about rhesus monkeys," I say.

"What?"

"Never mind." It's always around this point in her visits that I get weary of my sister. I start to crave my quiet house, the way I can talk to myself or to Sid out loud—yes, I still talk to him, even though he's been gone for three years—or shuffle around in my sweatpants eating peanut butter straight out of the jar. And that's how I feel after two days of Trisha. I can't imagine what it's like to live with her all the time.

It's still nice that she visits, though.

James brings us steak and martinis and we agree it is delicious. The casino is packed, hectic with lights and noise. It's the nicest place I've ever been around here, and as we start to gamble I'm feeling loose and happy. We play some slots, drink some cocktails, and then head over to the table games. I lose twenty bucks to an old dealer who calls me "ma'am."

We exchange a meaningful glance.

"Screw this," I say, and we hit another table where the dealer is cuter and younger. I don't mind losing money but I'd like to have a good time doing it. We order drinks and Trisha plays first. She wins fifty bucks! Like she even needs it. When she sees me glowering, she laughs and says, "The drinks are on me." Just our luck, the young dealer immediately goes on break, but the next one coming is young, too. He keeps his head down as he readies the setup, muttering his dealer patter, and at first I don't recognize him. Cyril.

Trisha doesn't notice that I've stopped talking. Listening's never been her strong suit. Of course he knows it's me and he won't make eye contact. He looks better than the last time I saw him—he's put on some weight and the acne's cleared up. His hair is short now, no more braids, and in his white collared shirt he actually looks semi-respectable.

"Place your bets, place your bets," he mutters. There's one other person at the table, a middle-aged guy wearing an Eagles shirt, and he stacks his chips, then looks at us expectantly.

I try to exchange a meaningful glance with Trisha, but she's not paying attention. She sips on her drink by lowering her head, without holding it in her hands. It would be cuter if she were thirty years younger.

"Hey," I say to Cyril. "I didn't know you were in town."

He mumbles unintelligibly and Trisha finally figures out something's up.

"How long have you been back?" I say.

"A while."

"Are you living at home?"

He shrugs like it's none of my business. My hands are trembling so bad that some martini sloshes on the table, and Trisha blots it with a napkin. "Sher," she says. "What's up?"

"This is Cyril," I tell her.

"Rose's Cyril?"

"The one and only."

Cyril must have pressed some button somewhere because a lady materializes beside the table, blond, name-tagged, a supervisor. "Everything okay here?" she asks brightly.

"Fine," Trisha says, also brightly. The lady looks confused—clearly she was expecting a couple of rowdy drunks. "We're just waiting for our dealer to, you know, deal."

The lady supervisor pats Cyril on the shoulder, and he lifts his head, shooting her a plaintive, panicked look. If I didn't hate his fucking guts I'd maybe feel sorry for him.

"Go ahead and deal, Cyril," I say. "We're here to play. We're here all night."

Trisha laughs her mean laugh, the one I'm sure drives her husband and kids crazy, and I laugh, too.

WE PLAY AND LOSE, PLAY AND LOSE. I'M IN THE HOLE A HUN-dred bucks, which is my budget for the night—Sid taught me that, that it's okay to lose as long as you prepare for it. He was a budget supervisor, so profit-and-loss sheets were his thing. But sometimes you have to throw the budget out the window. I'm playing until Cyril gets off his shift, that's my plan, then I'm going to follow him to the break room or the parking lot and beat the shit out of him until he tells me what I want to know. That's as far as I've gotten in my thinking when Trisha starts needling him. Are you working here full-time, Cyril, shouldn't you be in school, Cyril, do you make good money, Cyril, what do young people around here do for fun, Cyril? The way she says his name is like a swear. In answer to every question he mumbles until she asks him to repeat himself. It's fun watching her torment him, like swatting mosquitoes is fun. It's satisfying to see the blood squirt out of them, even if you know it's your own. Whether because of Trisha's questions or Cyril's weird mumblings, other people are avoiding the table and for ages it's just the three of us, losing, dealing, needling, rinse, and repeat.

I'm on my fourth martini and the air in the room feels hot and thick around me, propping me up. I used to drink a lot of martinis when Sid and I first met, before Rose was born. Then I gave them up for a long while. To be a mother you have to have your wits about you. Sitting here now with Cyril across the table from me, close enough to touch his arm, the wiry black hairs above his wrist, I start thinking back to that time, and even earlier, back to when I was his age. In college I used to have these dreams—I guess they were sex-guilt dreams, me being Catholic—that I'd gotten pregnant by accident and had to cover it up. In the dreams I always kept the baby but tried to hide it. I had this one recurring dream that I hid the baby by keeping it in an aquarium in my dorm room. I'd come home from class and sprinkle fish flakes over the water, my little fish baby rising to the surface to gobble them down. It looked just like a regular baby, fat cheeked and dimpled, but it happened to live in a tank of water.

Remembering this, I get a little weepy, thinking about all the years between then and now, about the dream of a baby that you could keep in your room, suspended in a tank, safe from the world. *What happened?* I think to myself. *Where did my fish baby go?*

It's possible I say this out loud.

Cyril looks at me and says, not at all mumbling, "Oh, shit."

"Where is she?" I ask him. I mean it to sound aggressive but it comes out drunkenly morose instead. "Where's Rose?"

He shrugs. "I don't know."

"When was the last time you saw her?"

"I don't know."

"Do you know how to get in touch with her?"

He shakes his head.

The whole time we're interrogating him, he never makes eye contact. This is different from before: he used to stare at me, defiant, or maybe numb, I could never tell which. His eyes were dark and featureless. He's not a particularly good-looking kid. I never heard him crack a joke or say an interesting thing.

I couldn't figure out what drew Rose to him, and I used to complain about this to Trisha, on the phone, until the day she snapped at me, "She doesn't have to think he's a genius, Sherri. He's her drug dealer, for God's sake."

See what I mean? The truth.

If you could have seen her as a little girl, my Rosie, then you would know what happiness looks like. She laughed all the time. Her bed was piled so high with stuffed animals you couldn't even see the blankets, but Rose insisted on taking each of the animals into bed with her, so none of them would be lonely. I still don't know how she went from that little girl to the teenager who skipped school and spiked her hair and pierced her tongue and lower lip and who just laughed at me when I told her the truth—"You're going nowhere, Rose"—and who grabbed my wrist and twisted it until my tears came and said, "*You're* nowhere, Mom, you're the definition of it," and who marched out of the house as she had a hundred times before during that long bad year, only instead of coming back at three in the morning, or the next day, she never came back at all.

She and Cyril were going to ride trains, her friends told me when I tracked them down. They said something about New York. They said they knew some people who lived in tunnels and that sounded cool.

They said they were going to California.

They said they wanted to see Spain.

They said they knew a guy who could get them work in Canada.

I thought she'd call or send a postcard, let me know she was okay. We'd been fighting for months over this and that, school, her friends, her clothes, but she knew how much I'd worry, right? She knew I'd need to know she was okay? I said this to

Trisha, on the phone, but it felt like a lie, because some things I'd kept even from my sister. Like how bad the fights got. The time she spat on me in the parking lot at the mall when I wanted to buy her some nice clothes. The time I found her passed out on her bed, eyes rolled back in her head, and when I shook her awake she smiled gently at me and said, "Hi, Mommy," and I was so happy to hear her talking sweet to me that for a minute I was *glad* she was on drugs.

Calls to police, calls to her friends, relatives, none of it turned up anything. Thank God Sid wasn't alive to see it, though I guess if he'd been alive, maybe it wouldn't have happened. Just the two of us together, me and Rose, was too much for that house. Sid diluted us; together, we were too strong.

"Listen, you little fucker," Trisha says to Cyril now, pointing her French manicure at him, "you tell us something about Rose or I'm going to kick your ass from here to Sunday."

She's all sparkly in her fancy dress and her jewelry and her shiny striped hair. In retrospect I can't 100 percent blame Cyril for what happens next, which is that he laughs.

"Oh my God, you little punk," she says, and hits him smack across the face.

"Trisha!" I say.

Cyril's standing there with his hand pressed to his cheek, very still, eyes blank. He looks like someone who has a lot of practice getting hit. I grab hold of Trisha's arm and pull her back. The supervisor is coming from across the room. I can see her making her way. I realize that I'm extremely drunk, like maybe going to be sick right on the table drunk.

"You're pathetic," Cyril says to Trisha.

"You're pathetic, you crystal meth–snorting piece of shit!"

Not for the first time I hear Sid's voice in my ear, calm and gentle. It's okay to lose, he used to say, as long as you prepare for it.

I look at Cyril. The room is swimming, the lights from the casino dancing unhappy steps. "She's still alive, right?" I say. "She's okay?"

He doesn't say anything. Those black eyes give nothing back. Trisha's expensive rings have cut a line along his cheek. By the time the supervisor gets to us, I am crying.

WE SIT IN THE CAR FOR A WHILE, OUR BREATH CLOUDING THE interior.

"God, I wish I had a cigarette."

"That was pretty *Cops* back there, Trish."

"What a punk. I used to think you were exaggerating, but now I know you weren't."

"I'm too drunk to drive."

"Let's just sit here for a while."

We turn on the radio. Trisha hums along off-key and if I were more myself I'd be irritated and tell her to shut up. I think of my daughter sleeping in a tunnel beneath New York City. I think of her in Canada, huddled in a snowstorm. I think of her with a strange man in a bad house in some dark city without a name.

I don't know how much time passes before I wake up. The radio is still playing and Trisha is still staring out the window at nothing, scratching shapes into the condensation. Suddenly the back door behind me opens and Cyril gets in the car. I don't turn around, just look at him in the rearview mirror. It's so dark that I can barely make out his face.

"Last time I seen her, we was in Baltimore," he says, speaking quickly and without any mumbling. "Staying with a guy named Hank. He was all on top of Rose and she left one morning, didn't say where she was going or nothing. We didn't get along too great by that point anyway."

I nod, though I'm not sure he can see me. "Was she still using?"

In the shadows, I imagine him smirking the way kids do when adults try to talk about drugs like they know anything. *Using*. But when he answers, his voice sounds sincere.

"Sometimes. She mostly stopped, though. After—"

"After what?"

He sighs, and then talks fast. "After one time in Newark when she OD'd and I had to take her to the hospital. She was fine, though," he says. "They fixed her up real good."

I'm holding my breath. Trisha seems like she's holding hers, too. Out of the corner of my eye I can sense her looking at me, and all I want is for her to shut up and keep out of it.

"Cyril," I say, and I try to pronounce it gently this time, as gently as if he were my own son, "do you think she'll ever come home?"

This time he doesn't even pause. "No way she coming back. She hated it here."

I flinch, but I know he's right.

He opens the door and gets out of the car. The last I see him he's running away across the parking lot, his white shirt ghostly in the headlights of my car. Jesus, I think, that idiot child didn't even put on a coat to go outside in January. I hope Rose has more sense than that. I don't know if she does or not.

Trisha clears her throat. I wait for her to tell me the truth: that Rose is probably involved in some terrible situation. That I might never see her again. That I'm the one who drove her away. *See, Sherri, see?*

Instead, she offers to drive home.

"I'm not sober yet but I'm close," she says.

I shake my head and say, "Let's just wait a bit." We sit in the parking lot, watching people stream out of the casino and into the darkness, heading to their cars. They're all bundled up against the cold, young people chattering, couples leaning against each other. It's funny how they all seem thrilled and happy, their breath like flags in the dark. How you can't even tell from looking at them whether they won or lost.

The Universal Particular

OF COURSE SHE'LL NEVER ADMIT IT TO ANYBODY BUT THE first thing she feels, seeing the girl, is relief: how awkward and homely she is, acne splattered, not to mention overweight, bent under jet lag and luggage, coming down the escalator at the airport with a glazed look in her eyes. She might even be a little cross-eyed. Tamar's holding a sign with her name—AZIZA—written in black marker, but the girl walks right past her. Maybe she's not familiar with the convention of sign holding. Maybe she's illiterate. That's unkind, and also impossible. Aziza and Albert have been messaging for months; obviously she can read. Many's the time, late at night, Tamar has watched her husband hunch over his phone, thumbing long responses to this girl who just marched by, a dirty green backpack strapped to her shoulders, like a soldier in a shabby army.

Tamar has to jog to catch up. The girl disappears into a restroom, and Tamar waits outside. She throws the sign in the trash. When Aziza comes out, Tamar, ready with a brilliant smile, calls her name.

The girl startles. Her first reaction is a kind of horrified grimace, which she smooths away slowly, without complete success. Tamar leans in, offers a hug. Aziza is stiff and Tamar's palms meet the backpack instead of her body.

"Welcome," she says. "Welcome."

"Where is Albert?" says the girl.

"He had to work, he's so sorry, his hours are super intense lately, he'll tell you all about it," Tamar prattles. She's trying to tug the backpack off the girl's shoulders but Aziza's fingers are curled tight around the straps as if she fears being robbed. Giving up, Tamar grabs an elbow instead, guiding the girl outside to the parking lot while keeping up commentary on the weather, the traffic, the nuisances of travel.

Aziza says nothing. She smells of sweat and plane air. There's a scratch on her arm that looks infected. They find the Honda.

Tamar says, "We're going to take good care of you."

As they drive, Aziza stares out the window at the airport terminals, the planes lifting and landing. It's a grubby airport, outdated and partially under renovation, and the car moves sluggishly past traffic cones and construction machines. On the steering wheel, Tamar's nails gleam fluorescent orange, like a warning. Her black hair is streaked with blue; on her right biceps is a tattoo of a tomato plant, faded red circles with green tendrils that swirl toward her armpit. Aziza can't imagine loving any vegetable enough to ink it on her arm. She wishes to be elsewhere, while knowing there is no elsewhere for her to be. Mainly what she feels is embarrassment. Why did she tell Albert so much, why did she beg for his help? In truth, a lot of the time she forgot she was writing to an actual person. She treated the messages like a diary, and into them she poured all her hatred of her mother, her anger, her fears. Her loneliness. She and her mother fought constantly, right up to the day of her death, and then all of a sudden Aziza realized that she had no one, no place to go. From a continent away, Albert's words bobbed into her in-box like a life raft on a stormy sea. *We're your family,* he wrote. *Why don't you come stay with us for a while? A change will do you good.*

A change will do you good. It seemed so optimistic, so North American. Aziza's life has consisted of nothing but changes, of which her experience has been less good or bad than crushingly inevitable. First her childhood in Somalia, where her birth father vanished before she could even begin to remember him, and then her mother meeting Alvin, who worked for a technology company with interests in Africa, and latching on to him with a desperation that was transparent to Aziza even as a child. But not, apparently, to Alvin. Or maybe he didn't care. In any case he took Aziza and her mother home with him to Stockholm and settled them in a quiet, boxy apartment in Djursholm. At the wedding she was introduced to Albert, her new father's cousin, although the day was a blur to her now. She learned Swedish and English. When she was twelve Alvin died of heat exhaustion on a business trip to Uganda. Abandoned, she and her mother turned on each other. Aziza stayed out late, got in trouble with boys. Her mother threatened to send her back to Somalia, which made Aziza laugh bitterly and say, "Go ahead." Her mother was a terrible liar. She lied the day she told Aziza she was sick but it wasn't serious, that everything would be fine. She lied when she said, at the very end, trying to make up for all their fights, that Aziza had made her proud. She wanted to stage some scene of kindness that would linger in Aziza's memory, even if it was a fiction. Then she died.

Aziza, eighteen years old, three times orphaned, responded to Albert's gentle inquiries with messages she spent hours composing. He told her about himself and Tamar, how they had longed for children of their own but weren't able to have any. Then: the invitation. Now: a car speeding along the highway as fat raindrops splash against the windows and Tamar hums a tuneless song.

ALBERT HITS THE GARAGE OPENER WITH ONE HAND WHILE turning the steering wheel with the other. He has it down to a science, knowing exactly how close he has to be to the house for the opener to work, how much he has to slow down to bring the car in. It's dumb but it makes him feel a little like Batman, driving his car into the bat cave. Also a perfectly coordinated docking in the garage, with zero lag time, saves him from conversation with his next-door neighbor, Oszkar, an underemployed "consultant" who seems to spend all day in his "home office," watching out the window for Albert to come home. Any time he catches Albert lingering in the driveway he's there instantly, with a hearty handshake and some pronounced opinions about the news of the day. Oszkar thinks we need to hit back hard against the terrorists. He thinks climate change is a myth—"The weather's always been changing, since the dinosaurs, no?"—and that immigration needs to be curtailed. "It's too much!" he says, clapping Albert on the back. "There are no more jobs!"

Albert usually nods and smiles, mumbles something about dinner. But every once in a while he has to disagree, for his own moral peace of mind or whatever, and then there goes half an hour, as they stand in the driveway and hash it out, knowing neither of them will change his mind. Oszkar loves to argue. "Good talk!" he always says at the end, after having yelled explosively at Albert for a while.

"Why do you even engage with him?" Tamar wants to know when he finally comes inside, and Albert says, "Some statements you can't let pass," and Tamar says, "The curry is cold," and Albert sighs and says, "We do have a microwave," and then they both start drinking.

Tonight's evasive maneuvers are successful, but still he sits for a minute in the darkened garage, door closed, before he goes in. He's nervous to meet Aziza. The last time he saw her she was a bright-eyed child of—what, seven? Now, he knows from Facebook, she's a young woman with long dark hair and her mother's scowl. It's possible he wrote her too much, and too often. It's certain he did. And he had a few too many the night he invited her to stay—*we'll get you a student visa, you can take classes for a while, have a great time!*—and when he woke up the next morning, furry tongued and regretful, she'd already begun making plans. Tamar was not pleased; but Tamar is rarely pleased.

Inside, he smells the tofu lasagna she always makes for guests. Aziza is asleep on the couch in front of the TV, which is showing news about a bombing in Europe. He frowns and turns it off, and the silence wakes her; she moves upright, wiping drool from her mouth, and sees him. She's both younger than he thought, and older.

"Hello, hello," he says.

Aziza struggles to get up off the couch, which appears to fight to keep her down. The couch wins. He sits down beside her instead and gives her a semi-hug, trying not to make contact with her surprisingly large breasts. What does he know of teenagers, especially girls? Not a thing. He'd been writing to an illusion, and part of the illusion was himself as a father figure, dispensing wisdom and care. "How are you?"

"Tired," she says. Her accent is straight-up British, as his cousin's had been.

"Did Tamar show you your room?"

"It's very nice, thank you." In truth the room intimidated her; it was enormous and carpeted in white, with a bed twice the size of the one she had at home. The posters on the walls were of rock bands she didn't recognize. She'd placed her suitcase against the wall and fled.

Tamar enters clapping her hands, saying, "Dinner's ready," then frowns as they both flinch at the sound. She is irritated by social awkwardness, despite often being the cause of it. They eat quickly and with little conversation, and then Aziza is released to the big white room.

SEVERAL DAYS LATER, TAMAR AND ALBERT HOST A PARTY AND invite the neighbors. Cindy and Mike, from down the block, bring their two kids, who are close to Aziza's age. Linda and Rafael bring their rambunctious ten-year-old twin boys, who will go through the bedroom, ransacking closets and medicine cabinets if given the chance (Tamar has learned this the hard way). And Oszkar—you might as well invite him, because he'll come over either way—brings his girlfriend, Tilda, who is from the Philippines and never says anything, though she seems to understand English just fine. They carry a platter of beautifully arranged tropical fruit and a large bouquet, presenting it to Aziza with ceremony.

"Thank you," she says woodenly, and stands there with the flowers gripped in her hands, clearly not knowing what to do with them. So far, saying "thank you" and standing still is how she handles most situations.

"Let's put those in water!" Tamar says cheerily, guiding her to the kitchen. Under Tamar's care, Aziza already looks better than when she arrived. She's wearing a well-cut sundress that flatters her hourglass figure, and the salicylic acid face wash is clearing up her skin. On their trips to the mall, the drugstore, the spa where Tamar works as a massage therapist and where she gets her friend Miriam to give Aziza a facial, Aziza has said next to nothing. She keeps her eyes down, though more than once Tamar has caught the girl studying her, her gaze fixed on Tamar's tattoos, her nose piercing, her hair. Surely they have piercings and tattoos in Sweden; for God's sake, she and Albert live in the suburbs and people here don't look twice.

Tamar is losing patience. Albert was the one who invited her, and of course Albert is now busy at work, monetizing his inexplicably successful blog, and the only time Aziza perks up is when he comes home. Sometimes they sit on the couch together late at night, whispering, looking up guiltily if Tamar comes in.

Albert, at her direction, is grilling veggie kabobs in the backyard. He knows nothing about grilling and doesn't care about it either, just turns the things over and over until Tamar tells him they're done. Mike lingers near him, drinking beer after beer.

"So she's, what, a refugee?"

"No, not at all. She's my cousin."

Mike belches discreetly. "But she's like African?"

"Somalian." Albert has to go through the whole thing, how his father moved here from Sweden, but Alvin was his Swedish cousin, who married Aziza's mother, and even though the story is clear and succinct he can tell he has lost Mike's attention, that all he heard was *Somalian*.

"She must be psyched to be *here*," Mike says, "after Africa."

Albert sighs. All the neighbors are idiots. He and Tamar bought this house years ago, for almost nothing, at a foreclosure sale. The schools were good and they were planning a family that never came. It had seemed like a joke, a role-playing exercise. *We're moving to the suburbs!* Albert at the time was still playing with his band and had started his website, *Beards of North America*, as a pastime during long bus rides. When he was on tour he would interview men about their soul patches and Vandykes and take their pictures, and he'd post the interviews in a serious, white-paletted layout, as if these dudes were talking about national security or famine or something. Then all of a sudden he had thousands of clicks a day and advertisers were all over him. He had meetings with venture capitalists. Boxes of sample grooming products kept showing up at the house. Now he has an office and contracted photographers who sell him images for the subsidiary sites—*Beards of Japan, Beards of New Zealand, Beards of Scandinavia*—and a twenty-four-year-old assistant who handles the social media accounts and flirts with him aggressively, enjoying how it makes him uncomfortable, which he actually finds pretty insulting. He and Tamar should have moved away a long time ago, but instead they slid into a static, low-grade misery that made planning for a different future impossible. Now somehow all he can do is keep rushing headlong into the days, no matter how stupid the days are.

He should slow down and focus, though, on Aziza. She's standing across the yard getting harangued by Oszkar about God only knows what, and he lifts a hand in her direction, then turns it on himself and pretends to shoot himself in the head. She looks alarmed, then laughs. When she laughs she's beautiful, with a wide, gorgeous smile that makes you wish it didn't disappear so quickly. She is a girl whose life has offered her almost no reason to smile like that, and still it's the moment when she seems most herself.

Tamar is dragging Tim, Cindy and Mike's son, across the yard by force. He's nineteen and shy, with shaggy dark hair.

From what Mike says, Tim spends all his time in the basement, obsessed with some online multiplayer game set in apocalyptic New Mexico. It's based on an ancient civilization with its own language, in which Tim, though he barely graduated high school, is fluent. Aziza nods at Tim, and he nods back. Tamar abandons them, a look of satisfaction on her face. Then she scowls at Albert and makes a gesture he understands too late. He has burned the kabobs.

IN THE DARK BASEMENT AT TIM'S HOUSE, HE AND AZIZA SIT with consoles in their hands. They don't talk, but Aziza doesn't mind. She has played the game before. People don't expect it from a girl—Tim, who invited her under duress, clearly didn't expect it—and she uses this to her advantage, playing timidly at first as she susses out his skill level, then venturing into a side canyon and stealing his stone weaponry when he least expects it. Some guys would freak out but Tim only glances at her with respect.

They break for soda and chips, which his mother brings downstairs on a tray. The look she gives Aziza broadcasts sharp betrayal; she wanted Aziza to lure Tim outside, instead of joining him here in artificial reality. But Aziza can imagine nothing more artificial than the reality outside, the hum of vehicles disappearing into garages, the angry wheeze of leaf blowers operated by men in masks, like a gardening militia. Here in the basement, her thumbs bent and ready, she feels invisible. Sweat gathers under her arms; she has to pee. She's more comfortable than she has been in weeks.

Only when Tim's mother comes back and tells her it's time to go does she understand that hours have passed.

"Bye."

"Bye."

Outside, it's somehow still light. The walk home is only three minutes but Aziza drags it out as long as she can, scuffing her new running shoes against the curb until the rubber frays at the tip. She dreads Tamar's cheerful cruelty and the long hours until Albert comes home. She's been treated worse— at school, when she first came to Sweden, girls asked if they could touch her hair and then whispered about it afterward. Once a boy in her class told her excitedly that he'd found a picture of her family in a magazine. It was a pack of dogs. But there is something particularly painful about Tamar's sugary care, her wide smile and dead eyes, her constant, unstated insistence that Aziza should be and look and act different than she does.

Can she dash straight from the front door to her room without seeing Tamar? She can only try.

But Tamar isn't home. No one is home. It's the first time Aziza has been alone all summer. Set free, she drifts around the house, snooping. Vaguely now she remembers Tamar saying she'd be working late, and that Aziza should help herself to the cashew nut casserole in the fridge. All the food Tamar makes is vegan and gluey, and anyway Aziza is pleasantly full of chips. She wanders into Tamar and Albert's bedroom. They have an adjustable bed. Tamar's half is propped higher than Albert's. It makes Aziza think of her mother's bed at the hospital, and she averts her eyes from it. Instead she runs her hands across Albert's shirts—he owns a ton of them, in endless variations of blue and white. She doesn't know what he does, something online; she pictures him in a loft office, cracking jokes with his employees, casual but businesslike with his sleeves rolled up. He looks like a nicer version of the Alvin she remembers. He's younger and fitter and also not bald, and his eyes are kinder and more wrinkled from smiling. She wishes he would put his arm around her sometime. She wishes she could curl up next to him like a cat and be petted, her body tiny like a cat's is tiny, tucked into itself. She would purr.

She runs her fingers through Tamar's jewelry, opens her bedside drawer: magazines, costume jewelry, lipstick. On Albert's side, the nightstand is covered with coins and crumpled dollar bills. She takes nothing. She knows she'd be suspected. She knows Albert and Tamar's carelessness is just a show they put on for themselves; they pay more attention to little things than they let on.

THERE HAD BEEN SOME TALK, OVER EMAIL, ABOUT HER EN-rolling in summer classes, maybe something with computers, that might help her in an eventual career. But deadlines were missed and paperwork unfiled. "I don't *know* what kids around here do," she hears Tamar telling Albert one night. Her tone is exasperated. "How am I *supposed* to know?" Albert's answer is low and unintelligible, as always.

Aziza decides to try babysitting. At the market with Tamar, she has seen flyers on the bulletin board, so she puts up her own, listing the number of the cell phone Tamar got her. Soon she has more work than she can handle; the parents are desperate, even willing to overlook the fact that she doesn't drive. She takes the bus all over, drags kids away from flat-screen televisions, makes them play in their lush backyards. She has no particular affection for children, but isn't scared of them either. "You're no-nonsense," a mother says to her. "I like that." Aziza repeats this term whenever she meets a new parent, despite not entirely understanding what it means. "I'm no-nonsense," she says. "Understandable, given where you're from," a father muses, and she doesn't answer. She has found that not answering is usually the best answer. Soon her own nightstand drawer is filled with bills, which she keeps tied in a rubber band; she has nothing to spend the money on except candy, which she buys from the convenience store and eats on the bus, the cheap chocolate dissolving fast on her tongue.

One evening, trudging home from the bus stop, she is accosted by Oszkar, who is out front spraying his flower beds with a hose. "My lady," he says to her, and she says nothing. It sounds sarcastic. He's a short hairy man wearing what look like pyjama pants, striped and floppy, and a T-shirt that hangs over his jutting belly like an awning over a porch.

"How's it going over there? You surviving the dungeon masters?"

She nods. He's trying to get her to admit something or confess something. She has seen him, at night, standing at his bedroom window, trying to see into Tamar and Albert's house.

"If it gets too much, feel free to come over and hang with me and Tilda. Pop a beer or whatever. Let off some steam."

"Okay," she says.

"You making any friends? Meeting any boys?"

"I'm quite busy," she says, and something about this—her accent? her gravity?—makes him laugh. His eyes graze her body hungrily. She's been flirted with before, but never quite so brazenly as this. It wouldn't be true to say she likes it; indeed she finds him disgusting. But she would like somebody else to look at her like Oszkar is, ravenous and direct. She'd like to hold somebody's attention so tightly that they can't look away.

As if sensing her desire, a car speeds fast around the curb and hurtles into the open maw of the garage. Albert gets out and heads straight for them, his face red and furious.

"Hey neighbor!" Oszkar waves.

Albert ignores him. "You all right?" he asks Aziza.

She nods. Albert puts his arm around her, a pressure on her shoulders turning her towards the house. Oszkar is unperturbed. He flicks the water across the heads of his pansies and grins at Albert.

"Don't forget what I said," Oszkar calls after them, and when Albert asks her what it was, Aziza tells him she can't remember, which only makes him scowl more.

ALBERT IS DRUNK. HE'S BRUSHING HIS TEETH TOO HARD, which always sets Tamar on edge. He killed most of a bottle of wine over dinner and Tamar watched Albert quiz Aziza about the creepy neighbor, what he'd said and done, while the girl grew first flustered, then sullen. Albert never knows when he's gone too far, doesn't understand that he's acting less like a protective patriarch than his own brand of creep.

"Let it go," she told him, only to have him turn on her.

"Like you care," he said, and she could tell from Aziza's brief, crumpled smile that she agreed. An army of two, massed against her. Tamar stood up, carried her plate to the sink, and left.

Now Albert sways as he gets into bed, lying on his side away from her. She places a hand on his shoulder and he doesn't stiffen, but he doesn't move either. He's numb to her. She lies on her back, looking at the red curtains, the dark blue wallpaper. They'd picked these things out together, years ago, when they still shared the same taste. In this bed she'd lain after the third miscarriage and told Albert she was done trying. *No more.* He'd nodded and held her hand, and she'd thought he understood, that he would not be angry. But she was wrong. In this bed, before that, she'd lain after sex, when they first married, astonished that he was her husband, and she was his wife. She'd wanted him so badly, had in fact stolen him from her roommate Brenda and burned up that friendship with zero regrets. *I got what I wanted.* Even after the wedding, she was still amazed. Now in this bed she lies still and feels him revealed as the stranger he's been for so long. He rustles and settles, snoring. She almost feels tenderly towards him, out of a habit of trying to keep loving him; then understands that the person she feels tenderly towards, the object of all her compassion, is herself.

TIM KNOWS TAMAR AND ALBERT DON'T KEEP THE BACK DOOR locked, just as he knows that Oszkar keeps a spare key under the doormat and Mrs. Cooper has an alarm system sign that's just for show. He used to go through all the houses in the neighborhood when he was in high school, an anthropologist of the ordinary. Creepy gamer kid is a cliché to which he strenuously objects, but sometimes he just got so bored. His sister Tanya came with him once, in between expeditions to smoke cigarettes in underpasses with her Goth friends, but all she wanted to do was look for booze and drugs and sex toys. He told her that her mind lacked subtlety and she rolled her eyes at him and left, which was how most conversations between them ended.

It's been a while since he visited the houses, but meeting Aziza has sparked his curiosity again. He wants to see her room, her clothes, the whatever-secret-inside she keeps hidden beneath her calm exterior. They've spent hours gaming together but still rarely talk. He needs a clue, some wedge of information he can use to pry her open.

The house smells dead inside; not dirty but too clean, uninhabited, despite the three people living here. In the recycling bin are a surprising number of empty wine bottles and a couple of pizza boxes. Tamar and Albert's bedroom is the only messy part of the house, with dirty laundry on the floor and dressers littered with crap. He picks up some stray dollar bills, a necklace, a tie, and stuffs them in his pocket. He doesn't want these items for themselves; he wants to have taken, to have rearranged the air around their possessions only enough for Tamar and Albert to sense the disturbance.

In Aziza's room he sniffs the air for the solution to the riddle of her. But he finds nothing. Her clothes lie neatly folded in drawers. She keeps no journal, reads no books. The place is emptier than a hotel room. She has perfected her own absence. He liked her before, but now, seeing this rigor and demarcation, the discipline of a ghost, he swoons.

THIS TIME IT'S TAMAR'S TURN. SHE ACTUALLY FORGOT ABOUT Cindy and Mike's party and had a drink or three at home after a long day at work. This guy Ruben, one of her regulars, was such a dick to her—he always was, grazing her body as she leaned over him; once he'd even stuck out his tongue and licked her hip. All he got was a mouthful of the apron where she stashed her lotion, so what was even the point? Being a dick was the point. She complained to her manager, Beth, and all Beth said was "Business isn't great, Tamar," and that was that. Today Ruben actually pinched her butt and she wheeled around and said, "What in the everlasting godforsaken fuck? I mean what fucking year do you think this is, Ruben?" and stormed out of the spa without finishing her shift. She probably didn't have a job to go back to tomorrow. So she'd downed some gin and chased it with tonic, too upset to even mix them in the same glass, and then, when she saw Oszcar and Tilda parading past her house, their goddamn fruit platter—did they ever bring anything else?—held aloft like an offering to the gods, she remembered. Albert was supposed to meet her there and who knew about Aziza; she kept her own hours these days. Tamar had asked Albert once, in the early morning, just how long the girl was going to stay, but things between them were so frosty that he hadn't even answered the question. She couldn't skip the party because then Cindy would ask why and if there was one thing she couldn't stand it was Cindy's Wrinkled Brow of Concern. Once, at the grocery store, she'd caught Tamar smiling at a toddler riding in a cart, and she'd placed her palm on Tamar's forearm and said sympathetically, "Albert told Mike about your trouble. It must be so hard," and Tamar, dark with heartbreak, had said, "Actually I'm relieved. Kids horrify me," and Cindy frowned with the greatest look of pity Tamar had ever seen. She can't go through a scene like that again. She must be unassailable. So she puts on a short-sleeved polka-dot dress and gels her hair into curls and walks very steadily down the street, carrying a bottle of wine in a silver gift bag.

In the yard, plastic sheeting covers the picnic tables, onto which Cindy is throwing down crabs and boiled corn. Albert and Aziza sit together at one end, wearing bibs and expressions of pliant misery. Tamar has never been less hungry, and she escapes to the kitchen, where Oszkar is mixing martinis. When he sees her, he leers, as he usually does; she has never actually seen him with a woman other than Tilda, whom she suspects is more a hired housekeeper than a girlfriend, so she doesn't take it seriously. She deposits her wine and picks up a martini instead. They cheers.

Tim and Tanya drift past, glance outside at the party, and refuse it, the girl going upstairs, the boy down. To Tamar's surprise, Aziza wipes her hands, comes inside, and follows the boy downstairs.

"Young love," Oszkar says knowingly. "The hormones do the talking."

"Don't be gross," Tamar says.

"What you call gross, I call beauty. Sex is nature's most beautiful invention."

"That's also gross," Tamar says irritably. "Where's your handmaiden?"

"My what?"

"Tilda."

"She went home to get more fruit."

"Of course she did," Tamar says.

Oszkar is standing very close to her, his spittle bursting against her ear. "You look very nice," he says.

"Are you hitting on me?"

"I've been hitting on you for years."

"Shameless."

"I notice you don't say gross."

Tamar flushes. Oszkar is disgusting, potbellied and scruffy bearded. To this party he has worn shorts that fall below his knees and a yellow T-shirt that reads "SILENCE IS GOLDEN. DUCT TAPE IS SILVER." Looking at him, she thinks about people interviewed on the news after their neighbor commits some terrible crime, saying, "He seemed like a nice guy. You would never suspect." Oszkar is not such a person. You would suspect him of anything.

Outside, Albert is talking to Mike, waving a crab leg around as he makes some point. He has become the kind of man who makes a lot of points, who cares about the winning of unwinnable arguments. Oszkar is kissing her, an attack on her person that she observes more than participates in, though she does not object. *I mean who even cares at this point.* There are arms around her, there are lips moving against her neck, her cheek, her earlobe. The sleeve of her dress slips off her shoulders. Over Oszkar's back some movement catches her eye, and she looks up to see Aziza and Tim watching her, both of their expressions neutral. Without saying anything Tim opens the fridge door, takes out two cans of soda, and leads Aziza back downstairs.

LATER, AT HOME, THEY FIGHT. "THIS IS LIKE SOME KIND OF parody," Albert hisses. "Suburban wife misbehaves. Is it a joke to you?"

"Yes, it's a joke," she says grimly. "It is beyond hilarious."

She wants to tell him that this is what adulthood is, to embody a role and not be able to escape it. Self-parody is inevitable. Instead she sits on the edge of the bed with hands folded contritely in her lap, a posture that also feels like self-parody, even though her grief and shame are real.

"Oh for Christ's sake," Albert says, and goes to sleep on the couch. But he can't sleep, and stays up too late watching talk shows. At a certain point Aziza pads into the living room wearing a hooded sweatshirt and yoga pants. He sits up and makes a space for her on the couch. She doesn't look at him or talk to him, just stares at the TV as if spellbound. He is not glad of the company. He has been mortified enough today.

"I'm sorry," he says finally. "I thought this summer would be better for you."

She shrugs. "It's no worse than at home."

He laughs. "You're a real diplomat."

She tucks her knees up under her chin, and he sees he's hurt her. "I'm sorry," he says again. "I appreciate your honesty."

She doesn't answer. On TV, an actress tells a story about eating too much cheese. The host guffaws. It's not a funny story, but Aziza smiles with what looks like real delight, the blue glow of the screen lighting her face with a spooky fire.

TAMAR'S HANGOVER IS EXTREME. SHE LIES BENEATH THE blanket as if entombed in concrete. Albert came into the room just long enough to dress, and then the front door closed a second time, when Aziza left. Now she stills in silence, her head deep in the pillow like a fossil in the dirt. She is bleached and dry; she is the long-ago dead. It's seriously time to stop drinking. Groping blindly she finds her phone and lifts it to her face. A text from Beth says, *Meet me at 10 if you want to keep your job.*

In the bathroom, she makes herself throw up, then swallows four Advils and a Ritalin. She can do this. She armors herself in makeup, then stops by the nightstand for her favorite necklace, the garnet pendant she inherited from her mother and which isn't there.

It is the absence that wakes her up. She stiffens, ransacks her jewelry box, calls Albert, who says he hasn't seen it. "It's probably in a pocket somewhere," he says.

"You know I would never put that necklace in a pocket," she says. Of course he does know; he knows the whole story of the necklace that came with Tamar's grandmother from Germany in 1936 and which her mother pressed into Tamar's palm before she died, requesting that Tamar pass it on to her own children, which her mother died believing Tamar would still one day have. Tamar doesn't need to voice the accusation; it's in the air between them.

"I'm sure you'll find it" is all he says. "I have to go."

In the guest bedroom, she parts the sheets, the pillowcases, opens the drawers, and finds nothing. Most of Aziza's things are still in her backpack; the only items hanging in the closet are the clothes Tamar has bought for her, barely worn and in some cases with the tags still on. Tamar is shaking. It is terrible to be invaded, and even worse to be refused.

ANGER DIGNIFIES HER. BRISKLY, WITH LITTLE EFFORT, SHE cows Beth, threatening to sue if she gets fired and making Beth promise to ban Ruben from the spa. She treats herself to an almond milk chai latte and then returns to the house and buys Aziza a plane ticket back to Stockholm. That evening, when Aziza and Albert are watching television, Tamar informs them both that it's time for Aziza to go home.

"Wait, what?" Albert says. "This is because of the necklace?"

"No," Tamar says. "It's because of everything."

Aziza doesn't know what necklace they're talking about. She thinks about the apartment in Stockholm, which still contains her mother's things, everything waiting to be sorted, sold, given away. The place is too big for Aziza to afford, and she will have to move somewhere. Lately she's been thinking of going to school in London. She's good with computers. She will walk in the rain to high grey buildings, where she will scroll through line after line of code. When she thinks about this distant future, she is calm. Only on the plane, a week later, after stilted farewells, does she burst into tears that disturb her seatmate, a businessman on his way to a sales meeting in Frankfurt.

"Are you all right?" he asks her, and she nods silently. She is embarrassed not because of the crying but because she is in love with Albert, and the thought of never seeing him again is more than she can bear. In her backpack, rolled into a tight tube, is one of his blue striped shirts, stolen from the hamper, dank with his smell. When she hugged him at the house, on her final night, she leaned into him, her cheek wet, and then lifted a hand to his face. She felt him go rigid. Now her grief and humiliation mix together, and she sobs into the tiny oblong window, barely noticing when they leave the ground.

At home, Tamar also cries. She and Albert sit on the couch together in the early evening upon their return from the airport, the windows open, a summer breeze tickling the curtains. They never found the necklace, despite ransacking Aziza's room and bag and asking her about it over and over, unable to make sense of her confusion. She acted as if she had no idea what they were talking about, but didn't defend herself either, seeming to accept their accusations as inevitable. "She must have thrown it away," Tamar says. Passing by outside on his way home, Tim sees Tamar lean her head against Albert's shoulder. He doesn't feel guilty about the necklace; he's forgotten he took it, and couldn't even say where it is. Years from now, his mother will sell it at a garage sale for fifty cents, believing it to be junk. Tim and Aziza will keep in touch for a while, sometimes finding each other in the canyons of that ancient online civilization, sometimes texting or Gchatting, until the too-clear longing in his messages makes her uncomfortable and she stops responding. Still, he continues to believe that, if only she hadn't left so abruptly, she would have learned to love him back; under very slightly different circumstances, he thinks, they would have stayed together forever.

Risk Management

LITTLE GOT EVERYTHING RIGHT. FROM THE DAY SHE WAS hired, she was perfect. The filing, the phones, the calming of patients made hostile by tooth pain: there was nothing she couldn't handle. Of course we all hated her for it, kind of, except the dentists, who loved her. You could see them congratulating themselves for hiring her every time they walked past the desk, where Little would be typing with blistering efficiency— she had those gel nails, and every week a different work of art was splayed across her hands, fireworks or hearts or skulls for Halloween—and simultaneously scheduling an appointment on the phone.

"You are very welcome," she'd murmur into the receiver while smiling at Dr. Pai. "We'll see you next Thursday at nine forty-five."

Her name wasn't really Little. It was something consonant-filled and Lithuanian the rest of us struggled to pronounce, and when Margaret, the office manager, clucked her tongue and said, "That's a big name for such a little thing," it was the little part that stuck. If Little minded, she didn't say so. In Vilnius,

I'd heard, she used to be a dentist herself, but here she had no license. Why she'd left her home, I didn't know.

At lunch we put the phones straight to voice mail and sat in the break room eating meals we brought from home. We made New Year's resolutions together, started salads in January, fell off the wagon like dominoes around Valentine's. Little never joined us. She put her coat on over her scrubs and disappeared, returning exactly forty-five minutes later with her frosty-pink lipstick reapplied. Then one day I was out running an errand and came upon Little sitting on a bench, a paper napkin tucked into the collar of her coat, eating a burger and fries. She smiled when she saw me. "Two things I can't live without," she said. "Fresh air and fast food."

She offered me a fry, and I sat down and took it. It was an ugly day in late March, windy and lusterless, spring hesitant to enter this unholy world. Little's long blond hair whipped against her cheeks. She wore turquoise eye shadow and dangling gold earrings, and her raincoat was dark, shiny red. There were fifteen minutes left of lunch, and I didn't want to go back. Margaret was on a tear about time sheets, and Caitlin and Alyssa, the hygienists, had been out drinking the night before; they kept laughing about how hungover they were and if you tried to talk to them they just shook their heads and rolled their eyes as if no one else had ever been young or drunk, much less both at the same time.

I'll say this about Little, she never rolled her eyes at anything. As we sat there, a man came out of an office building across the street and jogged straight toward us, pulling up short in front of the bench like a dog coming to heel.

"Sorry I'm late," he told Little. "I was in a risk management meeting."

Little held up a hamburger wrapped in yellow paper, and he grabbed it eagerly. She said, "It's okay. Who is at risk?"

"We're all at risk," he said cheerfully, and took a bite. "Who's your friend?"

"I'm Valerie," I said. "We work together."

"Josh," he said. "I'd shake your hand, but——" He shook the hamburger instead, indicating condiment spillage. He was wearing khaki pants and a white button-down shirt with a fleece vest on top. He seemed like the kind of guy who reads about extreme sports in magazines while doing a slow twenty on a bike at the gym. But Little was staring at him as if he'd invented the sun and made it rise on command.

"Are you coming to dinner tonight?" she asked him. "I'm making kugelis."

"Wouldn't miss it," he said. His hamburger was already gone, and Little handed him a napkin, which he used and then returned to her, along with his wrapper. He smacked his lips. I saw he was older than I'd thought at first. He was balding at the temples, and the khakis were tight around his hips, bought for a younger version of himself.

Little turned to me. "Would you like to come, too?"

I shook my head; it was clear she'd only issued the invitation out of politeness. We'd never socialized outside of work. In fact I didn't socialize with anyone from work, even Margaret, who was close to my age and lived in my neighborhood and whose cats I took care of when she went to visit her aunt in Nanaimo for two weeks every July. I liked everyone fine, but forty hours a week is already a lot of time to spend with people who've entered your life by happenstance.

I was surprised when Josh chimed in. "You should definitely

come!" he said. "The kugelis, man. It's a thing of beauty, not to be missed."

I was even more surprised to hear myself say yes.

THAT NIGHT I TOOK THE BUS TO LITTLE'S APARTMENT, FOL-lowing her directions. She lived in a terrible neighborhood, one I would have avoided in normal circumstances. Not two weeks earlier, five kids in their early twenties had been found dead in an apartment building nearby, having overdosed on heroin laced with fentanyl. I was an avid follower of this kind of news. My own son and daughter were busy and straitlaced and held bachelor's degrees and jobs, but I never stopped worrying about their lives going over a cliff. Every time the phone rang I braced myself for the worst-case scenario, and in this way I kept them safe.

I stood on Little's stoop, ringing her doorbell, and nobody answered. Behind me a car slowed menacingly, then sped up again. The building across the street had been boarded up, and on its front door was a spray painting that looked like a cartoon penis brandishing a knife in tiny hands. Just as I was about to turn around and go home, I saw Josh jogging up the block, waving.

"Her doorbell doesn't work," he said. He had a key and let us both in. "I guess she forgot to tell you."

I followed him up a set of damp linoleum stairs to the second floor, where he gave a cursory knock and then opened the door. Little was in the kitchen, wearing a frilly red apron tied about the waist, listening to Russian hip-hop. My kids would roll their eyes at me knowing about hip-hop, but Caitlin and Alyssa keep me up-to-date. Little's cheeks were flushed and I could tell that she'd been drinking, not that I cared. She and Josh shared a kiss that passed swiftly across the border from affectionate to uncomfortable. I cleared my throat. Little made for me next, pecking me on both cheeks. I handed over the wine I'd brought, and Little opened it and poured two glasses.

Josh grabbed a can of Coke from the fridge. "Here's to recovery," he said.

"Josh is three years sober," Little said sweetly.

"Cheers," I said, then flushed because it felt like the wrong thing to say.

We sat down in Little's tiny living room. She'd done her best with the place, arranging colorful slipcovers and sofa pillows and some pretty paintings on the wall. But instead of camouflaging it, her efforts only made the dumpiness of the place more obvious. It's like when I put on a dress—you think to yourself, *Aw, that middle-aged lady made an effort* and not *What a looker.* Sometimes it's better to accept limitations than to defy them. I wondered why Little didn't move. I wondered where Josh lived and why they weren't living together.

While I was wondering all this, Little brought out a tray of cheese and crackers, telling Josh about a patient this afternoon who'd gotten so loopy on anesthetic she'd put her hand on Dr. Ertegun's knee and stroked it. Flustered, he ran out of the room. "Poor man!" Little said, laughing. "He was quite unused to the attention."

I didn't think Dr. Ertegun was unused to attention from women, but I didn't say so. When I first started working at the practice, he was a young dentist with a beautiful wife who left him because he was quite happy to get attention from women, if you know what I mean. After his divorce he went off the deep end for a while, drinking and staying out late, and he developed a pretty serious coke problem. I didn't realize how bad it was until one Monday morning when I opened the office and found him lying on the floor in the waiting room. He'd voided his bowels. I called 911 and sat with his head on my lap until the ambulance came. His body was clammy and inert, skin the color of wet cement. I cleaned up the office before anyone else arrived and then went to the hospital; I was the first person he saw when he opened his eyes.

Afterward he went on a monthlong "vacation," aka rehab, and when he got back he started over. In time, he found one reason or another to fire everyone in the office except me. He kept me around not out of gratitude to me but as punishment to himself, a permanent reminder of how low he'd once fallen. I knew it and he knew it, but each of us kept it to ourselves.

Josh started talking about the intricacies of risk management. He seemed like the most tedious person I'd ever met, and I'm someone who spends most days listening to people's regrets about their inadequate flossing technique. He sat with his Coke cradled in both hands, his knees spasming up and down. The apartment was warm and his face developed a sweaty sheen; his glasses kept slipping down his nose. Instead of pushing them up with his fingers he scrunched up his nose to do it. Since they slipped often, this gave him a recurring grimace, like a man in perpetual vicinity of a bad smell.

"Dinner is served," Little said from the kitchen.

She didn't have a dining room, so we filed into the kitchen, served ourselves, and returned to the living room to balance the plates on our knees. The kugelis turned out to be a kind of pudding, and Josh wasn't kidding about Little's cooking—it was fluffy and rich, deeply comforting, the kind of food your mother makes for you in childhood and you spend the rest of your life trying to imitate and fail. My own mother was a terrible cook, as well as being not a very nice person, but I still thought about food and love this way, and when I ate a meal like Little's I sometimes found myself on the edge of tears. I took a break and drank some wine. The Russian hip-hop was still playing in Little's kitchen, low, rhythmic, and unintelligible.

"So," I said. "Is it true that back in Lithuania you were a dentist?"

"What?" Little said, and burst out laughing. "No! Who told you that?"

I tried to remember, but couldn't. It was one of those pieces of office gossip that had floated around so long its original source had evaporated.

"I was a hydrologist," she said. "For many years I worked for the government making a—what's the word?—a study regarding a proposed dam."

"She was also a dancer," Josh put in, between bites.

"You were a hydrologist *and* a dancer?"

Little nodded, nervously, I thought. Josh said, "Vilnius is some kind of town."

"You've been there?"

"No," he said.

"So why did you leave?" I asked Little.

"There was so much corruption," she said. "It was impossible to make an honest living."

Josh snorted, and Little shot him a glance. "Oh, come on," he said. "You've got to admit that's kind of funny, coming from you."

"It's not funny," Little said, standing up. "More?" she asked me, holding out her hand for my plate. It was an order, and suddenly I could see her in ten years, erect and scolding, ordering her kids around. I gave it to her, and she disappeared into the kitchen and didn't come back for a while.

Josh leaned closer to me, across the coffee table. "She catfished me," he whispered. I could smell his hot breath, sugary from Coke. "When she was back in Vilnius. That's how we met. You can't blame her for wanting a better life. Catfishing—"

"I know what catfishing is," I said irritably. Nothing is more aggravating than the condescension of younger people. "But I don't understand. Why would she pretend to be somebody else on the internet? She's what everybody wants to be."

"True," Josh said. "True."

"So what was she pretending?"

"She pretended she was going to marry me," he said. "My mail-order bride. Like in the good old days!"

"Which good old days are those?" I asked, but he ignored the question.

"After she got her paperwork and came over, she said she didn't want to get married after all. That it was all just to escape. But guess what? She figured out that I'm not such a bad guy. We might," he confided, lowering his voice, "we might even be falling in love." He sat back against the couch, raising his eyebrows at me significantly.

"Congratulations, I guess," I said.

When Little came back she was even drunker. I was alarmed. At the office she gave off an air of cool containment. She was never frazzled. When people flipped out, as they sometimes did, from pain or drugs or a bill they didn't want to pay, she never seemed the slightest bit disturbed. She had a way of smiling that made people feel she was on their side, even when she was ushering them out the door. It was a real talent. But right now she was bright-eyed in a bad way, fidgety with some emotion she couldn't get a handle on. She handed me my plate and more fell than sat down next to Josh on the couch.

"I also brought cookies," I said. "Sorry I didn't have time to make anything myself. But they're from the Italian place by the office. The people who work there are really mean but the baked goods are delicious." I was rambling.

"Thank you," Little said. "You're nice." Drunk, she seemed younger than usual. Or maybe it was her posture, slumped down on the couch with her knees slightly raised, twisting her hands in her lap.

Josh said, "You're the nicest one in the office, I hear. Some of those others sound like real witches. Is it a dental practice, or a coven? Ha ha ha."

"Josh," Little said warningly.

I put my plate down on the coffee table and smiled at Little in what I hoped was a placating way. "Every office has its politics, I think," I said, and she smiled back.

"Is it true," she said then, "what they say about you?"

I couldn't imagine what anybody at the office said about me. I'd been answering the phones there for more than a decade. I'd never missed more than a day due to illness. I had photos of my kids on my desk, childhood pictures even though they were grown. They'd always be babies to me.

"That you killed your husband," Little said.

"Wait, what?" Josh said. He was excited and his knees jerked even more than before. "For reals?"

Little was staring at me intently. Her palms lay flat on her lap, and her nails were striped green and yellow. The ring finger on each hand was blue. It seemed like a message in code.

"Yes," I said stiffly. The only person in the office who knew, who could have told, was Dr. Ertegun. When he hired me I'd had to indicate my background on my application. "I'll take a chance on you, Valerie," he said, chewing his pen, which I already knew was bad for your teeth. "I just hope you won't let me down." Oh, he was pompous back then! He was rich in self-regard! But he needed me to thank him for his generosity, so I did.

"Tell us more," Josh said, and Little laid a hand on his arm.

"There isn't much to tell," I said.

"Not much to tell!" he barked. "Let us be the judge of that."

I looked at Little. I was imagining the conversation she'd had with Dr. Ertegun, him leaning across her desk, filling her ears with secrets, anything to make her look at him twice. I knew how he was, how he still was, despite the second marriage and the three-year-old twins.

As for me, I'd grown up in a bad situation and escaped it for a worse one. My husband was a cruel man without a light in his soul. The day he came after my son, who was hardly more than a baby at the time, I stopped him. Even the judge, after reviewing the photographic evidence of my husband's brutality, said the situation was terrible. Sentencing was lenient. After I was released, I got my kids back from my sister and moved across the country and I made a new life for myself, one I'm proud of, which is not to say it's something I care to discuss over potato pudding, no matter how tasty it is.

To Little I said, "It's in the past."

She didn't look as ashamed as I thought she should. But she did say quietly, "I understand."

Josh said, "I'm the only normal person here!"

We moved on to dessert.

Over cookies Josh talked about his job, a promotion he anticipated, a place in Costa Rica he wanted to take Little on vacation. He wanted her to try zip-lining. He wanted her to see some particular kind of monkey they have there. He was on his third Coke, and talking fast. Little sat with a faraway look on her face, and I don't think she was listening to a thing he said. Was he the only person she knew in this country when she arrived? Had she clung to him the way I clung to my children when they were young, snuck into their rooms at night to hear them breathe? When Dr. Ertegun put his arm around me at work one day, early on, I shuddered as if electrocuted and slithered away. His face darkened, and I knew he'd fire me. But instead he waited until late that day, after I'd shut down the computers and was putting on my coat, to apologize and promise me it would never happen again. "I want you to know you're safe here," he said, and he placed his hand very briefly over mine, and never touched me again. There was goodness in him alongside everything else, and there must have been goodness in Josh, too, a hand held over Little's when she needed it.

When he finally paused to take a breath I gathered up the plates and took them into the kitchen. Over Little's protests, I started washing up. In the other room I heard Josh turn on the television. Little and I fell into the easy rhythm of women who are used to cleaning up after everybody else has gone to bed. Her kitchen was neatly organized, and she dried the dishes and put them away, and before long the work was done. I wiped my hands on one of her pretty dish towels and thanked her for the evening.

"I'm afraid it was a little strange," she said. She was still drunk, and the words ran together as she spoke in a way that never happened while she was at work.

"Yes, it was," I agreed. I didn't see any point in denying it.

Little came to me then, her movements sudden and impulsive; she wrapped her arms around me and laid her head on my shoulder. I smelled shampoo and boiled potatoes and wine. She lifted her head to gaze at me searchingly, as if asking me some question that couldn't be spoken out loud; and then she kissed me on the lips, deliberately and without haste; and then she stepped back and smiled at me as if we'd reached an understanding, as if whatever question she'd wished to pose had been answered to great satisfaction. I'd like to tell you that we became close then, that we ate lunch together on the bench outside every day and gossiped and went to the movies on Saturdays. But in fact the next day we showed up at the office, exchanged friendly smiles, and picked up the phones. Maybe we didn't have enough in common, or maybe we had too much. When she and Josh got married at city hall, a year later, the rest of us went in on a floral arrangement and a gift certificate to a nice restaurant downtown, and that was that. When I broke my ankle on sidewalk ice she brought me a card and some soup. I never went to her place again, nor did she ever come to mine. When she quit the practice, because she was having a baby, I wished her well and only later, in the privacy of my living room, did I sit and shake and allow myself to feel the loss of her. I had taken some comfort I can't even explain, some great and durable solace, from the sound of her voice, her swinging earrings and long blond hair. Her body next to mine, the brilliant clatter of her nails as they flew across the keys.

Money, Geography, Youth

I

Vanessa was home. She repeated the word to herself, tucked into her childhood bed, a twin with a pink comforter that barely covered the reach of her adult body and was somehow all the more comforting for that, hoping that if she whispered it often enough, the place would feel like it was supposed to. In Ghana, she'd slept on a cot in a room with three other volunteers, and when she closed her eyes at night she fantasized about luxuries she'd once taken for granted: a long shower, a sweating bottle of Arizona green iced tea. Every two weeks, when the NGO officer swung by and granted them each fifteen minutes of internet access on his laptop, instead of answering emails she browsed the Instagram accounts of her LA friends, gazing at their bright but bleary faces, their arms around drunk friends at parties in the first year of college they were all enjoying. On her own Facebook she'd quickly post some line about how Africa was changing her life, she felt so grateful and humble, and then she'd log off, hunger unmet.

Scrolling back now, she could see that Kelsey's Instagram had been sparser than usual, just an occasional picture of the beach or her cat Max—Kelsey wasn't in college either, unlike just about everybody else—but in Ghana she hadn't been online often enough to notice. Kelsey's emails were pedestrian and stilted *(How are you? I am SO PROUD of you for what you're doing! LA isn't the same without you)* but she was a terrible writer, always had been; Vanessa had been doing her English homework for her since they were twelve years old. Vanessa's father, by contrast, had sent paragraphs-long messages, three or four every time she checked, and which she zoned out while skimming, the same way she zoned out when he talked to her in real life.

Still, she was sure there hadn't been any clues.

When he picked her up at the airport, her father was dressed in his business uniform, a light grey suit with a blue shirt, no tie. He wrapped her in his arms, telling her she was too skinny but looked great, a mix of contradictory messages as usual, and she felt his stubble scrape against her ear; also as usual she felt overwhelmed by his body, his affection, while simultaneously wanting to be held next to it forever. Reflexively she thought, as she had since her mother left, *This is everything I have.* This five o'clock shadow, this not completely effective antiperspirant, this forced but genuine joviality, this *Dad.* They were happy to see each other but still ran out of things to say by the time they hit the 405.

"So your flights were okay?"

"You already asked me that."

"Sorry." He tapped his fingers on the steering wheel, smeared his chin with his palm. He seemed keyed up, thrilled to see her—almost too thrilled to speak—which was gratifying.

"So how's work?" she asked.

"Great. Hectic. Super hectic, really. Kelsey is a huge help."

"Kelsey? Oh, right. The internship. She hasn't flaked on you?"

Her father frowned. "Why would you say that?"

"Come on, Dad. You always said yourself she isn't the most reliable person in the Western world."

This tic of her father's, always to specify a geographical range, as in *This is the best hamburger in the Western world*, used to drive her crazy, until she ate at what she'd been told was the best burger place in Accra and thought, *You know, he has a point*. She meant to tell him this, once he laughed in recognition at hearing her use his own pet phrase. But he didn't laugh. Instead his expression turned serious, and he turned his head to look at her for so long that she was about to say, "Dad, the road—" But then he sighed, glanced back at the traffic, and said, "She's been a godsend," which was not a phrase she'd ever heard him use before in her life.

So she said nothing. The highway rose and fell, the stutter and swerve of traffic as familiar as her own pulse, and beside it palm trees and fast-food signage poked out from the June gloom. The sunset was ebbing, leaving flashes of neon as its hopeful replacements. She wanted a milkshake. She wanted a taco. She wanted everything ice cold or piping hot. To dip her toes in the ocean, to rinse the gunk from her scalp.

As he parked the car in the driveway her father cleared his throat. "There's something I have to tell you," he said, but then didn't say anything. Vanessa had her hand on the door handle, was halfway out of the car, saying, "Tell me inside," because she couldn't wait to see her room, the kitchen with its well-stocked refrigerator, the *bathtub*, and so when he said, "Kelsey's here," she only thought that he'd done this for her, what a sweet gesture, inviting her best friend to welcome her home, and she missed the part or maybe he mumbled it when he said, "We're together," and he had to repeat it on the threshold, as she opened the door to the house she used to call home.

Kelsey was standing in the foyer, wearing shorts and a hoodie, one foot overlapping the other, and she gave Vanessa a hug and said, "I guess he told you! I know, it's so weird," and held up her hand with the engagement ring.

Vanessa thought, *If she says, "We didn't plan it, it just happened," I am going to kill her or myself.*

"It just—" Kelsey started and Vanessa didn't want to kill anybody, so she interrupted and said, heading for the kitchen, "I'm starved."

WHAT FOLLOWED WAS THE LONGEST SHORTEST DINNER OF Vanessa's life: ten minutes spent picking apart snacks that Kelsey had arranged on a platter while Vanessa watched her move around the kitchen. The explanations tumbled out of her father and her friend, each of them completing each other's sentences, her father's large hands gently slapping the table every so often, keen to touch Kelsey's shoulder or hand but holding back, for Vanessa's sake, she could tell. Kelsey had started out working as an intern, become a trusted advisor, and somewhere along the way graduated to girlfriend. They'd kept the relationship secret, because they wanted to tell Vanessa first, and doing it long distance didn't feel right. But now they were happy, happiness spilled from them, sloshed like liquid from a drunk person's glass. Through the scrim of joyful phrases Vanessa eventually discerned that not only were they together, not only were they engaged, but Kelsey was living here; she had moved in months ago.

She ate an olive, a slice of cheese.

Her father said, "You must be exhausted."

Kelsey said, "I know this is a lot."

Vanessa couldn't have said how she felt. There were no words for it. At this same table, her mother had harangued her about grades and boys, had helped Vanessa and Kelsey frost cupcakes for an eighth-grade bake sale. Also at this table, she'd told Vanessa about the affair she'd been having, with a Swiss oncologist named Jonas—"*a man of great purpose and integrity*," she said, as if reading from a certificate of achievement—whom she intended to follow to Europe, to make a life of *intentionality*. Vanessa had been to visit them once, had toured the clinic where Jonas treated poor people who couldn't otherwise afford care, while her mother helped their families. Her mother had let her hair go grey and wore fuzzy sweaters that looked hand knitted, though Vanessa didn't know by whom. Before she departed, Vanessa's mother had kissed her and told her—her voice some-how both urgent and lazy—to let herself be happy. Then she'd added, like an afterthought, "Let your father be happy, too."

Vanessa stood and stretched, rubbing her eyes. "Congratulations, you guys," she said.

2

At least that's over, Graham thought, getting into bed beside his child bride. He didn't ever call her that out loud, of course— she would have been hurt, and rightly so, and anyway they weren't married yet—but he nonetheless thought of her that way, hearing Tracey's sardonic voice in his ear. His ex-wife's imagined commentary was a running counterpoint to his thing with Kelsey. You don't live with someone from senior year of college through your forty-sixth birthday without folding them into your brain. In the three years she'd been gone he'd come to realize that he depended on her judgment just as much as he had when she was still around; depended on it even when he chose to defy it. So he let her speak to him, chide him, mock him when he deserved it. Sometimes he'd be listening to her, and Kelsey would say, "What is it?" She was sharp enough to see through his muttered excuses, but young enough not to question them directly.

Of course it was possible he'd chosen her for exactly this reason.

So yes, okay, fine, Tracey, he was a cliché, patching his shattered ego together with the affections of a beautiful, dark-haired nineteen-year-old. But Kelsey wasn't just some kid. Her character was tough; her life hadn't been easy; she had essentially raised herself. To see how she responded to the simplest kindness was to understand how much had been denied her.

She's your daughter's age, Tracey's voice said to him at the office, when they first started bantering. *Picture Vanessa with one of your friends.* That had pulled him up short. But quickly—so quickly—Vanessa, away in Africa, became an abstraction. And anyway he'd never really understood his daughter, a fact he wouldn't admit to anyone, especially her, especially not after life had made him essentially her only parent. When he'd first met Tracey she was a feminist activist, she went to marches for reproductive freedom in Washington and argued politics for hours and the edge never wore off her, even after decades of marriage and home buying and social work and motherhood. She could always smite you with a phrase; she could wither the world with the moral force of her gaze. When she told him she was leaving, he wasn't surprised; he was only amazed that this restless and sharp-tongued woman had stayed put with him in one place for as long as she had.

Yet in Vanessa they had somehow produced a mild, biddable child, a girl who, when asked what she wanted to do, what her dreams were, once thought over the question and answered gravely, "I'm not sure . . . maybe . . . marketing?"

Then again, after Tracey's departure Vanessa had weirdly not struggled in school at all, had applied herself as diligently as ever, and she surprised everyone, the guidance counselors, Graham, by announcing her plan to do volunteer work in Africa for a year. She said she wanted to do something good for the world. So she deferred NYU and off she went and Tracey whispered in his ear, accusingly and correctly, *You're relieved to see her go.*

He drove her to the airport, he wrote her every other day, he followed the news about Ghana, asked questions about her activities to which he received only the most cursory responses. He worried about her constantly. And then he fucked her best friend.

Who was lying with her back to him now, hunched beneath the duvet, hiding the tattoo of a compass that reached across her delicate shoulder blades. When he'd asked her what it symbolized, she said, "That I have a sense of direction." Kelsey was thin but strong, with black hair that curled around her neck. He brushed it away and wrapped himself around her, feeling her relax back into him, her need soothing his.

"Maybe I should leave," she said. "Maybe it's too weird."

He knew she didn't mean it. He kissed the nape of her neck, the fine hairs there. "You're not going anywhere," he said. "You're mine."

3

In the morning Vanessa woke to a bright, empty house. Only when she walked into the kitchen did she realize that it wasn't morning, but two in the afternoon. The central air kicked on and off in a steady, plush rhythm. She poured herself a glass of juice and wandered around, touching her fingers to things as if to confirm their reality. The kitchen counter, the living room sofa, the bathroom towels. In her father's bedroom Kelsey's clothes hung on one side of the closet; her shoes stood in a rack on the floor. The bed was neatly made. In their bathroom she fingered the pill bottles: her dad's antidepressants, Kelsey's ADD meds. She took a couple of Kelsey's, washing them down with a handful of tap water. By the time she showered and dressed, her brain was pleasantly humming and the colors everywhere felt deluxe. She drove around for a while, just for the pleasure of driving, then stopped at an In-N-Out Burger and ate outside without sunglasses, squinting and chewing. Her teeth felt wooden in her mouth: uncertainly fastened, ready to splinter. She remembered as a child learning that George Washington had wooden teeth. She always wondered what kind of wood and how roughly hewn, and she pictured the first president grinning in lightly carved maple or birch, twigs and leaves gathering at the corners of his mouth. Later she found out this was a myth; Washington's dentures were made from the teeth of slaves. Her mother told her that. She drank a Coke down, then refilled.

"Look who it is," a voice said, interrupting her thoughts. "Miss United Nations."

With some difficulty she focused her gaze on the speaker, who was a boy with shaggy brown hair wearing a navy blue T-shirt with a picture of a baby on it. The baby was smoking a cigar. Out of context—and everything felt out of context at the moment—the boy was hard to place.

"You don't even recognize me," he said. "I'm wounded."

"Who are you?"

"It's Barry," he said. Seeing her empty expression, he switched to a reciting tone. "Barret Oliver Bernstein," he said. "You may remember me from trig, and AP history, and music camp between eighth and ninth grade, and also I think we spent seven minutes in heaven at Jane Rodriguez's thirteenth-birthday party. Man, Africa has made you a *snob*, Vanessa Palkovsky."

"*Barry,*" she said. "God, I'm so sorry. So very sorry. God."

"Are you high?"

"Kind of. Something."

"I didn't even know you were back."

"I just got here," she said. She stood in front of him, drinking her Coke, her mouth worrying the plastic straw, fixated on the almost painful burst of bubbles against her lips, the sweet acid of the drink coursing down to her gut. She opened her mouth to say something else but burped instead, and then shrugged. Her time in Ghana hadn't changed her vitally but it had rendered her temporarily immune to certain things.

Barry laughed. "I'd ask you to sit down, but I don't think you can." Only when she followed his gaze did she understand that her foot was idly kicking the stem of the plastic table where he sat, tapping it in concert with the sips from her straw.

"I was thinking of going to the beach," she said. "Want to come?"

He stood up instantly, crumpling his napkin into a swirl of ketchup. "No offense, but I'd better drive."

In the car he said he was going to community college, which

frankly sucked but was all he could afford after his dad lost his job and emptied Barry's college fund so they wouldn't lose the house.

"I didn't even find out until, like, the last minute," he said. "I thought he'd been working as a consultant for the past two years. He had a home office and stuff."

"Consultant's what old people say when they're unemployed."

"I understand this now," Barry said. They were on the freeway, not rushing freely but moving at a stately, caged pace through midafternoon congestion. Vanessa kept burping, a slow but constant stream. "I was packing for school when he came into my room and said, 'There's something I have to tell you.'"

Vanessa smiled at him for the first time. "Prefaces are the worst," she said.

"There's something I have to tell you," Barry repeated in a stagey tone.

"You're adopted."

"I've been earning a living as a male prostitute."

"Your grandparents aren't in Tacoma. They're in jail."

"I really am adopted, though. I just found that out, too."

"Wait, seriously?" She clapped her hand to her mouth.

"No."

She laughed. The beach was cloudy and windy, the surf flat, and a row of surfers paddled hopelessly in a line not far from shore. They walked for a while without speaking, then sat down in a sheltered spot in the dunes. Vanessa's stomach bucked unhappily. After a few minutes she stood up, walked quickly away from Barry, and threw up her hamburger by some rocks, wiping her chin with the hem of her shirt.

"I'm not used to the food here," she said, sitting back down next to him. Seagulls were already making a feast of her vomit, jostling each other angrily to get at it.

"You're a tourist in reverse," he said. "A stranger in a strange land. Et cetera."

"Don't say *et cetera*," she said.

Her lips were chapped, and she pulled at a shred until it bled, rubbing her reddened fingertip absent-mindedly on her thigh. Farther down the beach a big dog and a small dog were running into the waves, the small dog fearless, the big one hanging back and barking. Which seemed like a metaphor for something, but she was too tired to think of what. Kelsey's pills were wearing off, leaving a headache behind. Barry put his arm around her shoulder; he smelled—she couldn't have said what she meant by this, but the notion was clear in her mind—*American*. For a while she leaned her head against his shoulder, and then she leaned over into his lap and gave him a blow job. When he finished she rested her head on his legs, and he ran his fingers through her hair. It seemed funny that she'd forgotten him, when she'd known him for so long.

4

"There's something I have to tell you," Kelsey heard some-one saying outside. She wasn't eavesdropping—she had the kitchen window open because she hated central air, something she couldn't bring herself to tell Graham, who liked to cool the house to sixty-seven degrees. She'd confessed to him the great-est secrets of her life as if they meant nothing but found it almost impossible to share her small preferences, her littlest needs. Vanessa laughed, a brisk, knowing snort. Glancing quickly outside, Kelsey saw it was Barry Bernstein. Vanessa didn't ask what the thing he had to tell her was, and he didn't go on. She wondered why Vanessa was hanging out with Barry; he was nice enough, but they weren't close friends. He was a little bit emo, he drove a decent car, he wasn't completely unfortunate-looking. In high school he was just there, a landmark without distinction, like a Del Taco you passed every day in your neighborhood. Why would you suddenly stop in and eat?

The door opened, and her best friend came in looking red eyed and splotchy cheeked, her fair skin a collage of pinks. One day back in California seemed to have weathered her more than eight months in Africa had. Kelsey placed her hands on the graphite counter, spreading her fingers as if seeking traction; she'd thought about taking the ring off when she saw how Vanessa looked at it, but couldn't bring herself to. It was her favorite thing she'd ever owned or worn.

"You're allowed to make eye contact, dude," her best friend said. A few years ago they'd started calling each other *dude* in ironic imitation of the bros at their school and then found the habit had stuck with them for real.

"Sorry," Kelsey said. "Do you want something to drink? I was just getting some water."

Vanessa said breezily, "Let's have some wine." She came around the counter, jostling Kelsey casually with her hip, and pulled out a bottle, the opener, two glasses. As kids they'd snuck sips from whatever bottles were open, adding water to keep the levels up. She didn't ask Kelsey whether she wanted any now, just doled out two hefty pours.

"Cheers," she said.

"Listen, Van. I feel like we should talk, or whatever."

Vanessa took a long sip. Her eyes were hazel and steady, her pale hair lank. They used to dye each other's hair with box color but in Ghana her hair had gone back to the uncertain shade she called *blah blond*. She was the calm one, the one with the nice house, the girl adults always said had *a good head on her shoulders*. Kelsey wasn't any of those things. When Vanessa set the glass down, her lips were shiny and wet. "Okay," she said. "Let's talk."

"I just—" Kelsey moved forward into the impossible task of discussing the choice she'd made. "I'm sorry I didn't tell you."

It was the wrong thing to say, she knew, the wrong apology. The right apology was *I'm sorry I'm sleeping with your father and it will never happen again and things will go back to the way they were before*. But she wasn't going to say any of those things.

Vanessa said, "Does my mom know?"

Kelsey was startled. "I don't know," she said. "She didn't hear it from me."

Vanessa laughed. "No, I guess not," she said. She tilted her head to the side, surveying Kelsey, a serious, appraising look, and her eyes grew foggy. Kelsey knew that she was thinking about how long they'd been friends. She knew everything that Vanessa was thinking, just as she could predict that Vanessa would drink half her wine at once and then sip the rest; that Vanessa would buy time in the silence by pushing her hair behind her ears, and then clasping her hands behind her back. She'd seen Vanessa invent these gestures, cobble together a personality from them. Some gestures they'd come up with together; many of them they shared. They had the same handwriting. They wore the same size shoes.

They'd met in middle school, when Kelsey's parents moved to LA from Oregon, and Kelsey Parr was seated next to Vanessa Palkovsky. Was it a friendship, or a habit of long association?

Kelsey wanted to press forward, to dispel the fog in Vanessa's eyes. She wanted to be seen as she was now, an adult, not as the skinny, friendless kid in Walmart clothes on whom Vanessa— Kelsey knew this—had taken pity. "Your dad is such a good guy," she said stiffly. "We make each other happy."

"Dude," Vanessa said. Her tone was of arch amusement. "Keep it in your pants."

"I just wanted you to know," Kelsey said.

"And now I know."

She darted forward and kissed Kelsey on the cheek, the kind of kiss you'd lay on your grandmother or your aunt. Her lips were rough. And then she was gone, carrying her wineglass high as if keeping it above water.

Kelsey drank her glass down and poured another. She'd known things would be weird when Vanessa got back—how could they not?—and she wasn't going to panic about it. With Graham, last night, she'd asked for comfort, because she knew he needed her to; it reassured him to hold her in his arms, murmuring consolations. In the morning they had sex, quietly, and afterward he wore the same look of infused confidence as every boy she'd ever slept with.

In the months leading up to graduation, Vanessa had told all their friends that she was taking a gap year—she kept calling it that, in a pseudo-Euro affectation that Kelsey found more and more irritating—and Kelsey would say, "Yeah, me too. I'm going to spend a year working at the Gap."

"No, but seriously," Vanessa would ask when they were alone, "what are you going to do?" She couldn't fathom that there weren't any enriching life activities on Kelsey's horizons; she couldn't imagine a future that had no plan. The things that drove Vanessa—grades, extracurricular activities, the all-consuming goal of college acceptance—had always felt abstract to Kelsey, the staged rituals of some civilization to which she didn't belong. She wouldn't even have made it through senior year without Vanessa's help, plus the Ritalin, of course.

When her parents were still married, way back when, money was scarce, but then things got a lot worse later. Her mother moved in with a guy named Gary; they both started drinking every day at five thirty and didn't stop until they passed out. They had nothing in common except the drinking, but it seemed to bond them pretty tightly. Also, Gary paid the rent. One day in seventh grade her dad said he had a job in Vegas and disappeared for a year. When he came back, he took Kelsey and her little brother to the park, bought them ice cream from a truck as if they were little kids, and explained he'd done some work for the wrong people, and as a result of that work, he'd be spending the next five to seven years at a federal detention center in Stockton. "It's probably best if you don't visit," he'd said, although neither of them had offered.

When Kelsey discovered the Palkovskys' house, it felt like a TV set: rooms impossibly bright and large, people guffawing at familiar jokes as if on a laugh track. With an exhale of relief she began to spend all her time there, the de facto second child. She didn't cause her own family any trouble. She swallowed her ADD meds in the morning and some illegally obtained Xanax at night. After her high school graduation, she went out to dinner with her mom and Gary at Joe's Crab Shack and her mom said, "Maybe you should think about the army."

Kelsey laughed.

"What?" her mother said. "They pay for your college and stuff."

"I don't think she's interested in a military career," Gary

said. He was right, but everything he said was snide. He'd made it clear that she'd have to find her own place to live soon; he'd bought a pool table on eBay and wanted to put it in her room.

"Maybe Dad can hook me up with something," Kelsey said.

Her mother sputtered, as Kelsey had known she would. "Don't even *joke*," she said.

And that was the extent of their conversation about college.

Vanessa was so alarmed by Kelsey's lack of a plan that she arranged for Kelsey to work for her dad. He was a headhunter and most of his work involved meeting clients; he was always out for lunch, drinks, coffee. In his absence, Kelsey filed and answered the phones. She updated the website. She emailed follow-up surveys to recently placed clients and employers and categorized their responses. Despite her complete lack of invest-ment in the work, she looked forward to going to the office every day. When he came back from meetings, he'd rehash the meetings for her, imitating the clients, and he was really funny when he did it. She'd always thought he was kind of a fox—he was charming, and he worked out—although she would never have said so to Vanessa.

The first time they slept together, it was at a hotel, because doing it at his house would have been too weird. Afterward he wanted to take a bath together. She was afraid it would be infantilizing and awkward but he was right; it was romantic. Then she stood on the bath mat while he dried her off, working his way downward, until he got to her right foot and frowned. "What's this?"

Her pinky toe looked like it had been chewed on by a dog. There was a split nail that never seemed to grow right. Instead of trying to make it better, she allowed herself to make it worse.

She peeled the skin. She ripped the nail from its bed. As soon as it grew back she started over. The whole toe was always raw and red, rubbing against every shoe she wore, a slice of exposure.

"It's my worry toe," she said. "My theory is, everybody needs to destroy a little part of themselves. If you pick it right, like you do it consciously in a small way, then you're safe from doing it some bigger way. You get it out of your system."

He continued to look at her, his head tilted, as if he were listening to some sound outside the room. *If he kisses my worry toe,* she thought, *this thing is over.* But he didn't. He got a fresh towel, two towels, and wrapped her in both, then draped the hotel robe over that, and she was laughing and saying "Stop," and he wrapped her in every towel in the room, making her a terry cloth mummy, layers upon layers, heavy as a cast, and then he carried her to the bed and unwrapped her like a gift.

5

A month passed and Vanessa and Kelsey did not talk again. They spoke often—had dinner with Vanessa's dad, watched a movie together on the couch—but they never *talked* because, honestly, Vanessa didn't see the point. In high school their history teacher, Mr. Calderón, had habitually used an expression she hated: *It is what it is.* It's a fucking tautology is what it is, Vanessa had wanted to say, but didn't because she was an honors student and that kind of comment gave you a reputation with teachers. Mr. Calderón seemed to think this phrase would soften any terrible historical fact he was required to present to them. The Huns massacred their enemies and raped their women as a technique of intimidation. Not very nice, but *it is what it is.* It used to drive Vanessa crazy, but now it fit her circumstances perfectly. My best friend is going to marry my father. *It is what it is.*

Of course they weren't best friends anymore; now they were related instead. They were cleaved apart and drawn together at the same time.

A few weeks after her mother left, Vanessa dreamed she came back, full of apologies and regrets, a dream so vivid that when she woke up she couldn't believe it wasn't true. Bereft all over again, she padded through the house to her parents' bedroom. Her father, asleep in a T-shirt and boxer shorts, was curled in the fetal position on top of the duvet, the light still on. He'd made a ball of the clothes her mother had left behind and was sleeping with his arms around it. Vanessa could see her mother's blue cardigan, her Orioles sweatshirt, her bathrobe. Her remnants.

Whenever she tried to be mad at her father about Kelsey she thought of that moment and the anger dissolved, re-forming into some cluster of pity and betrayal and confusion that she held like her own ball of rags, thick in her arms.

And there was something else. To her surprise, she'd fallen in love with Barry, a development that soothed and preoccupied her. Barry was always available, as eager to get out of his house as she was hers. He was taking a couple of classes and working at a car dealership but somehow he always picked up his phone immediately, always texted back right away, was always interested in going to a movie or the beach or on a hike. Not that they did those things very much. Mostly they drove around looking for places where they could park and have sex in his Sentra.

They didn't discuss their families. Barry knew about Kelsey—everyone from school had heard, and she kept getting texts of fake concern from the most gossipy girls in her network—but he never asked her about it. In return, she never brought up college, even though she'd be leaving for New York in six weeks. They did each other the kindness of pretending their sore spots didn't exist. When he drove, he put his arm around her and she put her hands on his thigh, his knee, his hip. After they were done having sex they lazed around until they were ready to go again.

By the end of July she'd started spending nights at his house. His dad was too ashamed about the college fund thing to give Barry a hard time, and Vanessa's dad was in a similar state. So they'd crawl into his bed with takeout and watch TV, chewing messily, wiping their hands on the covers. His room, like hers, was schizophrenic, halfway done molting his childhood self. The shelves held old Legos and a chemistry set and a leather bound Torah he'd gotten for his bar mitzvah, and his desk held his work ID and car keys and macroeconomics textbook.

They were watching a TV show about a psychic who solved crimes. Vanessa liked anything about psychics; she was drawn to extrasensory information, any hint that the dead cared what the living were up to. She was lying on her stomach with her face too close to the screen; her mother would have scolded her for it. Barry rubbed her back with his knuckles.

The psychic accused a Botoxed woman in a short dress of having killed her husband. The woman burst into tears, though her expression remained the same.

"Do you think you'll go back to Ghana?" Barry said suddenly.

Vanessa blew some hair from her eyes. "That's a random question."

"I was just thinking. I've never been that far away from home. My mom is afraid of planes so we never flew anywhere, and now there's no money."

She made a vague sound in her throat. She wanted to hear

what the psychic was saying; she was pressing onward, showing the villainous woman no mercy, expositing the crime and
its motives.

"I think it's cool you went," he said.

She wished he would stop talking, and he did. He was sensitive to her silences, one of his many good qualities. She didn't
want to think about travel or departure, or planes, or her own
imminent trip to college. Ghana had been an exercise in failure.
She'd found the program herself, by googling "volunteer in
Africa," and the website had shown adorable children in polo
shirts and khaki shorts being read to by teenagers like her, in
rooms with brightly painted walls. Everyone looked clean and
happy. Of course she'd known the reality would diverge from
this advertisement. But what divergence! The orphanage was
dusty and falling down, and there were no brightly colored
walls with murals of fish and flowers. What she hadn't expected
was how much she hated it there, how tedious the work was,
how hard it was to entertain a sickly two-year-old. She experienced a visceral revulsion to the small bodies, their sores and
runny noses and tears. The other volunteers handled it better;
two of them were hard-core Christians and kept saying they
were so blessed to help God's little angels. Vanessa rolled her
eyes at this and one of them caught her doing it and that eliminated the possibility of friendship. The third volunteer was a
guy from Minnesota who never spoke to adults but came alive
around the kids, tickling them, picking them up and holding
them upside down, shaking them as if to see what would come
out. The children ran to him with their arms out, begging to
be upended. When they saw Vanessa, they stopped and stared
distrustfully, picking their noses. Sometimes she made faces at
them, not nice or funny faces but crazy ones, scary-on-purpose

ones, and they backed away, knowing with their unerring kid instinct that she was an adult to steer clear of.

In turn, Vanessa began to do anything to avoid spending time with them; she mopped bathrooms and built a latrine and peeled vegetables in the kitchen for hours until her hands were red and cracked. Still, she'd stuck it out, the whole seven months of the program, because she didn't want to admit how badly it had gone wrong.

She went to Ghana for her mother, who had always talked about *privilege* and *myopia* and the *cultural self-absorption of the American electorate* and who used to make Vanessa spend every Thanksgiving at the soup kitchen and every Earth Day picking up trash along the Arroyo Seco Trail. Vanessa had thought that going to Africa would get her mother's attention. But after an initial congratulatory email her mother's focus returned to her new life, the one that had so fully absorbed her. Vanessa didn't interest her anymore. And that was just as true in Ghana as it had been at home; she was motherless everywhere.

Barry kissed her neck. "Lie on top of me," she said.

"I'll crush you."

"That's what I want," she said.

He spread himself on top of her body, his hands on hers, his cheek against her ear. His legs on her legs. Her lungs contracted, shuddered with effort. She took short, shallow breaths and waited gratefully for the world to go black.

6

Graham and Kelsey were tasting cakes. They'd agreed on a small wedding, a simple ceremony on the beach. Kelsey had suggested eloping—she thought it would be funny if they got married at city hall and then went through the drive-thru at In-N-Out in a white dress and tux—but Graham was convinced that ultimately she'd look back on it with regret. He didn't want to begin their life together with no sense of occasion. He believed in the need for symbols and trappings, the consecration of moments. Otherwise life was a mess of emotions, fraught and terrible, lacking form to contain them.

Kelsey said, "If it means I get to taste a lot of cake, I'm okay with it."

She joked around about most things to do with the wedding but he sometimes caught her staring at the ring with a look of shocked and tender gratitude. He was sure she cared about all of it more than she allowed herself to show. At the bakery, he fed her vanilla bourbon cake with white chocolate ganache, holding the fork to her mouth, then kissing the crumbs away. The caterer averted her eyes with a politeness that seemed prudish. Anger rose in him, sharp and furious; he thought, *You don't know how I've been starved.*

Kelsey asked for the carrot cake—which was absurd, who would have carrot cake at a wedding, but she could choose whatever she wanted—and the chocolate, and the coconut. She was enjoying herself. The caterer had brought her a piece of paper and a pen to make notes on but she wasn't writing anything down.

"Don't you have any other kinds I can try?" she said.

The caterer was Graham's age, tastefully made up, her hair dyed purple-red like a turning bruise. She got up and returned to their table with two more samples. Kelsey exclaimed happily and set to eating. Sometimes he was amazed at the amount of food she could put away.

"Well," the caterer said, smiling tightly. "Any thoughts?"

"Let's have all of them," Kelsey said to Graham. "A cake bar."

"That sounds festive," the caterer said. "Might I suggest—"

"Or cupcakes," Kelsey went on. "With *sprinkles*." She gripped Graham's leg under the table, then moved her hand up his thigh. He sat rigid.

"Cupcakes are often popular as a second option. In addition to a cake for you to cut, of course."

Kelsey was nodding, smiling at the caterer. "His first wife left him," she said sweetly. "*I'm* the second option."

"Kelsey," he said.

The caterer opened and then closed her mouth. Kelsey said, "Babe, let's go."

In the car she put her legs up on the dashboard, her toes tapping the windshield.

"You're not—"

"Forget it." She waved her hand. "I just wanted to shut her up. Oh man, I ate too much cake."

Later, in bed, he was seized with his own appetite. He rolled on top of her and kissed her until she was ready, then slid inside. Her hands trailed across his back, so lightly he could hardly feel them, then gripped his shoulders as she shuddered. He was sure she enjoyed herself with him but she never seemed to lose control entirely; she stayed inside her body, somehow just beyond his reach. Afterward, doubt sat heavy on his chest. Maybe to her it was all a staged game, a sequence of skits. "Am I being played?" he said.

"Don't say *played*."

"Well, am I, whatever?"

She nestled against him, in the crook of his arm, fitting herself there. Tracey's voice was mute, refusing to guide him. He could not be abandoned to this absence. Kelsey told him not to worry; she was already falling asleep, which she did easily, every night; it was her most childlike attribute. Once he'd asked her what she'd dreamed about and she said she didn't know. "When I wake up, I never remember anything," she said. How he envied her. How glad he was to have her near.

7

Vanessa was leaving. In a week she'd be on the East Coast, a place she'd seen only once, on a brief college tour over a long weekend with her dad. She had a double off Washington Square with a girl named Megan from Philadelphia; they'd already shared pictures on Instagram and agreed on a color scheme for the room. Megan was going to major in art and she took aesthetics seriously. Vanessa hadn't known what to answer when Megan asked about her own major. But when she texted *Unclear*, Megan hadn't seemed fazed. *Excellent. You're opening yourself to the world*, she wrote back.

At home Vanessa repeated this to herself as she sorted and packed her things. She had to fit her whole life into what she could take on the plane. In Ghana, she'd grown wildly posses-sive of the few items she'd brought with her from home, her woven bracelet and track team T-shirt and notebook, things that when she got back to LA seemed shabby and dumb. The expe-rience had taught her that attachment was arbitrary and sepa-rate from value. Or so she thought. When she was with Barry, attachment didn't feel arbitrary at all. As their time together dwindled to weeks then days, they began to talk about the things they'd worked so hard, over the preceding summer, to ignore. Barry spoke about his father, who kept trying to make amends with misplaced gestures: tickets to Dodgers games and hamburger dinners, gifts to mollify a seven-year-old. "I can forgive him for taking the money, but not for lying to me," he said.

"Really?" Vanessa said.

"No. Fuck him for taking the money."

Vanessa told him how she tried to stay out of the house as much as possible but she couldn't not see Kelsey's sandals by the front door, her drink on a coaster in the family room, her dad and Kelsey together, a constantly airing TV show that she couldn't turn off. She could tell that her dad was happy with Kelsey; he cooked meals and asked questions and made jokes like he used to do when she was a kid. If their interactions were pleasant but awkward, they'd always been sort of pleasant but awkward, so it was only a question of degree. They were both watching the calendar, counting down the time to her departure.

She'd come back here. She'd come for Christmas and maybe spring break at first, and over the summers she'd find internships or research opportunities. She was good at applying for things. She'd go abroad junior year, and then grad school in something, anything. She wouldn't live here again.

It was what happened to everybody.

But when she thought about leaving Barry, panic squeezed her breath. On her last night, they drove around listening to music, not talking. Her father had wanted her to stay home and have dinner with him and Kelsey, but she'd said no; understanding that he no longer had any prerogative, he didn't argue. Vanessa was full of tears that somehow refused to fall; her head felt heavy with the quantity unshed.

Barry wasn't saying much, but he held her hand as he drove, curling her fingers up then uncurling them, counting them as if each time fearing a different result. She knew he felt like yet another thing was being taken away from him. But he would never ask her not to go. Like her, he'd been raised not to make demands.

"I want you to come with me," she said suddenly.

He didn't answer.

"I'm serious," she said. "Transfer. There are community colleges in New York."

"Where would I live?"

"I'll get an apartment. You'll live with me."

"Vanessa."

"We can do this," she insisted. Her voice was part whisper, part wail. "We can."

She waited for him to say the practical things: about money, geography, youth. To articulate the internalized thoughts of their parents. Instead, he clenched her fingers into a fist inside his fist, which hurt but at the same time was not unpleasant, and said, "Okay. Yes. Okay."

There would be a plan; they would be together. In a state of exhilarated relief they drove back to Vanessa's. Barry walked her up the steps and they lingered under the porch light, kissing now, sadness waylaid.

"There's something I have to tell you," he said in her ear.

"You've decided to become a woman."

"I am my own twin."

"You killed a man in Mexico."

"I want to marry you."

She stood circled in his arms. The future swept her like a fever.

8

In the bedroom, Kelsey heard voices. Graham was out with a client; he had dinners most nights, and he'd come home clutching his stomach, freaked out about having eaten too much, requiring Zantac and reassurance. She'd finally called her mother and told her she was getting married.

Her mother said, "You marry an older man, you'll wind up being his nurse."

"I don't mind being his nurse," Kelsey said.

"You don't mind *now*," her mother said.

Kelsey hung up. She liked making Graham happy. And she liked living in this house; she liked watching TV on the king-size bed while waiting for her almost-husband to come home. She had solved the riddle of her future, and she was pleased.

When she heard the voices outside—she had the bedroom window open, though when Graham's car pulled up in the driveway she would hurriedly close it, knowing that he'd strip off his jacket and say, first thing, "Is the AC not working? It's hot in here"—she knew it was Vanessa and Barry saying goodbye. Unable to stop herself, she went to the kitchen, closer to the porch, so she could see and hear them better.

Her friend stood in the porch light, wearing jeans and a purple T-shirt she and Kelsey had bought together at the mall before she left for Ghana. It had a spaceship on it, Kelsey remembered, which was funny because Vanessa hated anything to do with sci-fi or fantasy. She wouldn't see horror movies either. She wanted to be tethered to the real. The spaceship had an evil-looking alien inside it who was dropping bombs on a group of stick figures—mom, dad, two little kids, all cowering and running away. Underneath it said NOBODY CARES ABOUT YOUR

STICK FIGURE FAMILY. The T-shirt was so stupid that it made them laugh and laugh. They'd spent most of their time together looking for things to feel superior to.

Barry moved into the light and put his arms around Vanessa's waist. He whispered something in her ear. Kelsey leaned closer, trying to hear. But they'd stopped talking. Vanessa reached her arms around her boyfriend's neck and rested her head against his shoulder. They looked like kids at a middle-school dance, frozen at the end of a slow song. Then she raised her head, smiled at him sweetly, and they kissed. Kelsey held her breath, and it seemed to take all the strength she had to leave the kitchen, granting them their privacy. She walked quietly down the hall and into the bedroom, and although she closed the window and got into bed, pulling the covers over her head, still she could see them and hear them, rapt in the midst of a moment she'd never have.

The Woman I Knew

I FIRST READ MULVANEY'S BOOK, *THE WOMAN I KNEW,* WHEN
I was thirteen years old, an impressionable age. Although I
should say that I was impressionable at all ages, especially where
books were concerned. I wanted books to *press themselves* upon
my body and mind, to change me in every way a person could
be changed. I don't know where I got this idea, as I came from
a home almost devoid of books. My parents were from a small
town in New Hampshire, neither of them with much money,
and my mother worked as a waitress to support my father as he
went through medical school. He became an ER doctor who
tended with meticulous, coiled energy to people like those he'd
grown up with—people in exigent circumstances, with stark,
immediate needs. He bore down on the practicality of things.
Novels, if he'd thought about them at all, would have seemed
frivolous to him—and to my mother, too. In our home books
were instruments: there was a Merck manual, my mother's *Joy
of Cooking,* and not much else.

Mulvaney's book was what my mother called *smut,* though
it had won the National Book Award for fiction the year I was

born. I found it in the fifty-cent box at the local library sale. I was drawn first of all to its cover, which showed an ink drawing of a woman's body, her naked back arched in a parabola. The thick black lines of her shape communicated confidence, as if the artist were someone who understood exactly what he saw. At this time in my life, early adolescence, I was obsessed with the idea of an invisible, unknown spectator—that there was a person watching me, a man, older, who saw something special in me, who was my particular and desired audience. In retrospect I'm very lucky that this attitude didn't get me in more trouble than it did. I read Mulvaney's book over and over; it was how I learned about orgasms and blow jobs; it was also how I learned about language, because Mulvaney was an exuberant stylist, whose long and rhythmic and vibrant sentences cataclysmed into paragraphs, and even now, years after the last time I read the book, there are passages I can recite from memory.

MY PARENTS SENT ME OFF TO STATE SCHOOL IN VERMONT with the hope that my bookishness might transform into something vocational over the course of my degree. There was talk of my being a teacher or going into advertising. My two brothers were well on their way to practical careers; one was going to be a doctor like our father, and the other had declined college and gone to work at the car dealership, where he sold sedans and trucks with cheery, voluble aggression. He already knew he wanted to be rich. I didn't know what I wanted; to me four years seemed so long that there was no point even visualizing what might happen at the end of it. I took my classes, worked at the campus dining hall, and forgot entirely that once I graduated, my student loans would come due and there would be a reckoning.

My roommate was from Southern California, and once the spectacular Vermont fall gave way to cold, dark winter, she fell victim to seasonal affective disorder. She spent each day huddled under her duvet in our room, refusing to go to class, and then she went home in December, swearing never to return. I was thrilled by the idea of my own room; even though I still went down to the hall to the bathroom and showers, this was more privacy than I'd had at home. My family, who thought closed doors were weird, were forever barging into rooms. My brothers came out of the bathroom bragging about what they'd accomplished there; my parents walked around half-dressed and mid-change; they believed that nobody should be precious about the body, which was just another physical fact of the world. So I was disappointed when I returned to campus in January to learn that I'd been assigned a new roommate, also from California, named Iris Dolores. The fact that she had two first names—two *old lady* first names—seemed a bad sign.

But Iris Dolores was not old ladyish. She was twenty-one—having failed out of two previous schools, she was, she told me cheerfully, starting college for the third time—and a drug addict. She'd brought almost no stuff, and her side of the room was decorated only with the thin institutional blanket and pillow provided by the school. She had long dirty-blond hair and wore ripped jeans and a men's button-down shirt with a parka over it, even inside. "You don't mind if I fix, do you?" was the first thing she said to me, and she took out her kit and prepared a needle and shot heroin between the toes of her left foot. I'd been around drug users before—my town was full of them, my father's job was full of them—but I'd never lived with one before. When she was done she lay back against the flat pillow and smiled at me dreamily. "Tell me something good," she said.

I considered. I wanted to do something to jiggle her compo-
sure, while at the same time I resented the feeling that I was audi-
tioning for her. So I said: "Last year there was an avalanche."

She raised her eyebrows—I had gotten her attention.

"Three juniors were snowshoeing on the trails behind Massey
when the snowpack loosened and all of a sudden it just . . .
descended on them. They were buried for fifteen minutes but
fortunately they had enough of an air passage to breathe." It
wasn't technically an avalanche, the school had been at pains
to report, but it was nonetheless a dramatic story that had been
repeated to every incoming student by the current ones, and the
surviving students themselves walked around with an aura of
wan celebrity. Fear of being trapped in an avalanche was one
of the reasons my previous roommate had cited for not getting
out of bed.

"Just to be clear, which is the part you think is good?" Iris
asked. "The avalanche, or the rescue?"

"It's that when you step outside this dorm, anything could
cascade on top of you," I said.

Iris bit her lip, which was chapped, and chewed off some
skin. She did it slowly, as if she enjoyed it, and then she smiled
at me again. I felt I'd succeeded in wresting something from her.

"Anything could," she said.

IRIS AND I LIVED TOGETHER FOR THE REST OF COLLEGE,
first in the dorm and then in a drafty, noisy, second-floor apartment above a pub on Main Street in town. I'd initially assumed
that she'd failed out of her two previous schools because of
her drug habit, but this turned out not to be the case. She was
regimented about her using, compartmentalized and discreet.
With academics she was the opposite—spectacularly lazy and

undisciplined. She went to class spottily, and even if she liked the subject she rarely completed the work. She enrolled in a studio art class and spent hours painting, but didn't show the professor anything she'd done. "I'm not interested in his *verdict*," she said when I asked her why. I assumed that anyone who could afford to be so casual about school must be wealthy, but her financial aid package was similar to mine, and we both had work-study jobs. She used to watch me study at my desk, my head in one hand, my highlighter in the other, as if I were some kind of marvel. I was both embarrassed by her attention and pleased by it. I liked to think I was a good influence—after realizing she wouldn't be able to distract me from my work, she'd sigh and open her own books, at least for a while. At any rate she did better in school in Vermont than she ever had before.

Neither of us went home much. Iris's parents traveled often, and mine had already downsized, with typical practicality, to a two-bedroom condo; when I went back, I slept in the spare room like any other visitor. We nestled in at school. We ate dinner in our apartment by candlelight, drinking Sangre de Toro wine, and lining our windowsills with rows of the little plastic bulls that came with it. We read on the couch, our legs under a shared quilt. Sometimes she crawled into bed with me, and we kissed and touched each other and fell asleep that way, and sometimes we slept separately, and that was fine also. Each of us had boyfriends who came and went, and we never had any discussion about what our commitment to each other was or how far it should extend. It would have seemed beneath us, somehow.

At graduation my parents presented me with a check for five thousand dollars. It was my share, they said, of what they'd saved by selling the larger house I'd grown up in. They hoped I'd use it to get a foothold on my life after school, specific plans for which had yet to materialize. Iris was moving to New York, and I was going with her, because I had no other ideas. The money from my parents was a generous gift, and it was also, I understood, their final one. After this I would be on my own.

Iris's parents came from San Francisco. Her mother, Tamsin, was tall and thin like her, with the same aura of hanging back in judgment, waiting to be impressed, and her father, Gregory, was curious and bossy, wandering around our little apartment, making wisecracks. He laughed out loud at our collection of Sangre de Toro bulls, picking them up and setting them down, and I wanted to shield them from him as if they might break. Then he browsed the bookcase for a while, saying, "I'm guessing these are all yours, right? Iris never read a book in her life."

Iris ignored him. She had her dreamy armor on. She claimed her parents never noticed when she was high, and as far as I could tell, this was true.

"So you're a fan of Iris's dad, are you?" Gregory said.

I was confused. He'd pulled down Mulvaney's book, with the woman drawn on the cover, one of ten or so books I'd brought from home.

"My *bio* dad," Iris corrected mechanically, from the couch. When she saw me stare at her, she shrugged. "I hardly ever see him," she said.

"John Mulvaney is your father?"

Tamsin was sitting at our kitchen table, scene of all our candlelit dinners, smoking a filterless cigarette and picking the tobacco off her tongue with one long fingernail, which seemed both impossibly glamorous and completely affected. She'd been a model in her youth, and she still moved like someone who expected to be looked at.

Of course I'd told Iris how much the book had meant to me. In all our time together, there was nothing of myself—my earnestness, my confusion, my desire to have a different life than my parents', without any idea of what that might look like, or who I might have to be to inhabit it—that I had held back from her. I may even have talked about it while we were in bed together. It was impossible to me that she could have withheld this information.

That night, after her parents were gone, we sat among the cardboard boxes we had begun to pack and passed a bottle of Jägermeister back and forth. One side of the apartment was stacked with all the art Iris had made in college, her sculptures and ceramics and paintings, which she'd been required to clear out of the studio on campus. She wanted to throw it all out, and I'd been trying to convince her to keep at least some. It angered me that she cared so little for these things she'd made.

"You talk about him like he's a legend," Iris said without preamble. "To me he's pathetic. He's a weird little wreck of a man. I haven't seen him in years. I didn't want to ruin your fantasy of him."

I raised my eyebrows at her. I loved Iris, and she was many things—talented, affectionate, fun to be with—but she was rarely selfless. Like most addicts, she was a narcissist, and I'd never had any illusions that she placed other people's feelings before her own.

"What do you mean by *wreck*?" I said.

She pulled out her kit and I shook my head at her, something I never did, and she set it aside. Sighing, she told me things. Tamsin and Mulvaney—she called him Mulvaney, as I did, as if reading his name off a syllabus—had been together on and off throughout her childhood. (They couldn't agree whose last name Iris should have, so they left her with the two first names, Iris after Tamsin's mother, and Dolores after Mulvaney's.) They moved around either for Tamsin's modeling jobs or Mulvaney's writing and research—Paris, Buenos Aires, New York—fighting and breaking up and then reuniting in some new location they thought might solve the problems between them, whatever they were. When Iris turned ten Tamsin declared she'd finally had enough. She moved to San Francisco with Gregory and quit modeling. What Iris remembered from this time was Mulvaney coming to the apartment in Pacific Heights begging Tamsin to take him back. He was homeless, Iris said, and drinking heavily, and his beard was scraggly and he smelled rancid and unbathed. Tamsin, wearing a short purple dress, went down the steps to the sidewalk and told him to leave. He kneeled down on the pavement and took the hem of her dress between his fingers, rubbing it. Tamsin was unmoved. Iris watched him from the window, wanting only for him to disappear.

Which he did—he went to Mexico to dry out and didn't come back for years. She'd seen him only occasionally since then, and they had little to say to each other. For a while he wrote her letters, in ballpoint pen on lined notebook paper, and she found the letters condescending and didn't answer. She considered her father nobody who should offer her advice. He was back in California now, living in Los Angeles, and once or twice they'd had coffee, facing across a small table, making small talk like strangers.

"I think he means less to me," Iris said, "than he does to you."

I didn't know enough then to dispute this statement. Or maybe I couldn't afford to. Iris was my path forward in life, and I took it. We moved to New York together, and Iris got a job at an art gallery and I went into teaching, as my parents had suggested. I taught at a high school in Brooklyn that was under-resourced and overcrowded. The students slept in class, they fought each other, they were angry and often hungry and when they didn't see the point of being in school I was hard-pressed to explain it to them. I came home at the end of each day more exhausted than I'd ever been in my life. Iris went to parties, and I did lesson planning. There were no more candlelight dinners. She stopped doing heroin and started taking Adderall, which helped her stay up late and charm buyers and artists. She was very good at it and soon got promoted. She had beautiful clothes. I wore chinos and cardigans from Old Navy, and every month I swore I wouldn't dip into the savings account I'd started with my parents' money, and every month I did. Some people swim in New York and others drown, and Iris and I no longer made sense together as we had in school. I lasted in the city eighteen months before I moved home.

PEOPLE USE THE PHRASE *LOST TOUCH* AS IF IT'S A CASUAL negligence instead of what it can also be: a grief, a lack. At least that's how it was for me. Iris and I lost touch when I left the city, because whatever strands wove us together in college no longer held, and as much as it felt inadvertent—there was no falling-out, no ill will—it also felt deeply sad. I lived in New Hampshire, not far from where I'd grown up, and taught middle school, and it turned out that I was better with younger kids, at ease with their awkwardness, their protean flashes between childhood and adolescence. I saw my parents every two weeks and babysat my brothers' children. I started paying off my student loans; I joined a food co-op; I wore clogs. I dated a few women, and then I was with a man named Lucas for five years and almost married him, and then he got a job in Chicago and asked me to move with him and I realized I didn't want to go.

I heard from Iris occasionally, enough to know the facts of her life if not the animating spirit inside them. She returned to California to direct an art gallery there. Tamsin and Gregory divorced, and Tamsin remarried another wealthy businessman Iris called the Oligarch instead of using his name. She never mentioned Mulvaney. I was buying groceries at the co-op when I saw a flyer on the community bulletin board advertising a talk at the local college. They often put posters up for their chamber music concerts or history lectures, and I would glance at them on my way out, thinking I should go and then never going. But this poster was for a reading and talk with their visiting writer, John Mulvaney, celebrated author of *The Woman I Knew* and other novels. Next to the author photo—a serious, bearded man in a turtleneck—was an image of the same book jacket that had mesmerized me at the age of thirteen, the woman seen from behind, her rounded back, its thick black outline.

I had to go. I drove to the college on a Wednesday evening in March. It was just after the time change and the lightness in the sky felt like an astonishment, a reprieve. My hands on the steering wheel prickled with sweat. The talk was held in the library, in a small room with an unlit fireplace. I sat at the back, the oldest person there. When Mulvaney entered with a professor and they took their places in two wing chairs by the fireplace, I scrutinized him intently. He was stooped—he must have been seventy-five—but he looked prosperous and healthy, in a collared shirt, cable-knit sweater, and corduroy pants. He could have been a retired oncologist. There was nothing in his posture of the derelict Iris had described, down on his knees on a San Francisco sidewalk. In his introduction, the college professor described Mulvaney's career and all the books he had published since *The Woman I Knew*. I had never read or even thought about his other books—they never existed to me—and I was brought up short by this evidence of my lack of curiosity. Mulvaney read for fifteen minutes from his latest novel, about a man whose son commits a crime, and who covers it up. The man and his wife disagree about the ethics of this, and in the passage he read, the two of them fight toward the brink of divorce. The wife was described as elegant and stubborn and I couldn't help but wonder whether she was based on Tamsin, even knowing that there were vast swaths of Mulvaney's life I knew nothing about, perhaps even other wives.

Mulvaney's voice was rich and melodious. When he read the dialogue, he shifted tone slightly so that it was perfectly clear which person was speaking. He was a practiced reader of his work, and the room was silent in that specific way that indicates collective attention. I felt utterly immersed in the story, wondering what I would do in the situation he described, and also judging the characters as if they were real people—I found the husband bullying, and the wife high-handed, and my sympathy with each of them wavered and revolved. When he stopped reading, I let out an involuntary groan—an *oh!*—because I wanted the scene to keep going, and the students in the audience turned around to look at me, and I flushed.

Then there were questions. Evidently the students had been reading Mulvaney's work in class, and their questions extended beyond what they'd just heard. Some asked about his writing process, and his influences. Others picked apart the themes and subject matter of his work, with impressive sophistication. I was taken aback by the breezy confidence of their tone, which I could never have adopted when I was in school. A young woman with purple hair asked him about the objectification of women in his books, specifically *The Woman I Knew*, and how it reduced the main character to the sum of her sexuality and nothing more. Hearing it phrased that way, I couldn't deny it was true. The novel follows a woman who has an affair with a man at a hotel where they're both staying for a week. She is younger, less experienced, at times even unwilling. The man pursues her, then abandons her. Much of the book is devoted to his ambitions as a painter, and how the affair galvanizes his creativity; there is nothing in the book about her ambitions at all. And yet—when I'd read it, as a young teenager, I'd noticed nothing of that. I'd read the sections about the woman's body, her frank and complete enjoyment of sex, how the affair, to her, had nothing to do with wanting love or marriage or romance but about *feeling something important*, a craving for experience for its own sake. To me it had been a manifesto, an instruction manual, enlarging rather than reducing the possibilities of my life.

And what had my life actually become, as a result? Was I so free, so full of possibilities? Maybe I'd read it wrong. I felt angry at the student then, a fury that escalated fast, arising out of defensiveness—not about Mulvaney but about my own young self.

Mulvaney wasn't angry. He answered each question openly, wittily, often making the students laugh. To the young woman who asked about objectification, he nodded in agreement.

"You're absolutely right," he said. "I don't disavow the book, but I see it as an artifact of its times, and a very limited one at that. I would write a different version of it now. But of course that kind of book, a novel exploring female sexuality, isn't mine to write anymore, if it ever was. It's yours. I look forward to reading it."

The student tilted her head, if not persuaded, then silenced.

Afterward there was a book signing. I hadn't brought my copy of *The Woman I Knew*, which I still owned. Instead I lined up behind the students and bought the new one, about the parents with the criminal son. I kept letting other people in front of me, and watching how Mulvaney interacted with them. He took his time with the students, often following up on a question they'd asked, or asking about their own writing. They seemed less flattered than accepting; they took his attention for granted.

When at last it was my turn, I gave Mulvaney my name. "Are you a student here as well?" he asked.

"No," I said, my throat constricted. "I live nearby . . . I know Iris. We were at school together."

A slight ripple passed across Mulvaney's face before he smoothed it away.

"Ah," he said. "Lovely of you to come."

He asked my name, and wrote it in firm, blocky handwriting, in a blue ballpoint pen. Then he signed his name in much larger, firmer flourishes, and handed the book back with a smile, looking for the next person in line. But I was last. The professor-host hovered anxiously at his side. I thought of what I might say to him, how to explain everything his book had brought me, or failed to. Perhaps every reader felt this deeply about his work, but I refused to believe so. There had to be something between us that was entirely mine.

"How is she?" I said.

Mulvaney sighed and capped his pen. "I suppose she's all right. As you know it has not been easy for her. And the child's condition came as a surprise, so there weren't supports in place at first. I'd suggested she take advantage of the prenatal testing, given her habits . . . Well, as you know, Iris does as she wishes. I just try to be as helpful as I can."

"Yes," I said. The ripple crossed his face again, and he looked at me doubtfully. I could see that he was tired, and had talked too much that evening, and probably regretted what he'd just said. In her emails to me Iris had never mentioned a baby, or a troublesome diagnosis, or a closeness with Mulvaney that would involve him helping her. But she'd always shared with me only a part of her life, whichever part she chose.

"Thank you for coming," the college professor said, and whispered something to Mulvaney about a dinner reservation. He stood up, gripping the arms of the chair for support, and in that moment he seemed a great deal older, and more fragile. I couldn't bring myself to leave. I watched them edge away from me in discomfort. The students had already gone. I was alone in the library, holding the copy of Mulvaney's latest book, and I found I didn't want it. I left it there.

Something About Love

LEWIS DARK LOST HIS WIFE IN A FIRE. LESS THAN A YEAR later he was living with Vicky, who was divorced and had primary custody of three children aged four, seven, and ten. People said—sometimes to his face—that she was taking advantage of him in his state of grief; that she was after his money, which he made selling high-end espresso machines to restaurants. People said she didn't even try to control the children, who ran and shouted through the rooms of his now-crowded home. It was true they were noisy, but Lewis liked noise. It drowned things out, and he wanted to be drowned.

People didn't know that he had pursued Vicky, not the other way around. He was driving home from work one day when he saw a woman standing at a bus stop, crying. Traffic was heavy and he edged alongside her, registering the scrunched spasms of her face. It had rained earlier in the day and she leaned on a long, rolled-up umbrella as if it were a cane. To cruise slowly past a stranger crying seemed to him heartless. At the next light, he turned and circled around the block, but by the time he made it back, the bus had ferried her away.

The next day he drove past the bus stop again, at the same time, but she wasn't there. He spent his days in the car, driving from one restaurant to the next, taking meetings and arranging demonstrations of the Mostro Dolce, which was a sleek steel behemoth retailing for twenty-five thousand dollars. The machine's espresso was so good it spoke for itself, Lewis always said, but he spoke anyway, to earn his keep. He'd make a single espresso for the restaurant owner and point out the velvety *crema* at its surface. He talked about authenticity and depth of flavor. And then he would point at himself, with a self-deprecating smile, and tell the owner that the machine was idiot-proof: "I just made you a world-class espresso, and I am an idiot."

The owner would laugh a little.

"Trust me," Lewis would say. "I really am."

The crying woman at the bus stop roosted in his thoughts. She was not an especially attractive woman—thirties, wan—dressed in a bulky cable-knit cardigan and jeans. He took to driving past the bus stop at different times of day, sometimes going far out of his way to do so. It was weeks before he saw her again, and at first he wasn't sure it was the same woman. She was wearing a flowered dress and vaping, and only her hair, blond and curly, was the same. When he pulled up in front of the bus stop and rolled down the window, strawberry vapor wafted into the car.

"Excuse me," he said, "do you need a lift?"

The woman did not make eye contact. She lifted her mouth to the sky and exhaled fruit.

"I'm not a psychopath," he said, wondering, as he spoke, whether this was something a psychopath would say.

She ignored him, and he flushed.

"Sorry," he said, and rolled up the window. He sat in the car with his hands shaking on the steering wheel. The light turned red and stayed red for ages. He was about to press the gas when there was a tap on the passenger-side window and the woman slid in beside him.

"You don't look dangerous. Your car smells like coffee," she said.

"It's espresso," he said.

"Well," she said, "tell me all about it. Who are you? What is your story? Tell me everything. And don't lie—I always know when someone's lying." This turned out to be true. He once saw her reduce a store manager to tears as he admitted that an item had been mis-tagged.

THEY MOVED IN TOGETHER TWO MONTHS LATER. VICKY WAS not at all the dowdy, depressed woman he had first imagined. She was the kind of woman of whom her friends said, "She's a force of nature." She started him on kombucha and took him off dairy. She was stricter with him than she was with her children, whose autonomy she stoutly defended. "They're free to make their own mistakes," she often said when they refused to go to bed at a reasonable hour. He didn't want to admit that he'd seen her at the bus stop weeks before they met, for fear of seeming like a stalker, and so he could never ask her what she'd been crying about. It was all right, he thought, not to know everything about a person. To save a little mystery for later.

VICKY WORKED AS A WAITRESS BUT HER PASSION WAS POD-casting. She wanted to be the Beyoncé of podcasting, or the Kim Kardashian. She converted the garden shed in his backyard into a recording studio, and she spent hours back there working on her programs. She had several different podcasts: one was about cooking, one about celebrity crushes. The most successful one was called *My Terrible Family*, and in it she interviewed people about their awful childhoods. A steady stream of people tromped through the backyard to share their stories. Lewis tried to listen to her podcasts, to support her—he played them as he was driving around in the car—but there was something strange about Vicky's recorded voice, how it varied in tone and pitch depending on which podcast she was hosting, as if she were a different person each time. Every episode of *My Terrible Family* opened with a monologue that was intimate in the extreme. Once she told a long, explicit story about how bad the sex had been with her ex-husband. "Do you think he'll mind?" Lewis asked her.

"Mind?" Vicky burst out laughing. "Mind! You don't know him." She walked out of the room, still laughing.

The ex-husband, Stan, was a chestnut-haired Pole who had worked as a plumber before a back injury put him out of work. He subsisted on disability checks and defaulted on his alimony, but lavished his children—he came to pick them up on Wednesdays from Lewis's house—with a tenderness of affection that was almost embarrassing to watch. He caressed their cheeks with his fingers, and sometimes he wept. "I missed you, my darlings," he would say, grabbing at their hands. The children ran from him, laughing, and Lewis was never sure whether they were being cruel or whether it was a game. Or both. Stan was very friendly to Lewis, whom he thanked for putting "such a nice roof over kids' heads." He was friendly to Vicky, too, and never said a bad word about her. "I am happy," he told Lewis gravely the first day they met, "that she meet a rich man."

Lewis had never thought of himself as rich—the restaurateurs he saw at work were so much flashier, with their gold watches and sports cars—but in comparison to Vicky and Stan, who had lived lives of struggle and want, he knew that he was. He enjoyed bringing home toys for the children, and buying them the particular brands of shoes they believed were crucial to their social success. In return, the children seemed to like him. The youngest hung on him, sometimes clinging to his calves as he walked, shrieking with pleasure. The ten-year-old asked for help with homework, money for lunch. "Thank God," he said drily one day, "there's finally a grown-up around here."

Lewis could see what he meant. Vicky *was* like a child at times: bossy, impetuous. He understood why his friends, who were long settled in their marriages and routines, couldn't see her appeal. But Lewis liked everything about Vicky, her weird opinions and fearless enthusiasms; how she brought him bee pollen tea before bed, swearing it would cure all his ailments; how she kissed her children good night and then blew on their hair, so that the wind would carry them to sleep.

ONE NIGHT, WHEN HE WAS HAVING A BEER WITH HIS FRIEND Brian, he ran into Stan, who was sitting at the bar staring at an empty shot glass. He looked so lonely that Lewis invited him over to the table. Brian was an investigator for the government—he always called himself an investigator, though really he was a data analyst, combing through documents for patterns that might indicate tax corruption—and he shook Stan's hand with a quizzical look.

Stan sat down, muttering thanks. "It's a bad night," he said. "My wedding anniversary."

"Oh," Lewis said.

"Too awkward to say? Sorry," Stan said. "I hope you know, I am happy for you and Vicky. She and I—it wasn't good."

"But you can still be sad."

"Yes," Stan said, his eyes watering. "I can still be sad." Lewis went to the bar and bought him another drink, and when he came back, Stan and Brian were talking about women. Brian was married to Aviva, whom he'd met at camp when they were both fourteen years old. He'd never been with anyone else.

"You regret this?" Stan said.

"Never," said Brian. He sat back in his chair, rubbing his chest. "Oh, we have our issues. I don't make the bed the way she likes. She talks too much in the morning. She's always trying to tell me her dreams. *What do you think it means?* It doesn't mean anything, it's a fucking dream, it's your brain having a garage sale, getting rid of stuff it doesn't need. But you know what"— here he pointed a finger at Stan—"that's life right there. That's life." He was drunk.

Stan nodded slowly. "I often dream about my mother," he said. "She has been dead a long time but I loved her very much."

"My friend," Brian said, "you're missing the point."

AFTER THIS NIGHT, STAN BEGAN TO JOIN THEM REGULARLY. IT was a strange friendship but Lewis welcomed it. Brian grated on him, always leaning forward precisely twenty minutes into the conversation to ask him, in a meaningful tone, how he was. With Stan there, the conversations shifted. Stan was a philosophical person. You asked him how his day had gone and he'd respond with some thoughts on the meaning of life. He didn't follow politics or sports. Once he reached into the pocket of his shirt and unfolded a piece of paper on which he'd written a poem. He read it to Lewis and Brian, but it was in Polish. Nonetheless, they praised its musicality.

Lewis had worried that Vicky wouldn't approve, but she only waved her hand and said, "Go with God." The children loved that he was friends with Stan. They called Thursdays "Dads Night." "The dads are going out!" they said. Otherwise they called him Lewis, not dad, and hearing this made Lewis feel warm, a warmth that was part shame, because it did not yet seem deserved.

Stan told him and Brian details of his marriage to Vicky that would have bothered Lewis if he hadn't already heard them on the podcast. He talked about their sex life, about explosive fights they'd had. "Are you saying you were abusive?" Brian asked, sitting up straight in his chair. He was always on the alert for malfeasance. Stan shook his head.

"One time only, she slap me and I punch a wall," he said. "Still, it was very bad. Kids say, why is there a hole here? I say there is a plumbing problem but it's fixed. We hang a picture over it." The picture now hung in Lewis's living room. It was a watercolor Vicky had made, of a bowl of fruit, washed-out apples and oranges floating against a dark background as if in space. Stan was crying again. He told the story of how he hurt his back, falling down a flight of stairs at work and fracturing two vertebrae, and how he remained in pain that doctors said would never go away. It was such a woeful story that it sobered them up. When he saw their sad looks, Stan grimaced as if their pity were worse than anything else that had happened to him. "Now I no work, I cannot pick up my little boy. I am less a man."

"You're still a man," Lewis said.

"I said *less*," Stan said.

When the evening ended they stood up and shook hands gravely. This was a formality instituted by Stan and which they now all three observed. Lewis thought he and Brian both could learn from Stan. Despite his sorrow, he maintained certain graces.

AT HOME, VICKY WAS JUST COMING IN FROM THE BACKYARD. She'd been recording the celebrity podcast, in which people recounted real or near encounters with the famous.

"How was it?" Lewis asked her.

She rubbed her eyes. "Ridiculous. This guy I met, he wants to tell a story about being pulled over by a cop who looked like Erik Estrada. I try to tell him, this isn't about people who *look like* celebrities. It's about *real* celebrities. I mean, it's not that hard to understand, is it?"

"You met this guy where?"

"On the bus. So then he tells a story about meeting Boris Johnson at a bar in New York. I go, 'Who is Boris Johnson?' He goes, 'It's a British politician.'" She said *British politician* like a swear. "I say once again, 'Guy, this is a show about *real celebrities*.' Then he storms out."

"Weren't we talking about getting you a car?"

"You know I don't mind the bus. It's a cross-section of humanity, and I can fall asleep if I'm tired."

"A lease is pretty affordable, car-wise."

"Oh Lewis," she said, leaning across the bed and kissing him. "You are too much."

At night Vicky turned her back to him and faced the wall. She slept deeply and well. He often sat up in the dark, not reading or watching TV, so as not to disturb her. He could have gone into another room but her presence soothed him, her nighttime smell of strawberry and light sweat, even when he couldn't himself sleep. Sometimes he put a hand, very gently, on the small of her back. Once she'd turned over and asked him what he was doing. He answered honestly—knowing she'd detect any lie— that he was making sure she was breathing. Vicky nodded and went back to sleep. She didn't mind being watched over. She let him study her, and all through the night he quietly attended to the slope of her shoulders, the pump of her heart and lungs.

IT WAS LEWIS STAN CALLED FROM THE HOSPITAL. LEWIS WAS in the car, on a high after having sold three Mostro Dolces to a restaurateur planning to open a mini-chain of steak houses. The restaurateur had insisted they sample the grappa he'd brought back from Italy, and Lewis knew better than to say no. The restaurateur poured shots and chanted numbers: the exact temperature to which a grill should be heated, the perfect climate to grow grapes, the number of minutes that pizza dough should rest. He believed all food was numbers. Lewis said that Vicky would love to interview him for her podcast. "Her what?" the restaurateur said, and Lewis dropped it. Now he was sitting in his car, drinking a slushie and sobering up.

On the phone Stan's voice was somber, but his voice was always somber. It took a while for Lewis to understand what he was saying. "Was there an accident?" Lewis said. His heart was beating too fast, and his ears felt clogged.

"No accident," Stan said. "Sad to say. You please come to the hospital."

"I can't," Lewis said. "I can't drive right now."

"Okay," Stan said.

"Can you call Vicky?"

"Vicky!" Stan said. "Vicky!" It was the exact same tone in which Vicky had said "Mind!"—an impossible astonishment garnished with love.

Lewis gave in. "I'm on my way," he said. When he looked in the rearview mirror, he saw his mouth was ringed with blue from the slushie, and his eyes were bloodshot. He looked like the site of an accident himself. He drove carefully along side streets, already regretting his actions. The hospital was west of downtown, in a seedy area populated with check-cashing stores and methadone clinics. One time Vicky had told him about walking through that neighborhood with her kids, on the way to the hospital—the youngest had an appointment with a doctor there. There were people hanging around the entryways and street corners and when they saw Vicky coming they called out "Kids! Kids!" so that everyone would stop doing drugs as the young ones passed by. Today he didn't see anybody doing drugs; it was rainy and he couldn't make out much of anything through the whir of his wiper blades. He texted Vicky to say he'd be home late. *Picking Stan up from the hospital.* When he went inside, he couldn't remember Stan's last name.

"He's Polish," he told the receptionist, who rolled her eyes.

Eventually they worked it out. Stan was on the second floor, in a room with three other men. He had an IV but no signs of injury. As Lewis walked in, his phone beeped with a text from Vicky. *Don't bring him here,* it said.

Stan was pale, reclined. Reddish-brown chest hair sprouted above his hospital gown. He acknowledged Lewis with a grave nod, like a dignitary. "I had no one else," he said.

Lewis would have liked to sit down, but there was nowhere to sit. The other men in the room were silent, eyes closed, medicated or comatose. "What happened?" he said.

Stan said, "I took pills. Not the first time. This, you know, is why Vicky left me. She said bad for the kids. I agree with her."

Lewis had a hard time absorbing this information. Vicky hadn't told him anything about it, nor had she ever mentioned it on her podcast. Stan's tone was resigned and impartial, an observer to his own behavior. "I have some problems," he said simply.

"We all have problems," Lewis said. Anger welled in him, thickened his voice. "You have children."

"True, true," Stan said.

Lewis had the urge to punch him. He looked around the room, as if searching for a weapon—there was nothing on the walls, the floor was dirty, it was not a good hospital, it was a hospital for people who couldn't afford to be in the hospital and ought to do anything to avoid it.

"You know my wife died," he said to Stan.

Stan nodded. "Vicky told me."

"She was on vacation with her sister, in the Bahamas. They got a deal on a vacation package. A cheap hotel without proper fire exits. Her sister was downstairs in the bar. She made it out. My wife didn't."

"I am sorry," Stan said.

Lewis stepped closer to Stan. He could see large black pores on Stan's nose, a streak of grey in his eyebrows. He didn't talk about how he and Gabrielle had fought on the way to the airport, how he'd felt abandoned and she'd said he was controlling, how they'd made up on the phone later—this was why her sister was downstairs in the bar, giving them some privacy—as he told her how he missed her and her body, and her breath came ragged and heavy and beautiful in his ear, and how she said abruptly, "I should go, something's going on here," and he didn't hear anything from her the rest of the night, only waking to the news the following morning, and he hated almost more than anything the fact that he had slept through the hours of her death. He said to Stan, "You are an asshole."

Stan nodded. "I am an asshole," he agreed.

There was no fighting with him. A nurse came and disconnected the IV. Stan signed some forms and was released. These seemingly simple actions took hours to accomplish and it was midnight by the time they pulled up to Stan's apartment. Lewis's drunkenness had dissipated, leaving behind a strangely giddy mood. Sometimes he felt this way, when especially sleep deprived. A sort of buoyancy would set in, an exigent positivity about the world. He followed Stan inside and drew out a chair for him, like a host. "You should have something to eat," he said. Stan, meek and docile, agreed, and Lewis found a can of Campbell's soup to microwave. On the yellowing refrigerator Stan's kids smiled gamely in school photos, their hands positioned on weirdly staged props—a steering wheel, a tree branch. They had Stan's reddish-brown hair but Vicky's small upturned nose and round eyes. It must be weird, he thought, to see parts of yourself replicated in another person. Like catching a glimpse of your future, a ghost haunting you in advance.

"I want to give you something," Stan said behind him. "As thanks." From a bookshelf in the living room he pulled a thin blue paperback. It was in Polish. On the back, there was an old black-and-white picture of Stan, reedy and windswept, standing on a bridge in a peacoat. His legs were crossed at the ankle and his crooked smile, half a grimace, was recognizably the same.

"These are your poems? I wish I could read them."

"Just take," Stan said. "Please. I think I will sleep now." He staggered to the couch, where he evidently slept, and lay down with his hands beneath his cheek, like a child. Lewis found a blanket and laid it over him. Stan was already asleep, his breath deep and regular. Apparently like Vicky he was a good sleeper. Their marital nights must have been peaceful, Lewis thought. He found himself imagining them in bed, young and undisturbedly asleep, and the thought was pleasant to him. Picturesque. For a while he sat next to Stan and listened to him snore, and then he went home, thinking of Vicky crying at the bus stop, probably after a night like this one.

His house was quiet and full of people. He turned on a lamp in the living room and opened his laptop. He tapped at the keyboard, putting Stan's poems into an online translation program. The results were fractured and metaphysical. Something about a moon and a garbage truck. Something about love. Something about a woman in an apartment building, cooking, and he wondered if this was Stan's mother, back when she was alive. A clown pulled on his shoes and danced. It wasn't clear to Lewis whether this image was happy or sad, what it was supposed to mean. Maybe a clown dancing was an expression in Polish, like a fat lady singing. Lewis found he preferred not to know. He was not the slightest bit tired. He was awake and alive. He was going to stay up all night.

FMK

WE'D BEEN TO THIS FUNERAL HOME TWICE BEFORE—AT
least, I think we had? I guess it sounds heartless but they blend
together, the signs calligraphed with the family name, the floral
arrangements and folded programs, the standard chairs in the
standard rows. Even the silence feels uniform in these places.
They must all use the same soundproofing.

I followed Cat inside, making intermittent eye contact with
strangers and smiling a closemouthed half smile, the facial
expression that is also uniform at funerals. Mr. Braverman's
service was standing room only, and we took positions at the
back. It was nice to see an overflowing crowd; I hate the funerals with just a few souls huddled in their misery like animals
outside in a storm. Here I saw little kids dressed up and fidgety
in the second row. Some people don't like children at a service
but I think it helps everyone to remember the promise of youth
in the world. I don't know what it's like for the kids. An elderly
woman in pearls entered the room, and from the way heads
swiveled in her direction I took her to be Mrs. Braverman. Her
clothes, though elegant, looked at least a size too large, bought
for a woman she used to be. Her eyes were hooded and vacant

until they lit on Cat, who stepped forward, and they hugged for a long time.

"Thank you for being here," Mrs. Braverman said as they let go, and Cat said, "Of course."

The widow's eyes grazed across me and Cat added, "This is my friend Sonia."

Mrs. Braverman bobbed her head and moved on. I didn't bother to tell her I was sorry for her loss; my presence didn't matter and neither would my words. We came for the hug between her and Cat, who had located Mr. Braverman's most accommodating vein and rubbed his necrotic feet and emptied his catheter bag and washed his wasted body and left the imprint of Mrs. Braverman's lipstick kiss on his cheek when he died. Cat was here for Mrs. Braverman. I was here for Cat.

THE FIRST TIME I MET CAT SHE WAS OUT WITH HER WORK friends at the Red Sombrero and they were all drunk off their asses. I was with my work friends, too, but we were admin assistants too poverty-stricken and subservient to cause much of a ruckus—if one of us spilled beer on the table another would rush to wipe it up. I'd been at the job a month and wanted desperately to be promoted, if I didn't die of boredom first. I'd spent my twenties playing in a band, with nothing to show for it, and now I wanted a steady income and benefits, I wanted to buy a condo and adopt a dog. Sleeping in a real bed night after night still seemed like a luxury to me, a dangling prize that could be snatched away at any time.

Nonetheless I couldn't help turning my head when I heard those women whooping and hollering on the other side of the bar. They were playing the most reckless and violent game of darts I'd ever seen. Darts bombed the wall below the target.

One woman took a hit to the thigh, howling with pain, and the others only shrieked with laughter. When our waitress, with whom I'd been low-key flirting, brought our second round, I tried to offer her some sympathy.

"Rough customers over there?"

She glanced over, shrugged. "Every Friday they tear the place up. You can't say anything to them, though."

"Why not?"

"Because of where they work." She jerked her head to the side. "Up the street. You know they have to cut loose."

I didn't know what she meant—this wasn't my neighbor-hood—but Molly, who sat in the cubicle three down from mine, was nodding vigorously. "Makes sense," she said.

"What makes sense?" I said.

Molly dropped her voice. "Hospice."

A dart sailed across the bar and landed near my shoe. I picked it up and carried it over.

"You have a license for this thing?" I said. The nurses were busy yelling at each other about what shitty throwers they were, and not one of them acknowledged me or took the dart back. I lingered there, like an idiot. Finally one of them turned and said, "Oh shit, sorry," and grabbed it, but I held on. She was wearing dark blue scrubs with a long-sleeved white T-shirt underneath, and shiny white soccer shoes, and she had long straight black hair that was also shiny. In my memory all of her was gleam-ing. She tried to take the dart from me and I wouldn't give it until she told me her name. When I let go, my palm was pricked with blood.

We live together now in Cat's condo with a dachshund named Murray who has hip dysplasia and a terrible personality and whose presence in our lives is my greatest regret. I know

I'm lucky to have such a manageable regret. I'm lucky in a lot of ways.

MR. BRAVERMAN'S SERVICE WAS DELAYED. SOME PEOPLE UP front were fiddling with a laptop, conferring in anxious whispers. In my opinion multimedia at a funeral is always a mistake. Cat was humming a low tuneless song. She can walk hand in hand with someone to their last breath on this earth but funerals give her so much anxiety she takes a shot of NyQuil and a Xanax before we leave home. One of the little kids started crying and complaining, there was a scuffle involving a folding chair and the harsh whisper of a mother simultaneously pissed off and embarrassed, and around us people shifted uneasily. The mom gathered the kicking kid in her arms and tried to exit the room, but they were on the far side, away from the door, and the kid wasn't going easily, and he was too big and squirmy for her to carry, and he kicked an old lady's chair and *that* was a thing—but then the strains of Barber's Adagio for Strings issued into the room and people sat up straighter and quieted. The mom rounded the back, dragging the kid, who was trying to plant himself on the floor or something, and I could feel Cat trembling with discomfort, her hands fisted like grenades. No one was helping the mom, who continued scolding her child ("Jake, you are in *serious trouble*") at escalating levels of shit-losing.

I don't know anything about kids, but I've hauled many a drunk douchebag out of a bar show. I grabbed the kid's legs in one hand and his arms in the other and ferried him out to the hallway. He was so shocked by the rough treatment that he shut up. I kept going until we were all the way out of the building, then let him down on the sidewalk, where he stood frozen in grievance. Snot bubbled out of one nostril, and he just left it there.

The mom came up behind us. "Sweetie, are you okay?"

She kneeled down and hugged him like I'd tried to abduct him. No gratitude. I was about to head back inside when she met my eyes and abruptly stood up. She had gold highlights and a wavy blowout but still I knew her: the Fox.

"Sonia, Jesus," she said.

I didn't say anything. She looked herself but not herself, or in fact exactly herself, in a transformation I could never have predicted but now, on the sidewalk in front of the Dickinson-Donavalli Funeral Home, seemed inevitable. When we were together, years ago, the Fox wore muscle shirts and Doc Martens and shaved her head. I used to love to rest my palm on the soft stubble and tell her I was feeling her thoughts. We met at a show and were madly in love for six months. My friends called her the Fox as in crazy like a, though I told her it was because she was so sexy. Both were true. We were about to move in together when she announced she'd discovered herself to be the reincarnation of a Hindu priestess and was going to an ashram to worship a hugging guru. Also she changed her name to Alisha, which she said meant "protected by god." I told her she was running away from reality, by which I meant me, and she said her reality wasn't mine to dictate, and I told her she was desperate to be different, just not in the way she already was, and she never spoke to me again.

"Alisha," I said now, and she looked like she had no idea what I was talking about. She was wearing a black suit, very mom-as-executive, and a diamond on her finger the size of a Ring Pop. Her given name was Jennifer.

"What are you doing at my grandfather's funeral?" she said. "Is this some stalking thing?" The Fox was also a narcissist, by the way.

"What? No. I didn't know you'd be here," I said. "My girl-friend—" I looked down at the kid, unsure how much to say about end-of-life care. The Fox put her arms around him pro-tectively, although he was busy excavating the snot situation in his nasal cavities and wasn't paying attention.

"She's a nurse," I finished. "Cat."

The Fox nodded. "Oh, *Cat*. She was great. The best one."

Yes, I hear it now, a fox and a cat, and all I can say is that I've dated plenty of women without animal names. "Yeah," I said.

We paused for a moment, each gauging whether it was worth going into more of a catch-up and deciding it wasn't.

"We should head back in," she said, still without thanking me for my help I might add, and I put my 50 percent smile on and nodded, and that would have been the end of it except that her kid said "No!" and sprinted away down the sidewalk, hell-bent for I don't know where, and the Fox hissed at me with familiar anger, for all the world as if we were still a couple, *"Help me, for God's sake,"* and I obeyed, and we followed him down the street together, while Cat was alone at Mr. Braverman's service, probably wondering through her medicated haze where I was.

I DATED CAT FOR THREE MONTHS BEFORE SHE LET ME GO OUT with her and her friends again. Since I'd already met them the first night, I didn't understand the holdup. I didn't think she was ashamed of me or us—she brought me around to her family, the lovely and rowdy Zhangs, early on—so it had to be something else. I worried she was dating other people, that she didn't like me as much as I liked her. She said it wasn't any of that.

"I'm not sure you can handle it," she said.

"Handle a bunch of nurses?" I said. "You know I toured Norway with a metal band, right? I pumped a guy's stomach with a homemade siphon?"

She gave me the look "a bunch of nurses" deserved and rolled her eyes at the rest, which admittedly were stories I had a tendency to tell too often. "It's not that," she said. "I just want to wait a while."

"How long is a while?"

She pulled out her phone, tapped, swiped. "Three months."

"You wrote it in your *calendar*?" I said, although I shouldn't have been surprised. Cat, an exact person, measured her life in the appropriate units. She piled coffee grounds on a food scale before brewing; she used a bullet journal. There was no budging her from the preset conditions, which helped her tread the chaotic border between life and death. When the day I met the nurses arrived, she wasn't nervous, because she'd planned for it; I on the other hand was sweaty-palmed and stuttery and immediately drank too much, although it didn't matter because nobody cared about me or paid me any attention at all—they were already drunk and deep into a game of fuck, marry, kill. I didn't recognize any of the names, and it took me a few minutes to realize that they were playing FMK with the patients, the dying ones at the hospice.

Cat tipped a tequila shot down her throat and said she'd fuck Mary Delozio and marry Jefferson Johns. Her friend Jennie said she was crazy to fuck Mary Delozio, Mary Delozio was a clear kill and Ayelet Sabarsky was the only fuckable patient in the place. Someone high-fived her for that. They dissected the gymnastic possibilities of an adjustable hospital bed. They brainstormed how you'd use a bedpan in the weirdest of scenarios. It was the most profane conversation to which I've ever borne witness and I once rode a night bus to Croatia with a band promoter who bragged of operating a lucrative prostitution ring in Dalmatia and urged me to invest. Two hours later my shiny Cat was drooling and puking in the street, and I stroked her hair and put her to bed and that was the first night I told her I loved her; even though I know she doesn't remember it, I still count it as our anniversary, in whatever private, messy version of a calendar I keep in my heart of hearts.

THROUGH SOME UNCANNY INSTINCT THE FOX'S KID LOCATED a playground in the neighborhood of the funeral home, and when we finally caught up to him, the Fox hobbling in her corporate heels, he was hiding inside a plastic house with window shutters just small enough to make it impossible for us to extricate him.

"Jakie," the Fox said, "you need to come out of there *this instant.*" It was an empty threat and Jakie knew it. I rattled the house a little, to see if I could lift it up around him, but it was bolted to the ground.

"I can't believe you're making me miss Great-Grandpa's funeral," the Fox went on. "That is *so selfish.*"

Jake sniffled but didn't answer.

She looked at me, evidently wanting me to contribute.

"I think there's going to be snacks after?" I offered. "I saw some brownies."

The Fox's reaction was of barely controlled fury. "Jake has food sensitivities," she hissed, as if I was supposed to know.

"I can't have gluten," Jake said from inside the plastic house. "If I do I get diarrhea."

"Sorry to hear that," I said.

"It's okay," Jake said. "They make pizza and spaghetti without gluten in it so I can still have them whenever I want." Talk of gluten seemed to lighten his mood.

"Maybe some of the snacks at the funeral will be gluten-free," I said.

The Fox looked even madder. She plopped herself on a bench and kicked off her shoes, scowling. "Don't make promises you can't keep, Sonia. That was always your problem."

First of all in no way was that always my problem, and second of all—oh, whatever. "I said *maybe*," I pointed out. I sat down next to her on the bench, entirely because I didn't want to give her the satisfaction of having it all to herself. She sighed irritably and I sighed back. Our fights were always like this—circular, subtextual, impossible to resolve, and I was forever returning to her to clear up some misunderstanding that only deepened the more we talked, until it was the misunderstanding itself that seemed to bind us together.

From where we sat on the bench we could see only the very tip of Jake's brown head. A chilly but not unpleasant wind ruffled his hair. I could smell the Fox's perfume, a leafy, citrusy smell which seemed the same as when I knew her years ago, although I didn't remember her ever owning perfume, so maybe it was her shampoo? I couldn't remember what shampoo she'd used, and this made me sad, to think that I lived with her for all those months, a time that was fraught and turbulent yet crucial to my history—I would never have had the good sense to fall in love with a woman like Cat, I believe, had I not learned the hard way to avoid women like the Fox—and now so many details of it were lost and would never be found again. In this nostalgic mood I moved closer to her and as if she were feeling the same way she leaned her head against my shoulder and I put my arm around her and then she was crying, and it might

have been a sweet moment, I guess, had Jake not said, "Guys?
I peed in my pants."

EXCEPT FOR THAT GAME OF FMK CAT NEVER TALKED ABOUT
her patients. With the same exactitude that governed her scheduling she refused to bring her work home. I only ever learned
that someone had died when she told me the date of the funeral;
then I'd think back in my head about the previous week and
wonder which day it had happened and if Cat had seemed different that day, but she never did. She was the same every day.
Maybe it sounds cold, but it isn't. When I introduced Cat to
my friends, I saw how they reacted to her profession. They
said things like "I could never do what you do" or "That's so
intense" and then they recoiled from her like dying was a virus
she might transmit to them. After a while I stopped saying "hospice" when I told people what she did for a living, and eventually I stopped talking about what she did at all.

The first funeral we went to was Maureen Stella's. She was
in her forties, divorced, cervical cancer. Cat told me when to be
ready, what to wear. She was her usual controlled self until just
before we left the condo, when she gripped my arm, hard, and
said she didn't want to go. "I hate this," she said.

"You don't have to go," I told her. I mean, hadn't she done
enough? Her whole job was doing the things that other people
couldn't or wouldn't do.

"That's not what you're supposed to say. You're supposed
to make me go."

"But why?"

"Because I was invited."

"Okay, but—"

"Because I was *invited*."

"Okay."

Maureen Stella, it turned out, had no partner, no children, no surviving parents or family. But her funeral was packed to capacity. She'd befriended the waitstaff at all her favorite restaurants. She'd kept in touch with her best friend from kindergarten, had driven her elderly neighbor to physical therapy appointments. She'd sent flowers to people *just because*. Also, she had been really good at dying. By which I mean: she'd told people what they meant to her; she'd been honest about her suffering; she'd held on to whatever small joys she could. She sounded amazing. Though I'd never met her I couldn't stop crying throughout the service, while Cat, densely medicated, sat stone-faced and composed. I thought this was what she wanted me to see: that the world was a worse place with the loss of each and every person, and that the moment of this loss deserves its due. That to run away from death was to refuse value to life. As it turned out, I was wrong. After the service we went to a sports bar—Cat likes sports, she isn't athletic but scorekeeping appeals to her—and drank a pitcher of beer and she asked me politely never to cry at a funeral again. She didn't want me to grieve. She wanted me to hold her hand tightly and dig my fingernails into her palm so deep it hurt. She wanted me to stand still and rigid and as silent as possible. She wanted me to wear the same thing every time, to drive the car, to take her there and back. She was asking me, I finally understood, to be her container, her calendar, the system of measurements that holds the moment in check. I agreed, and I kept my promise, until the day I saw the Fox.

THE FOX WAS CROUCHED NEXT TO THE PLAYHOUSE, PEERING through the tiny windows, trying to get Jake to hand her his wet pants. Crying had messed her eye makeup so that she looked a bit ruined, in a sexy way, and I'm sorry to say I could feel my old attraction to her reviving from its dormancy. I felt guilty and ashamed, which only had the effect of magnifying the attraction further.

"I can't get them off," Jake said. "They're sticking to me."

"Just peel them."

"What do you mean, *peel* them?"

"You know, start from the top and work them down."

"That's not peeling, that's pushing."

"Okay," the Fox said. "Then push."

"Doesn't he need to take his shoes off first?" I said. The Fox looked at me, her mouth a straight line of aggravation. I decided not to make my next point, which was that taking a pants-less kid back to a funeral was perhaps as great an offense as a pee-stained one.

From inside the playhouse, Jake burst into loud, theatrical sobs. "I don't want to take my shoes off!" he cried. "My feet need to be *protected*."

Parenthood seemed like a drag. "What's with you, anyway?" I asked him.

"I can't control my feelings," he said.

I mean, I bought it, as an explanation. I've been there myself. "What about your mom, though, and the rest of your family? Why are you making today all about you?"

"For God's sake, Sonia," the Fox said. "He's six years old."

"Plucky six-year-olds in movies are always doing cute stuff and saving the day. Have you ever saved the day?"

Through the window, he looked at me with interest. I'm not suggesting I'm any kind of child whisperer, only that the novelty of the conversation was making an impression.

"Saved the day how?"

"I don't know. By rescuing a stray dog. By booby-trapping a house when it's being burglarized. By not being an asshole on the day of a funeral."

"Whose house is being burglarized? Where?"

"No one's house is being burglarized," the Fox said. "And please don't use bad words."

"I bet Jake hears bad words at school all the time."

"Yeah," he said resignedly. "I do."

"Which ones?" I asked. "Out of curiosity."

"Poop. Fart. Stupid. One time Raffi said *bitch*."

"You go to school with some potty-mouthed kids."

"Grandpa said it's because media is ruining our minds."

"Probably true," I said. As we talked I'd noted that the playhouse, while bolted to the ground, was snapped together at the top and sides without screws—designed for simple assembly without tools. What can be simply assembled can be simply disassembled, and I'd once, while on tour, taken apart an entire drum kit in seconds under the barked orders of a German customs official who was convinced we were smuggling drugs inside our snares.

"Watch out," I said to the kid, and braced my knees; then I wrenched one side of the roof from the wall, and then detached one wall from its neighbor, so that the kid was exposed, mouth agape, inside his yawning shelter, as if after a tornado. The plastic had been loosened and whitened by the weather and the walls only came up to my waist, but I still felt like a superhero. It's so fun to destroy things; no wonder people do it so much. Fortunately I didn't expect the Fox to be impressed, because she wasn't. She said, "What the hell are you doing? Jakie, are you all right?" without addressing me at all. It was important to her to see threat in any given situation, I remembered that, so that she could preserve her sense of victimhood. She pulled her kid to his feet and embraced him.

"Well, I'm going back to the funeral home," I said. "I'm going to hug my girlfriend and find the brownies and whatever other snacks they have, gluten-filled or gluten-free. I'll see you guys around."

"See you," Jake said.

I was halfway down the block when I heard the combined skip-shuffle of high heels and kid sneakers, the two of them following me, Jake with his hands in his wet pants, the Fox with a frown on her face, as if I hadn't just saved her ass.

THE SERVICE WAS DRAWING TO A CLOSE. CAT STOOD RIGID, her hands clasped in front of her crotch, her legs partly spread, like a bodyguard. When she saw me she looked neither relieved nor angry. She looked as if I meant nothing to her at all. I knew better than to run over and start with apologies. I took my place beside her without saying anything. "In My Life" by the Beatles was playing, and people stood up, blowing noses, smiling weakly.

A middle-aged man made his way over to Cat, extending his hand. "Good of you to be here," he said. "Recognize you from the place. I bet you don't do this for everybody."

Cat smiled thinly, said nothing. When her anxiety peaks she has trouble even talking, but the guy didn't seem to notice. "I'm Tony," he said to me. "He was my uncle. Great guy."

I knew his type, the glad-hander, the strong handshaker, the guy who acts like being in the room with death is not a big deal. "I'm sorry for your loss," I said.

"Well, thanks, but it wasn't exactly a life cut short. A life cut long, if you will. The way we'd all like it to go."

"Right," I said. I was thinking that there was no way anyone wanted to go, that no matter the terms and circumstances, each of us is ripped with violence from the fabric of the living. That's why Cat is so anxious at funerals. She can make it as easy as possible for a person, but a service brings out all the calculus that extends beyond the body, everything that refuses her control.

"How'd you get into the death biz anyway?" Tony asked Cat. "Sorry if that sounds bad, death biz. I'm an insurance adjuster myself, so I face disaster ratios all day long. You get a certain skin."

Cat said nothing.

It was my job in that moment to ferry her away. I was distracted, though, because the Fox brushed past me, along with Jakie and the wafting acridity of his pee-smelling pants, and she squeezed my arm and mouthed "Thanks," and Jake whispered very loudly, "They *do* have gluten-free snacks!" which made me laugh. And then Tony said, "Jenny! You look a right mess," and the Fox said nonchalantly, "Fuck off, Tony," and I laughed again. Cat dropped her hand from mine.

I picked it up again; I guided her to the door and out to the car. We went to the sports bar and split a pitcher. We watched a team in grey defeat a team in blue. Cat said nothing. I said nothing. We went home and found Murray had eaten part of a couch cushion while we were gone and was languishing in a corner. I took him to the emergency animal hospital and spent $500 to have his stomach pumped. Past midnight I came home and curled up next to Cat and fitted myself to her. We lay in bed together and I didn't ask for her forgiveness and she didn't offer it. We slept soundly, stonily, like our lives depended on it. Like we were in the room with death.

The Brooks Brothers Guru

JOHN LORIMER WANTS TO BE FRIENDS ON FACEBOOK.

Amanda isn't sure whether to accept. It's a long night like any other, her bedroom blue-lit by devices, laptop and phone and iPad scattered on the comforter, earbuds nestled as she listens to Folk and Singer-Songwriters on Spotify; this is how she goes to sleep. She has three or four windows open on the computer; she's watching a movie and reading reviews of it at the same time.

They have zero mutual friends.

In his profile picture, John stands, left knee bent, hands on hips, on a rock rising jaggedly from the ocean like a broken tooth. His short haircut looks military, his posture commendably rigid. He smiles like he's never been happier. Amanda's own picture shows a cartoon cat with its back rounded, fur up. She doesn't like to give too much away. In John's square jaw and dark brown hair she can barely make out traces of the gawky cousin she last saw—when, exactly? It would have been that summer in Virginia, when they were sixteen, both of their mothers sucking down gin and tonics as if alcohol were oxygen—years ago. Then John's mother died, then hers, sisters so close they succumbed to the same disease within a year. The funerals were blurred and washy to her; when she tries to remember them, she can summon only feverish sweat and a churn in her stomach, no visuals at all.

Now she spends summer vacations with her father's family in Delaware, those cheerful extended relatives with healthy genetic history and aged grandmothers and aunts, a family where nobody knows what BRCA stands for, where nobody has been getting yearly mammograms since they were twenty.

She doesn't think they look alike. She confirms his request.

IN EASTERN PENNSYLVANIA, SPRING BARELY REGISTERS. WINter hangs on for weeks, overcast and determined, until one day you wake up sweating and sneezing, all the flowers in bloom. Amanda lives in the house where her mother grew up, which her father believes is a sign of some great disturbance in her psyche. He thinks it's weird that she telecommutes to the design firm instead of working at the open-plan office in Philly, around other people her age. Amanda may be disturbed—she quite often feels disturbed—but the house is neither the symptom nor the source. She loves the place, and always has. It sits just outside Bethlehem, in an area that used to be organized into small farms but is gradually being developed into subdivisions. Though her mother found the transformation tragic—she was nostalgic for the rural existence from which she herself escaped as soon as possible—Amanda doesn't mind it. There's a feeling of nervy anticipation to the neighborhood, like being the first person at a cocktail party, waiting to see who's going to show up. She likes being in on the ground floor. She's only thirty, and already she's seen the tail end of too many things. Soon there will be major roads here, and kids and schools and malls. For now, though, you can still see for miles over cornfields, and the night dark is bitten by thick strong stars. Inside the house, the flowered wallpaper peels back from the walls, the paint on the moldings is chipping, the appliances are mottled and yellow. But she wouldn't, doesn't, change any of it. The house has everything she needs.

JOHN LORIMER TURNS OUT TO BE ONE OF THOSE FACEBOOK friends who lack restraint. He plays a lot of games. He sends relentless invitations. He requests her birthday, her zodiac sign, her signature on social justice causes. They never contact each other directly. She considers unfriending him, but then the requests stop, and without the daily reminders she forgets he exists.

She spends the summer working on the house. She gets an electrician in to bring the wiring up to code, and has the outside repainted, and she feels diligent and adult. "How are you going to meet someone living all the way out there?" her father sometimes nags her. "You're hiding yourself away." He keeps mentioning Emily, a cousin on his side, who's getting married in December. Amanda tells him she isn't hiding; she's feathering a nest. When she mentions this phrase to him over Skype, he rolls his eyes.

In late August, John sends a message to all his Facebook friends, fifty-eight people. Amanda reads it on her phone, while running a bath.

Dear cherished friends.
Sorry for the mass email, but this seemed like the easiest way to let everybody I care about know about

some important things that are happening in my life.
As some of you are aware, I've spent the past six months
studying with Jason Wilson, one of the great thinkers of our
time. My education has opened my eyes to a deeper, more
rigorous and profound way of seeing the world, and together
we have decided that I'm ready to progress to the next level.
So starting tomorrow I'll be living on the Landau in upstate
New York and pursuing my education full-time. This feels
like a dream come true for me. I won't be on Facebook or
email for an indefinite period of time. No phone either.
I'm very excited about this next phase of my life and I
look forward to telling you all about it, my dear friends,
whenever I see you next. Be well.

John

On Skype, Amanda tells her father about this message and its strange vague rhetoric, thinking he'll find it an amusing anecdote. *Jason Wilson, one of the great thinkers of our time?* (She googled him and found nothing.) But as has happened so often over the past decade, she and her father are out of sync. Instead of being entertained, her father coughs once, a dry husk of sound, then lapses into silence.

"What?" she says.

"Your mother always worried about it. He was such a quiet kid. Never had a lot of friends. Your aunt was kind of like that, too."

Amanda swallows the urge that always falls over her at moments like this, which is to say, hungrily: *But what about Mom, what was she like, let's talk about her, let's beckon her into the room.* Hoping that there might be some shred of information she hasn't yet heard, some fresh drop from the well. Her father doesn't approve of this. He thinks grief can be put to rest, tucked into bed at night like a child.

So instead she says, "It does sound weird."

On the screen her father's face pixelates, freezes, then releases. "We should have kept in better touch with them," he's saying. "It was just so hard at the time. And John's father was sort of difficult."

"There's nothing about the dad on John's Facebook. It's like he doesn't exist."

"This is a sad story," her father says, and they move on to happier things.

AFTER THEY HANG UP, SHE CHECKS HER COUSIN'S FACEBOOK page to find that it has exploded with concern. His friends are posting like crazy, some supporting his "brave alternative life choices," others worrying about his state of mind. A woman named Meg writes, "Don't you people understand that this Landau place is a cult?"

A chain of comments unspools beneath this post:

It's not a cult, it's a utopian community.

He's not allowed any communication with the outside world—
tell me what's utopian about that.

If John wants to try something different, why shouldn't he?
Life in this capitalist gun-infested hellscape of a country
isn't for everyone.

Please don't make this political.

Where's his family in this, anyway?

We need to save him. Intervene.

John, can you tell us more about this Landau place?

I don't know why you guys are even posting here since John
  isn't checking his page anymore.

Amanda clicks over to something else, and she's watching
TV when she gets a message from Meg, who is apparently John's
ex-girlfriend and knows that Amanda is his cousin. She says that
John isn't in touch with his father, who now lives in Orlando,
remarried, with two young children. John's been having a hard
time lately, she reports, has been out of work for a while. She
repeats the claim about the cult, then says she'd go check on him
herself, but just had a baby. (Not John's, she writes, then adds,
Long story, as if Amanda had pressed her for details.)
  Can you go? You're close by.
  Amanda writes, *I haven't seen John in almost fifteen years.*
  Meg writes, *But aren't you family?*
  Amanda contemplates the absurdity of this. Then she thinks
of the Labor Day trip she's supposed to take, with her family
at Rehoboth, everyone hugging her, the smiles and laughter
and music, talk of Emily's wedding, new babies, and dogs, how
perfect Labor Day is there, with the late-summer light dazzling
on the water, and she writes, *Yes.*
  Somehow Meg has located an address for "the Landau," but
no phone number. Maybe there is no phone. Cults in general
seem anti-phone. If it is a cult which, Meg's concern notwith-
standing, she isn't convinced it is.
  As she gasses up the car, stocking Red Vines and Diet Coke
for the journey, her mood is buoyant. The weather is road-trip

perfect, sunny and clear, made for blasting tunes and singing along with the pure abandon of the solo driver. One summer in college, she drove from Boston to Florida to visit a boyfriend who had an internship in marine biology. When she got there, he wasn't all that happy to see her, and they had an awkward dinner at a crab shack—all that sucking, all those napkins— before he told her he was seeing somebody else and asked her to drive home. The humiliation was major and yet, oddly enough, ephemeral. What stuck in her mind from the experience was the image of herself she'd held in her mind all the way down: she'd stand on a dock in a white dress, hair fluttering in the wind, the picture of lovely, vulnerable romance. When she thinks of it now, she remembers the billowing optimism of the trip and not the deflation of arrival.

She still likes road trips. She likes how being in the car makes you live in the moment, suspended between two points. She also likes grilled cheese sandwiches eaten in diners, gas station snacks, tacky billboards, and cheap sunglasses. For an hour or two, outside Scranton, she even forgets where she's going.

NERVES DON'T HIT UNTIL SHE EXITS THE HIGHWAY AND LUM-bers through a slow succession of pallid, downtrodden streets. This isn't the upstate New York of antique stores and farmers' markets. These are places abandoned by industry, previously whole mansions carved into Section 8 housing, Main Streets half-filled by obstinate stores. The address she's been given is on a rural route and she almost misses the turn at a Stewart's. Whatever spontaneous impulse guided her to accept Meg's challenge—because that's what it was, a challenge—has ebbed, and she wonders what on earth she's going to say to this cousin she hasn't seen since they were kids.

But she isn't going to turn back, either; she's always been stubborn. When she was little, her mother used to tell her: "Don't be like the stubborn oak, bow and bend like a willow tree." It was from a Shaker song. She remembers that.

So deep is she inside her thoughts that she's surprised to discover she has arrived, all of sudden, at a lovely old farmhouse that looks recently restored. Freshly painted white, with green shutters, a vegetable garden off to one side, a set of Adirondack chairs on the expansive porch: it ought to be a bed-and-breakfast. It ought to be an ad for something. It is what her own house ought to look like, but doesn't. The only strange thing about it is a kind of stillness: no movement, no sound. She slams the car door, hard, and stands for a moment, looking around.

Knocking on the door, she feels sticky in the humid, windless afternoon and finds herself, inexplicably, shivering. The place is too quiet. She can't hear anything from inside, and the windows are all closed, curtains drawn. She knocks again, waits, knocks again. Maybe the cult isn't home. Maybe they're out running cult errands. Finally some soft footsteps thud toward her, and a young man opens the door, around twenty years old and so good-looking that for a second she doesn't know what to say. He's wearing a crisp white button-down shirt and khakis, like a Gap ad. His blond hair is slicked on the sides with gel.

"Mr. Wilson doesn't speak to visitors," he says with a poised, regretful smile.

"Oh, I'm not here for Mr. Wilson. I wanted to see John? I'm his cousin."

A gentle silence greets this statement. She tries to press, to seem unthreatening and naïve. "I was in the neighborhood, well not exactly the *neighborhood* but not far from here, visiting a friend, and I heard he'd moved up here, and I really wanted to see him, you know, it's been years?" The eyes that meet hers are blue and blank, a computer program lacking algorithms for these particular inputs. So she steps closer, tilts her head to the side, going for girlish. "I just wanted to say hello."

He shuts the door, but politely, managing to communicate a pause in the action rather than a refusal. On the porch, she turns around and surveys the property. There is an apple tree on the other side of a clearing. Still no sound, not even birds. Her car is the only one here.

Behind her, the door opens again and when she looks around the blond guy is smiling. "You can follow me." They thread their way along a dim hallway until they reach a sitting room. Or is it a parlor? *Living room* is too banal a term for this place, which is furnished out of a different era, with different vocabulary. A chesterfield. A phonograph. Two brocaded armchairs with arched legs. A bookshelf with leather hardcover editions, titles stamped in gold. All this she takes in as her blond guide breathes, "Take a seat," and evaporates.

But she's still standing when John comes in and she's glad she is, because he wraps her in a bear hug and lifts her several feet off the ground. There's too much of him to take in at once, his big eyes, his smile, the fact that he's also wearing a white-collared shirt and khakis, apparently the house uniform, as if they're about to go to church or casual Friday at an uptight office.

"I knew it was you. I just had a feeling," her cousin says, and they smile at each other, Amanda so glad to see him that she's suddenly almost in tears. As a teenager John was sullen and acne ridden, but as children they'd often spent weeks at the beach together, collecting shells and jumping in the water, and some vestige of that time seems to hang in the air between them.

"I wanted to see you," she tells him, and it's the truth.

They sit down on the chesterfield, and the blond guy brings them drinks in tall frosted glasses. The air is cool as a cave. "So," she says, "what is this place?"

Her cousin smiles, looking not at all self-conscious or suspicious about why she's here. She remembers that he probably never even saw all that debate on his Facebook page. Instead of answering the question, he offers to take her on a tour. If he thinks it's odd she's come to see him unannounced, if he anticipates some kind of intervention or conflict, he doesn't show it. His happiness to see her seems pure, and she feels retroactive guilt for how irritated she was by all his Facebook activity. "Here, this is cool." He pauses in the hallway to show her an oil painting of the house's original owner, some angry-looking colonial guy with chins bulging down his neck. A minor Revolutionary War battle apparently took place in the backyard; Hessian mercenaries once camped out in the parlor. Upstairs is his room, with a plain white coverlet tucked neatly over a twin bed and a small desk with a notebook and pen on it. There is nothing on the walls. From the window, he can see an apple tree outside.

Standing in his monastic room, Amanda is struck by something she hasn't felt in years: a keen, swelling balloon of envy. She would give anything to live here, in this simple, quiet place. Beside her John nods, as if he has eavesdropped on her longing. "It's the best place I've ever been," he says.

He shows her to another bedroom, which looks very much the same as his, and offers it to her for the night. Instantly she accepts. They'll continue the tour later, he says, after dinner, and she nods. "For now, why don't you rest?" She nods again, already drowsy. She kicks off her shoes and sits on the bed; it's possible she's asleep before he closes the door.

WHAT WAKES HER IS A CHIME. FOR A LONG MOMENT, SHE HAS no idea where she is, and the experience is strangely pleasant. The indeterminate light could mean dawn or dusk. Then she hears the chime again, and remembers. In a bathroom down the hall, she washes her face and makes a lame attempt at fixing her hair. She pulls a wrinkled sundress from her bag and adds a cotton cardigan, feeling a desire to impress. Her phone buzzes; it's a text from Meg, wanted to know what's going on; she drops the phone back in her bag and heads downstairs.

In the parlor she finds five clean-cut, well-dressed men of varying ages holding cocktails who smile at her genially. John, who has been leaning over the record player, lets the needle drop on some classical music and then joins her, introducing her to the crowd.

"Everyone, this is Amanda." He rattles off names in quick succession; there's a Luke and a Michael and she loses the rest. As he presses a drink into her hand, everyone comes over to say hello and ask, solicitously, how her trip has been. She feels gently fussed over, as if by grandparents.

"And this," John says, "is Jason Wilson."

One of the great thinkers of our time is a slight man in a blue shirt, with dark brown hair and happy-looking brown eyes. "We're delighted you're here. You found us okay?" he asks, as if he'd sent directions. She says yes. Wilson is also wearing khakis, and bucks, less guru than Brooks Brothers. The Brooks

Brothers guru. She laughs a little, to herself, and Wilson laughs, too, as if he understands.

"Come to dinner," he says, touching her elbow softly as he guides her. He is a gentleman.

AT DINNER, THE TALK IS OF BRAHMS AND EMERSON AND JOHN Singer Sargent, who once painted a portrait of Wilson's great-great-grandfather, or maybe it was his great-grandfather, or maybe somebody his great-great-grandfather knew. She's had a few cocktails and can't keep up. But the five men—including, to her astonishment, her cousin—all hold opinions on these topics, on how Brahms constructs harmony in his piano concertos, how Sargent illuminates the details of clothing. Is this a cult, or is it college? Wilson introduces each topic, drawing connections between one thing and the next, referencing Joshua Reynolds's theory of the aesthetic or linking Beethoven to the sublime. She spends some time trying to remember what John majored in— she wants to say computer science? Across the table, the guru catches her eyes.

"Perhaps this all seems quite strange to you," he says, "but this is the home we've made. A place where those of us who care deeply about *classical knowledge* can come together to discuss it. The outside world"—he doesn't even gesture toward it, merely lifts his eyes in the direction of the window—"cares little. But here we are passionate."

They smile at each other. "I, uh, kind of wish I knew more about all this stuff," Amanda says.

"Then you should stay." His warmth is unmistakable. "We could use a woman's touch."

The blond guy who answered the door clears the plates; he

seems the youngest, and Amanda wonders if he's an intern, or a servant. But John gets up and pours more wine, and someone else carries in dessert. Amanda drinks it all, eats it all. Her cousin presses his lips against her ear, fleshy and wet with spittle. "I'm glad you're here," he whispers.

And maybe that's why later, in the twin bed, in the airless bedroom, she dreams of him. They are teenagers on the beach in Virginia. This could be a memory. Certainly she's aware, even in the dream, of the physical reality of her cousin: his frightening, newly adolescent body, skinny and tall and sprouting wispy hair at nipples and armpits. As if to deny these corporeal facts, they run into the waves together, like they used to when they were kids, but it's not the same. After splashing each other for a minute or two with listless self-consciousness they turn back to where their mothers are watching, high up on the beach under umbrellas, drinking their cool drinks. They decide to dive. The ocean is empty of seaweed; the sand is smooth and fine. Underwater she feels her cousin reaching for her, clawing at her arms as if he's drowning, and she can't understand what he's doing, raking his large hands across her chest, pushing her down or away. She chokes and kicks, the water a churn of salt and white, and then she wakes up sweating in a mess of sheets and no one is watching her and she is all grown, and motherless.

IN THE MORNING, CLAD IN SHORTS AND PLAIN WHITE T-shirts, the men fan out around the property, doing chores. From her bedroom, she hears hammering, the buzz of a mower. When she takes a shower down the hall, she runs quickly back to the bedroom in her towel, but encounters no one. Downstairs, Jason Wilson sits alone in the dining room, drinking coffee and reading *The New York Times*. She joins him hesitantly, serving herself coffee from a white urn on the table; without speaking, he finishes the first section of the paper, folds it, and passes it to her. The coffee is strong. When she looks up, he's staring at her, a gaze whose force is palpable, discomfiting, and yet very clearly not sexual in nature. She doesn't know what the look is or what it means.

Thank God her cousin arrives, smelling of sweat and grass, pouring himself orange juice from a jug on a side table. Though she hasn't heard a bell or a command, it seems clear to her that he has been summoned, and sure enough Wilson says, "I thought you two could go the store today."

"Sure," she says, and watches as he hands her cousin a list. Then he exits the room. He's the only one who isn't wearing shorts. John disappears and returns in ten minutes, wearing another clean white shirt. In her camp shirt with its bright pink retro '70s slogan (SUMMER FUN!) Amanda feels kitschy and commercialized. Unpure, maybe. Working from home, she has little need for formal clothes and still dresses basically the way she did in college, which has always seemed like an advantage, until now.

At the grocery store, they divide up the list, each taking different sections, though her cousin often frowns at her choices and sends her back for others; they want European butter, organic eggs. The brand requirements are specific. There is also a long list of alcohol. In the end the cart is piled so high they have to get another one. At the checkout, her cousin says, "Since you're staying with us, would you mind?" So Amanda pulls out her card and charges five hundred dollars and it doesn't feel any more surreal than anything else that's happened in the past twenty-four hours.

On the way back, at her suggestion, they stop at the Stewart's and pick up ice cream sandwiches, which she pays for also, and sit on the hood of the car, eating and looking at the parking lot. Even at the gas station the air smells good, fir scented and clean.

"So you know your friends are pretty worried about you."

Her cousin looks surprised. "My friends? Who?"

"There was a whole Facebook thing, discussion, whatever." She gestures vaguely at the parking lot, as if social media were lurking beyond the cars. "People wondering what you're doing up here, exactly."

"Ah," John says, noncommittal.

She decides to press. "Meg Patterson is particularly concerned."

He barks a short gulping laugh. "Meg and I went out for maybe six months, a couple years ago. She used to pack me a lunch when I went to work. She used to fold my underwear. She's sweet, but she's too much, you know? There's caring about someone, and then there's . . . whatever it is that she does."

Amanda tries to imagine what it would be like to have a boyfriend make her lunch, or do her laundry. The last guy she dated, Shamir, was a computer programmer who put his jeans in the freezer instead of washing them, claiming the cold killed the bacteria just as well. He was smart and funny and perfectly happy to eat delivery pizza every single night. They didn't break up because she was annoyed by his habits; they broke up because each of them preferred to stay at home, in front of a laptop, and driving all the way over to the other person's house took too much effort. They still Gchatted sometimes.

"It's nice she cares about you," she offers to John, who barks again.

"That's what women always say."

Meg's most recent text, ignored this morning, buzzes inside her head. *What are you finding out? Hello??* "So this house," Amanda says, "with these dudes? You're happy here?"

If she expected defensiveness or euphoria, she is disappointed. He only shrugs, crumpling the sandwich wrapper into a ball that he tosses, tidily, into a trash can on the other side of the car.

"It's a lot better than where I was before."

"Which was where?"

He shrugs again. "By myself." For a second she thinks he's going to turn the question back at her, and girds herself to answer; but instead he cocks his head at the groceries in the back of the car, as if the food might be impatient to get home.

AS THEY UNLOAD THE GROCERIES, THEY REMINISCE ABOUT meals from their shared summer vacations, and Amanda relaxes until Jason Wilson comes in and starts talking to her about pie. He seems to think that as a woman she should have some intrinsic expertise. "I know nothing," she tells him, "except how to order pie at a bakery," and he stops and gives her a long look. She realizes that he doesn't expect her to *know* how to make pie; he expects her to *learn,* because it's the task he's giving her. That's what he does: he assigns. Somewhere in the middle of this her cousin disappears, and she and the guru are alone in the kitchen.

"Don't worry," he tells her, "I'll help you. We'll do it together."

Though it's only ten thirty in the morning, he pours them each a shot of vodka from a bottle he pulls out of the freezer. The alcohol shivers down her throat, bringing cold and heat at the same time. As he sets out ingredients, he asks her to read from an ancient cookbook he produces from some pantry shelf. It's the kind of recipe written by women in the early twentieth century, with inexact measurements and instructions that assume a certain familiarity with the kitchen. Early in the process, she is drunk and lost. At one point she's standing with her elbows in a bowl of shaggy, sticky crust, her shirt ghostly with flour, her nose itchy, while the guru frowns at her, displeased.

"I don't think we had the butter cold enough. It says the butter should be cold."

Does he know, she wonders, that they stopped for ice cream? She swallows the urge to apologize. She doesn't understand how he manages to exert such authority; he's soft-spoken and not exactly frightening. But she knows she doesn't want to displease him.

In the end he adds some milk and she's able to work the dough into a rough, chillable ball. Then he takes over, cutting the fruit while she slumps on a stool, her elbows on the counter. He's not unattractive but there's something fussy about him, an old bachelor in the making, a man who will complain when things aren't done just his way.

Late-morning sun invades the kitchen, already oppressive with the oven's heat. Wiping his hands, the guru smiles at her.

"You know, Schopenhauer loved pie," he says. "It was one of his weaknesses, his sweet tooth. One of his unpreventable desires, you might say."

From his tone she guesses this is a joke, though she has no idea why. She could ask, but doesn't. He leans back against the counter, crossing his feet. "Schopenhauer knew that human desire caused pain and difficulty in the world, but our will is intractable. We want what we want. So what do we do about this? How do we find relief?" He pours them each another shot. "The only sublimation is through the aesthetic. Through the appreciation of art. Especially music."

Amanda listens to this dreamily, thinking of her mother and aunt, who sometimes danced together in a theatrically romantic fashion, their arms around each other. Sometimes her aunt laid her head on Amanda's mother's shoulder. When her father saw this, he'd tell them to quit it; it embarrassed him.

"My mother loved music," she says. "Especially the Beatles. George was her favorite. She said the mark of a sensitive person was to pick George." What she says next makes her realize she's drunk. "I wish I knew things like you do."

The guru smiles again, and now he seems not fussy but gentle, and kind. "You could learn them, if you joined us here."

The idea that she would stay here, with these khaki-clad scholar-men, Wendy to their Lost Boys, Snow White to their dwarfs, is so absurd that she can't even think of how to answer. And yet she doesn't say no. To learn about art and music and literature and philosophy, wouldn't it be a good life?

And also: it's like a drug, to be wanted.

AFTER THE PIE GOES IN THE OVEN, SHE HEADS UPSTAIRS WITH a book Jason Wilson loans her, *An Essay Concerning Human Understanding*, which puts her to sleep, and wakes ravenous and thirsty in the late afternoon. From downstairs comes a tinkle of glasses, and classical music. She puts on the same dress as last night—she brought only one—and makes her way down. Almost immediately, the young blond guy, whose name she was told but can't remember, hands her a gin and tonic, and she sips it while taking in the scene. Her cousin is changing a record, and two men are talking by the bookcase, two others seated on the

Chesterfield; Jason Wilson reclines in an armchair, smoking a cigarette, his eyes meeting hers neutrally. The smell of after-shave wafts through the room.

As she starts to take in more of the conversation, she under-stands that a debate is at hand, between the two men on the sofa and the two at the bookcase. Nietzsche is mentioned, and the nature of the will, and something about the representation of the world, and though she tries to get a handle on it, she's both sty-mied and bored. She wishes she hadn't left her phone upstairs; she needs to google everything they're saying. Twice Wilson intervenes to redirect the conversation, or ask some dense ques-tion ("But what of . . ." the question usually begins) and the men scramble after it like seagulls over scraps.

She guesses they're smart; it's hard for her to tell, just like it would be hard to tell if a crowd of Italians were smart. All she'd know is that they could speak Italian. She has the same feeling she used to get in high school English classes, when the A stu-dents would get worked up over *The Great Gatsby* or *Pride and Prejudice*, waving their hands in the air. Amanda could never understand how something so abstract, these words on a page, could inspire such interest. She'd daydream and draw, until by the end of the period she'd have made a landscape or a castle or a city, and even though she almost failed English she'd always wind up feeling satisfied with herself, thinking, *Hey, I made something.*

Without looking at him, she can sense the guru's eyes on her, again that penetrating but not sexual gaze. The two men closest to her are arguing about "the sponsorship of the elite." Cocktails are being refilled; there's no sign of dinner.

"What do you think?" Wilson has materialized beside her, his tone quiet but clear.

"I'm out of my depth."

"But the conversation interests you?"

"I don't know," she says honestly. "I guess the idea of it interests me. The idea that a place like this exists, where a conversation like this is happening, that sort of interests me." She's slurring her words.

He nods gravely. "That was *exactly* my feeling. What I wanted to do. I was a teacher before, you know. A high school teacher. Spending year after year hammering ideas into the heads of children who couldn't care less. Then they'd graduate and whatever tiny bit of knowledge they'd absorb along the way would just . . . evanesce. So I decided to *make something*. I made this."

This repetition of her own internal thought, her memory, is so uncanny that she can't help staring at him, wondering whether he'd heard her say it out loud. His brown eyes are intent on her. "You could make something, too, if you want."

She both wants and doesn't want it. She opens her mouth without knowing what she'll answer, and is saved by her cousin, who enters and announces dinner, shepherding them from one room to the next. He's been the one cooking, she sees now, and he has made roast chicken and salad and new potatoes, all of it delicious. She eats too much of it, and drinks three glasses of wine. Over dinner, Mozart is discussed, and Schrödinger's cat, and briefly the Obama administration's assassination of a terrorist who was an American citizen, but Amanda notices that the guru doesn't care to talk politics. He steers the conversation to the history paintings of Delacroix. Could she become a person with opinions on Delacroix, too? She slumps in her chair, knowing she looks glassy-eyed, as the river of talk wends around her.

The pie is served. It's edible, so far as she can tell, but everyone makes appreciative noises like it's the second coming of pie, and she takes a few bites, the peaches slippery and gelatinous down her throat, and then she's choking, and she has to run upstairs and rid herself of all of it—the pie, the wine, the chicken, the conversation—because she can't stand it, this thing they made.

WHEN SHE WAKES UP, JOHN LORIMER IS IN HER ROOM. HE'S sitting in a chair by the window, not staring at her, not reading a book, just sitting. Her mouth tastes like chalk and fur.

"Sorry," she mumbles. "I'm not used to drinking so much."

"It's okay. Do you feel better?"

"I must have embarrassed you."

"I'm thirty-two, Mandy. I'm an adult. I can handle it."

"This place is a little much," she says, because she's still drunk. "I can't wrap my head around it."

"Jason told me he asked you to stay. He likes you."

In the darkness she can barely make out his face, but his voice is steady, serene.

"How long are *you* going to stay here?"

"I don't know. I put enough in that I can stay indefinitely. You could, too, I think."

Something cold pierces her skin through the gauze of alcohol, and Amanda sits up in bed, propped on her elbows, squinting at him. "What do you mean, you put enough in?"

"This place doesn't pay for itself, obviously. What Jason has built—it costs money to create and maintain. You can't just be here and not contribute. That's not how it *works*."

"I see," she says. "And what did you contribute?"

Her cousin leans forward, and there's enough moonlight that she can make out his eager, childlike expression. She remembers him one long-ago summer, beckoning her behind his house, where he opened his cupped palms to show her, trapped in his hands, a brown frog.

"You remember the beach house we had. Where we used to go in the summer."

"Of course I do."

He flings his hands out in the air, palms up, as if releasing that frog he held when he was ten. "I sold it."

Amanda's elbows give out and she lies back down. "John."

He smiles. "She left it to me, and that's what I wanted. You still own the place in Bethlehem, right? I saw the pictures on Facebook. I told Jason about it. If you sold it and put the money in, you could stay here, too."

"But that's crazy. I'd never sell my house."

"Sometimes the best thing is to give up everything, you know," he says. From beneath the chair he pulls something out. "I want to share this with you." She can't see, but a rustling sound alerts her that he's turning the pages of a notebook. The room spins a bit, but lazily, like a merry-go-round someone stopped pushing a while ago.

When he speaks next, her cousin's voice is quiet but compressed with the importance of what he's about to say. "This is what I've been working on. It's a collection of poems. Every morning I get up at five and write for two hours."

"You write poetry?" Amanda says. When she closes her eyes, all she can see is the beach house in Virginia, her mother and aunt cooking dinner in the kitchen, the floor gritty with sand she and John were supposed to rinse off their feet.

"It's a book, about her. Some of them are about your mom, too. A lot of them are about those summer vacations. I'm pretty sure that's when my mom was happiest."

Amanda swallows, her throat constricting. Her tongue is thick, inert.

"Do you want to hear some of the poems?"

His reedy voice pokes through Amanda's ears, past her skin, past every defense she wants to erect. She wants to run outside but she can't get out of bed; she can't even open her eyes. With chill and silent precision, she knows that this—*this*—is the reason she left home to look for her cousin. Here's what she came for: to be with the person in the world who remembers what she does, who needs what she needs.

But now that she's got it, she can't abide it. The strain of her two desires—to seek the connection and to reject it—paralyzes her, and she lies rigid, every muscle tensed. If she were to speak, she would dissolve, or break in half.

Don't be like the stubborn oak, bow and bend like a willow tree.

"Amanda, are you still awake? Amanda?"

She says nothing and the silence grows long and longer until there is nothing else. And then there is a shuffle in the dark, and her cousin is gone.

WHEN HER MOTHER DIED, AMANDA'S BACK WAS TURNED. After the months of chemo, after the multiple consultations with multiple doctors, after her mother smoked pot for the nausea and smiled at her family through the haze of it, after she squeezed Amanda's hand, her thin fingers like a baby's grip, after months of preparing to say goodbye, she slipped away while Amanda was out running errands. Amanda didn't know that the end was near. When she came back to the hospital, carrying a CVS bag of lip balm and magazines—these little, little offerings—her father's eyes were hooded slits and he met her outside the room. Death was a secret he and her mother kept between them. Amanda found she could not forgive him, could not forgive her mother, and most of all could not forgive herself for missing the moment she had dreaded for so long.

SHE DOESN'T KNOW IF JOHN WAS THERE WHEN HIS MOTHER died, if he'd been holding her hand as she drew her final breath. If he got to be there—this is how she thinks of it, *if he were that lucky*—she'd be jealous. She plans to talk to him about this as she pulls her hair into a ponytail the next morning, now that she's sober and awake. But when she goes downstairs, the house is empty. She helps herself to the coffee, reads the newspaper, hears no hum of mower or clang of tools. She goes for a walk around the grounds—though it's only nine in the morning, the heat is already thick and strong—and sees no one.

When she comes back, though, the men are gathered on the front porch, some sitting, some standing. They are all dressed exactly alike, blue button-downs and khakis, hair wet and combed. The guru sits at the center, in an Adirondack chair. She's halfway up the steps before she understands that this is a line of defense. She pauses, one foot raised on a step, and glances questioningly at her cousin.

The look he gives her is beyond cool; it has eliminated expression altogether. There was a test, and she failed it. But how could she have failed it when she was drunk and unprepared? When she had received no warning?

Jason Wilson makes some gesture, and the young man who answered the door on the first day disappears inside the house, returning moments later with her bag, which has been packed for her. She doesn't have to look inside it to know that the clothes are neatly folded, the toiletries zipped into their kit. The guru puts his arm around Amanda and leads her back down the steps, his tone as warm as ever. "It was wonderful to meet you, Amanda," he tells her as her bag is stowed in the trunk and the door opened for her. "I hope you'll come see us again sometime." Nothing in his manner betrays upset.

"Wait," she says. "Wait."

"Oh, you're right," the guru says, "We forgot something important," and her heart lifts with the reprieve. He sends the young servant running back into the house. When he comes back, he's bearing a silver shield that glints in the high sun; it's the leftover peach pie, wrapped in foil. "Take this," Wilson says, resting it on the passenger seat. "For later."

Amanda, defeated, gets in the car and turns the key in the ignition. What sends her away isn't the brush-off; it's the expression she sees in all their eyes, which is not anger but pity. She has been cast out.

"Tell him—" she begs the guru, who smiles kindly, his face armored in friendly wisdom, and says, "I know."

The Detectives

WHEN I WAS TWELVE YEARS OLD MY FATHER HIRED A PRIVATE
detective to follow my mother around. He believed she was
having an affair, which she was, and he wanted proof to show a
judge, in order to fight for custody of my sister Nicole and me.
The detective was a short, dark-haired, overweight man named
Sam Postelthwaite, who came to our house one evening with a
manila envelope clutched in his meaty hands. My father introduced him, stupidly, as a colleague—stupidly because my father
kept the books for a few local businesses and didn't exactly have
"colleagues"—and then hustled him into my parents' bedroom,
where they spoke in whispers for a few minutes, then emerged
with somber expressions on their faces and hugged goodbye, as
if they'd been attending a funeral service in there. Years later
I waited on Sam Postelthwaite at the Blue Dragon Café. He
was even more overweight and had not aged well, and I knew
he could sense me staring at him from behind the bar while I
pulled his beer, but he didn't seem perturbed by it. Probably it
happened to him a lot, in his line of work.

Like a lot of my father's schemes this one both backfired, and
didn't. When confronted with the photographs, my mother was
so angry that she ripped them up and left: him, us, town. We

never saw her again. He got custody, and Nicole and I lost our mother, whom we spent the rest of our teen years idolizing as a free spirit who threw off the shackles of the ordinary world. She was our hero, despite having abandoned us, and every time we defied our father, which was often, we did so in her name.

At a certain point, though, I saw how foolish this was— which is to say, I grew up—and came to appreciate our father and his dogged affection for us, which endured the rocky years of our adolescence and was still there, waiting, when we became adults. After I went away to school and came back home (returning to work at the Blue Dragon, as if my education had never happened), I often had dinner with him and his girlfriend, Noriko, who was a stylish, successful real estate agent and whom both my father and I thought could probably do a lot better than him.

Nicole struggled more than I did. She inherited our mother's dark brown hair and her restlessness and her love of attention. At nineteen she went off to Los Angeles, wanting to be famous. And she sort of succeeded; she appeared on one of those reality shows where she competed alongside twenty other reasonably good-looking girls for the attention of a man with highly defined abs and no personality. When she didn't win, she came home, in debt and with a drinking problem, and got a job as a kindergarten teacher. She was the most famous person in our town, and people often turned to look when they recognized her at the gas station or the grocery store.

There was no party Nicole wouldn't go to. She had a string of short relationships, if you could call them that, and she often stumbled over to my apartment on a Sunday morning, still wearing her clothes from the night before, to complain and confess. She wanted me to make her eggs and tell her to straighten up. She had become our mother, and I our father, the two of us performing a script that had been written before we were born. It didn't feel fair to me, and I told her so; we fought, and then the following Sunday she'd show up again, and of course, I'd let her in.

It was nine o'clock on an April Sunday when the doorbell rang, which was early for Nicole, but I'd been up for hours, drinking coffee and reading the real estate section of *The New York Times*. Moving to the city was a fantasy so long ingrained in me that I couldn't let it go, though I had lost any intention of actually doing it. It was an unusually warm spring after an unusually cold winter, and the cardinals and robins were singing loudly, as if both pleased and alarmed by the extremities of temperature.

At my front door stood Sam Postelthwaite. He was an old man now, thinner, his cheeks sunken and wrinkled like a deflated balloon, but I still knew him instantly. He was wearing tan pants and a blue plaid shirt and holding something in his hands. For a second, I thought it was the manila envelope he'd brought to my father all those years ago, and I frowned and said, "Is this about my mother?" and he said, "No."

I saw then that he was holding a woman's purse, which was light brown and expensive and which I had given to Nicole the previous year for Christmas, and I said, "Is she all right?" and he said, "I'm here to take you to the hospital," and I nodded and got dressed. I suppose it was odd that I didn't ask him anything else. I knew the situation must be horrible, and that soon I would be required to face that horror in its entirety. When I was ready to go, he showed me to his car, a Ford Taurus that smelled like French fries, and I sat in the passenger seat with my sister's purse in my lap. My mind wouldn't go to her, not yet. Instead it kept dwelling on the strangeness of my being driven to the hospital by Sam Postelthwaite. "Why are you the one who came to get me?" I asked him.

"Your father was worried about your sister. He asked me to keep an eye on her, so I've been doing that. Trying to, anyway."

I glanced at him, then out the window, at the quiet streets with budding trees, the drab early grass just starting to recover from the weight of snow. We'd been pummeled that year.

"Your father and I have been friends for many years," Sam Postelthwaite said, answering a question I hadn't asked.

"Is he already at the hospital?"

"No," he said, which was also strange; but he didn't elaborate. We rode the rest of the way in silence, and then he pulled up in front of the hospital and didn't park, and I understood he wasn't coming in, whether because he had somewhere else to be, or didn't think he was invited, or for some other reason that I couldn't possibly calculate. The whole morning felt beyond my calculation. I opened the door. "Good luck," he said, and drove away while I was still standing in the parking lot.

THE WOMAN AT THE RECEPTION DESK HAD GONE TO SCHOOL with my mother, and when I was a teenager I sometimes babysat her son; that's the kind of town this is. When she saw me she said my name and tutted sympathetically and told me that my sister was in the ICU on the third floor. Upstairs, I followed the signs to my sister's room. She lay with her eyes closed, breathing through a respirator. Her left arm was in a cast, and the right one was hooked up to an IV. The hospital gown they'd given her was too big and slipping off one shoulder; it almost looked lewd, and instinctively I reached over and pulled it up. "Nick," I said.

"She don't hear you," a voice said behind me, and I turned to see a man sitting in a chair. I'd been so focused on Nicole that I hadn't even noticed him, even though he was quite imposing, and, when he stood up, well over six feet tall.

"I'm Lord," he said. "You must be Amber." He was wearing a blue T-shirt and dark jeans and a thick cluster of necklaces; one of them was made of shark teeth, and another one had a gold cross. His hair was in tight glossy cornrows. He reached out a hand, but I didn't take it. I didn't mean to be rude, or maybe I did; I'd never heard Nicole mention his name.

I turned back to Nicole, placing a hand on her arm.

"She's under sedation," said the man. "It's standard, they said."

"Standard for what?"

"A contrecoup lesion," he said. "That's when the brain gets jammed against the inside of the skull. They sedate the patient while waiting for the swelling to go down."

"I see," I said, though I didn't. Inside I was already blaming him, whoever he was, already organizing the categories in my mind. Nicole: the victim. Lord: a mistake she'd live to regret. All my sister's friends were delinquents.

"They think she was hit by a car," he said. "Walking home last night. They called me because mine was the most recent number on her phone. We talked most nights before she went to sleep."

"I'm sorry, who are you again?"

Lord faced me across my sister's bed. "A friend."

There was too much mystery to him, to this. I left the room and tried to flag down a nurse, but they all strode past me busily, shaking their heads and not making eye contact as if I were begging for change, and I was left in front of the nurse's station, starting to cry angry, confused tears.

Just then a pair of arms circled me, and a voice I knew said, "Hush, hush." It was Noriko. We'd never hugged before— Noriko, my father had once explained to me, "does not enjoy casual bodily contact"—and this more than anything made me grasp, all at once, the gravity of the situation. I stopped crying, and asked her where my father was. She just shook her head and held my left hand in hers, firmly, and then pulled me in the direction of Nicole's room. There, she exchanged introductions with Lord and summoned a doctor, who gave us a weary, terse recap of Nicole's condition: a traumatic brain injury, prognosis unknown. For the moment, drugs would keep her from moving. It was important that she remain immobile while her brain healed. I asked the doctor if we should speak to Nicole, and he said, "Sure," in a dismissive tone that made me hate him, and then he left the room.

Lord rubbed his eyes, like a tired child. I told him, "You don't have to stay, you know," and only when he flinched did I perceive what a mean thing it was to say. I just didn't know him, he was a stranger to me, and I was full up with strangeness, that day.

"I'm going to stay," he said quietly, and I shrugged.

Outside the door a shadow loomed, disappeared, passed by again, and then there was a quiet knock. I slipped outside to see Kevin Hewey, who was a police officer, waiting for me with a notebook and a wincing expression designed, I guess, to convey sympathy. In high school Kevin had been good-looking and a bully, and I was pleased to note that he was losing his hair.

"Hey Amber," he said. "How you holding up?"

I was irritated by his concern. Kevin and his fellow cops would sometimes come into the bar and get rowdily drunk and make lewd comments, on top of which they were mediocre tippers. "Never better," I said.

He didn't even register it. "I need to take a statement from you if you've got a minute."

I told him I didn't know anything about what had happened, and he nodded his chin at the door. "Who's that?" he said.

"Some friend of Nicole's," I said.

"Was he with her last night?"

"I don't think so, but you'd have to ask him," I said.

Kevin frowned. "I don't recognize him," he said. He made to open the door, and I stopped him with a hand to his arm.

"Do you think you can find the person who hit her?" I said.

He gave me his wince-face again. "We'll do everything we can."

Then Lord came out of the room, closing the door gently behind him, and Kevin's demeanor changed instantly. "Sir," he said, "could you step this way?"

Lord nodded. "Of course," he said mildly.

Kevin led him past the nurses' station to a bench in the hallway; I assumed he wanted to make Lord sit down because Lord was so much taller than he was. I couldn't hear what he asked, but I could see Lord shake his head, over and over. I remembered, watching them, that Kevin's brother Stu had taken Nicole to the junior prom. They'd gotten high in the parking lot and stumbled so badly, walking up the steps to the gymnasium, that the principal wouldn't let them in. I didn't know where Stu was now. Lord stood up then and Kevin barked at him—no other word for it—"Sit down, sir!" Lord sat down.

"Is everything okay?" I said.

Kevin glanced from Lord back to me, then nodded. "Don't go far," he said to Lord, and then gave me his card. I thought it was sort of funny he had a card. It said OFFICER KEVIN HEWEY, and below that the number of the police station, which anyone in town would have known to call already. Lord and I watched him walk off, saying nothing.

We spent the rest of that day, and all that evening, at the hospital, until the nurses kicked us out. Noriko and I—Lord slipped off separately, without saying goodbye—took the elevator downstairs and walked out to the parking lot together. The night was clear, the stars hectic in the sky.

I asked her where my father was.

I'd called his cell phone three times and each time it went straight to voice mail. Then I turned my attention back to my sister, to silently willing her recovery, which felt like the more pressing task. In the parking lot, Noriko held her car keys in one hand and her purse in the other. I was still holding Nicole's. Noriko and I liked each other—I was pretty sure—but we rarely spent time together just the two of us, and we didn't share confidences. She and my father had been together five years. They'd met when he bought some rental property on the edge of town, based on a rumor that a tech company was going to be expanding to our area; he was convinced that a boom was about to begin. The boom never happened, and half the rentals were empty; but he'd met Noriko, so it was, we all felt, a net gain. I knew little of her life before they met; she had a grown son in Seattle who visited once a year, in summer, during which time my father and Noriko did not sleep over at each other's houses. The son was a lab tech at a fertility clinic; he spent his days measuring hormones in blood. "These women think they can wait forever and still have kids," he'd told me once, rolling his eyes. "That's not the reality." I wasn't a fan of his.

"Your father is very upset," Noriko said now. "He can't handle seeing Nicole in this condition."

"Can't *handle* it?" I said. It didn't make sense to me. Our father had raised us on his own after our mother left; he bought us tampons and bras and didn't flinch when we screamed at him that our lives were ruined, because as teenagers we always thought our lives were being ruined. When I needed money for school he refinanced the house, and when I came home from school and went right back to waitressing, he didn't ask for any of it back.

"It reminds him too much of your mother leaving," Noriko said, "which was very traumatic for him."

"Noriko," I said. "His daughter is in the *hospital*. You agree that it's crazy that he didn't come, right? I mean."

"Of course I do." She opened the door to her car. "People can surprise you with their weakness, can't they?" she said. She hugged me again, awkwardly, with both the purses between us, then got into her car and drove away. I sat in my own car, rifling through my sister's bag, which I hadn't thought to do earlier. There was nothing of note in it: her driver's license, lip gloss, a pack of cigarettes. Her phone, which was dead.

IN THE MORNING I DROVE TO MY FATHER'S HOUSE. HE'D bought a small condo—Noriko also serving as the agent—and Nicole and I had helped him decorate it. None of us wanted the things that had been in our old house, and we laughed with a sort of hysteria as we took truckloads of knickknacks and old clothes and sports equipment to Goodwill. The theme for our father's condo, we decided, would be Clint Eastwood Unwinds at Home. At the same Goodwill we picked up some pictures of old gas stations and restaurants, which I framed to look arty. Nicole found some throw pillows with horses on them. Our father laughed, but he liked it, or he said he did, anyway.

Now he came to the door wearing a dark blue bathrobe and let me in without speaking. In the kitchen, he poured me a cup of coffee and listened while I harangued him. He just kept shaking his head. A few strands of his comb-over stood up on his head, waving slightly, like aquarium plants. It made him look wild, but his eyes were distant and dull.

"I'm going to need you to be understanding of this, Amber," he finally said. "I'm going to need you to find some room in your heart."

This was not the way he usually spoke. It was not the way anyone I knew spoke. I put my undrunk coffee down on his counter with a clunk, and it splashed. "If you care about her, you'll come with me right now."

"I do care," he said, "and no."

On my way out the door I passed Noriko coming in; she widened her eyes in a question and I rolled mine in answer. She pressed her lips together. I stood on the front porch for a minute after she entered, listening; but all I heard was silence.

WHEN I GOT TO THE HOSPITAL THE ONLY OTHER PERSON there was Lord. My sister looked the same, the same hushed pump from the respirator guiding her breath. A nurse came to check her and make notations on the chart.

"Such a beautiful girl," she said to me. "I used to watch her on that show. Couldn't believe it when he chose Courtney instead."

"Courtney was a bitch and a nympho," I said, and she looked startled and left hastily.

Behind me, Lord snorted.

"Well, I mean, come on," I said.

On the nightstand next to Nicole's bed I set out the things I'd brought: a CD player, some music she liked, a scented candle, some copies of *People* and *Us Weekly*. Nicole loved celebrity gossip. When she was in LA she was forever texting me about seeing somebody famous at the grocery store and what they had in their carts. After she came back home, broken and broke, I tried to cheer her up by taking her shopping at the mall, the big one an hour away, and she got so bummed out by it that we just turned around and came home. This whole life was her second choice.

Having Lord in the room made me self-conscious, but I wanted Nicole to know that I was there, so I read the magazines out loud to her, describing what people were wearing in the pictures, what they were buying at Trader Joe's. Who looked good and who was too fat or too thin. Every once in a while I'd glance over at Lord; he was reclining in the chair, which was too small for him, looking up at the ceiling. He seemed to be listening. For all I knew he was also a celebrity gossip fan. After a while my voice wore out and I took a break.

"Do you mind?" Lord said, and I shrugged.

He moved closer to Nicole and clasped his palms together. It took me a while to realize that he was praying. Our family had never gone to church—a total disinterest in religion was one of the few things our parents had in common—and I felt ill at ease. I went down to the cafeteria and got something to eat, and when I came back, Lord was standing in the hallway, doing a series of stretches. He was a big guy, solidly muscled, and when he reached his arms over his head he practically touched the ceiling. When he saw me, he dropped them back down.

"How did you meet Nicole, anyway?" I asked him.

The pause before he answered made me suspicious. "It was at the Lutheran church," he said.

"Nicole didn't go to church."

"Not usually, no," he said.

His presence made no sense to me. At first I'd thought he was one of her party friends, or a sometime or would-be boyfriend, and now I had no idea who he was, except an unwelcome guest at my sister's trauma. A rubbernecker.

"She was trying, you know," he said. "To change her life."

"I know," I said. Every Sunday morning Nicole would tell me she wasn't going to party anymore, and she meant it, too; she just couldn't act on it. I'd told her there were things she could do, people who would help, that she didn't have to do it all by herself, and she'd say, "It's not that easy, Amb," and I thought that she preferred the drama of it, the allure of her own misery, which at least made her feel important and alive. And then, in the hospital hallway, I put it together.

"The Lutheran church has AA meetings," I said. From the expression on his face I knew I was right. "She didn't tell me she was going."

He shrugged. "She was private about some things," he said. "I know that much."

It almost made me laugh. My sister was the least private person I knew. She'd been on television crying, drinking, making out with the guy who was the star of the show; she'd been photographed for a magazine shoot with the other contestants, all of them wearing lacy bridal lingerie, which was supposed to signal their hopes for a sexy wedding night. She said things out loud

I wouldn't have whispered to my closest friend. Then again, she'd surprised me earlier that year by showing me a printout from the internet of all the women in North America who had our mother's name. "She could be in Seattle," she'd said, "or Toronto. Or Des Moines."

"I don't care where she is," I'd said, which was the truth. "I don't need her for anything."

"How do you know what you don't need?" Nicole had said, folding the paper and putting it back in her purse.

"I just do," I'd answered, and she went quiet. I'd been surprised that she was even looking for our mother. I'd always thought we had an unspoken pact to let her go, to match her strength and defiance with our own. A while later I asked her if she'd contacted any of the women, and she shook her head and never brought it up again.

KEVIN HEWEY CAME BY ONCE MORE, BUT ONLY TO ADMIT THAT they had no idea who had hit my sister and would likely never find out; she'd been discovered well after the accident by some high school kids dazed and jubilant on Molly, who'd called the police in between giggles. They hadn't understood how serious her injuries were and they were not helpful witnesses.

Noriko visited every day, bringing thoughtful, useless gifts for Nicole—a throw blanket, fancy hand lotion, an audiobook called *The Power of You* which I refused to play—and food for me and Lord. Muffins she'd baked from scratch. When I asked her about my father, she hesitated and then shook her head. I was so angry at him I didn't know what to do, except to shelve my anger and deal with it later. Instead I focused on Nicole; Lord and I took turns reading to her, combing her hair, lotioning her hands. Her nail polish was chipped, and I took it off and applied a new coat of pink. It was something to do. During the long hours, of necessity, Lord and I got to know each other a bit. He'd been living in town for around a year, he said; he'd moved here from Glens Falls to start over after he got sober. Despite his name, he hadn't always been religious; for the longest time, he said, his teachers and social workers would shake their heads at him and say, "I wonder how you got *that* name."

"How did you?" I asked him, and he said he didn't know. He couldn't remember his birth parents, who'd named him; he'd spent his childhood bouncing around foster care until he wound up in a semi-permanent situation with an aunt and uncle. Then they got divorced, and Lord was on his own again, and there were a few years of his life that he clearly didn't care to discuss. He worked at Foot Locker at the mall, and when I said it was nice of them to give him time off, he shrugged and said, "I'll find something else." I nodded. At the Blue Dragon, I'd gotten people to cover my shifts so far but the weekend was coming up and my manager, Doug, was starting to make noises. Doug knew Nicole—they'd even dated for a while, a couple of years earlier—and said he wanted to be sympathetic but "you know Saturdays, Amb, we need all hands on deck." I hung up on him.

Of course we talked about Nicole, me more than Lord. I told him how Nicole was my best friend, how because our mother had left, we'd each acted as mother to the other; we'd taught ourselves about makeup and boys, we'd shared every morsel of information we found out about the world. The bond between us felt so solid that when Nicole came back from LA, plastic and haunted, with a fake bubbling laugh that hurt my ears, I assumed it was only a matter of time before the closeness between us would return. And when I saw her on Sunday mornings, her makeup smeared, scratches on her knees from

God only knew what Saturday-night events, I couldn't see her for what she was, for her trouble and pain. I saw her as my little sister, my partner in harmless crimes, and I believed against evidence that she would be restored. I had refused to understand how far gone she was, and now—I said this to Lord, crying, while he listened silently—it was too late. Lord didn't deny it.

THREE DAYS PASSED AND MY SISTER'S CONDITION DID NOT change. My father still refused to come to the hospital. When I called him with updates, he said, "Keep me posted," as if Nicole's injuries were a party I was planning. I was furious with him, and when I yelled he didn't yell back or excuse himself or explain. It was like punching a pillow, all give. Needing an outlet for my fury, I went to see Sam Postelthwaite. He lived in a run-down house near the old glove factory, where men of my father's generation had worked straight out of high school and which now stood abandoned. People missed the jobs but not the gloves themselves, which had been cheaply made and caused rashes. When Sam saw me, his whole face wrinkled in chagrin. "Come in," he said.

In the living room, he gestured towards the couch, and lowered himself down into a green armchair with the air of a man whose bones hurt him all the time. I told him I was there about my father, and he didn't seem surprised.

"I've known your father a long time," he said. "He's a decent man."

"I know he's decent."

"He's under a lot of stress."

The look I gave him must have been severe, because he wiped his palms on his pants as if I made him nervous. I went to his kitchen without asking him. It was the home of a man who fended for himself well enough: neat stacks of canned food in the cupboard, a freezer fully loaded with microwave meals. On a small shelf next to the fridge I found a bottle of whiskey. I wasn't much of a drinker—I saw too much of it at work—but I was craving alcohol, and I brought the bottle back to the living room, pouring us two glasses. By the time Sam had raised his glass to toast me, I'd already drunk mine down and poured a second. I examined his old man's face, the folds of flesh, the dark hairs on his bulbous nose. His skin hung on him like a bigger man's suit. He cleared his throat.

"I'll admit I feel responsible for your sister," he said. "I was supposed to look after her, but I couldn't be there every minute. She kept late hours, and I'm not as young as I used to be."

There was a pause in which he waited for me to say it wasn't his fault, and I didn't.

"Nicole is a wonderful girl," he went on. "But troubled, as you know. In the past two years she'd been badgering your father for information about your mother. She wanted to find her."

I remembered the printout she'd shown me, the list of names and addresses.

"Your father told her he didn't know where she went, but that's not entirely true."

"What do you mean it's *not entirely* true?"

He poured another shot and drank it down. I took another, too, which was more than I usually ever had. I didn't feel drunk, though, just flushed with an anger I didn't know where to direct—at my father, my sister, the car that had hurt her and then disappeared.

"I mean it's not true at all," he said. "Three years ago your father came to me and asked me to track your mother down. For you girls' sake. And for his own, too. So I did."

"You found her?"

I had always thought of our mother's disappearance as magical and complete. In my mind she'd reinvented herself so thoroughly that she belonged to a separate dimension. She owned a bar in Mexico and went by the name Dolores. She lived on a pot farm in the mountains and made millions, which she kept under the baseboards because she didn't trust banks. She was the wife of a gangster or a cult leader and everybody called her Mia. (Her real name, which she'd always hated, was Gwen.) Sitting on Sam Postelthwaite's brown tweed sofa, whiskey in my veins, I couldn't bring myself to ask him where she was.

"She died, Amber," he said. "She died five years ago. She had a hard life after she left here, I think, though I don't know the whole story. She was involved with drugs and, well, things caught up with her after a while, I guess."

My anger was a furnace inside me, glowing with impossible heat. I put down the glass of whiskey because I was afraid I might shatter it. I looked at my shoes.

"Here," his voice said. He was holding out a photograph of a woman I didn't recognize. She had my mother's eyes but her hair was blond and frizzy and her appearance was one of disturbed neglect. Her teeth were dark with rot. In the picture, she was wearing a blue dress and smiling sloppily at the camera—it may have been taken at a party—and these festive touches made the picture altogether sadder and worse than it would otherwise have been. I didn't take it from his hand.

"Your father couldn't bring himself to tell you," he said. "And now he thinks that maybe if he had, your sister . . ." He trailed off. I understood that our father had tried to allow us our fantasy of our mother, just as he used to let us eat all our Halloween candy on the first night, even though it made us sick. He had always been soft-hearted, unlike our mother. "Now look what happened," she used to say sternly when Nicole and I fought and ran to her, wailing from the injuries we'd given each other. "Look at what you've done."

WHEN I LEFT SAM POSTELTHWAITE'S APARTMENT I WAS exhausted and drunk, and I made it only a few blocks before I pulled over and laid my head on the steering wheel and cried. The night was dark and it was still cold enough that when I turned off the engine my breath plumed around me, boozy and visible. I called my father, and reached his voice mail. "Daddy," I said, and I had not called him that for many years, "I need you. I know everything and I need you." Snot bubbled out of my nose and I wiped it on my sleeve and dropped the phone under my seat. As I was bent over, a wave of lights strobed over the car. They almost instantly gave me a splitting headache. There was a hard rapping sound at the window, and I rolled down the window to see Kevin Hewey.

"Jesus Christ," I said. "Aren't there any other cops in this town?"

"I'm going to need you to step out of the car, ma'am," he said, and the *ma'am* was a rebuke to every sarcastic answer I'd ever given him, every time I'd stepped out of the way as he grabbed my ass at the bar. I got out. He took my license and then came back with a Breathalyzer test, which I took and failed. Then he turned me against my car and ran his hands up and down my legs, my shoulders, my back and stomach, my breasts, my crotch. I didn't make any protest. In my head I saw my ruined mother and my ruined sister, my companions, all of us ruined together.

PEOPLE CAN SURPRISE YOU WITH THEIR WEAKNESS, NORIKO had said, and Kevin Hewey surprised me with his. He finished his rough inspection of my body and then turned me around. He put a hand on my cheek. He had affection for me and he wanted me to know it. "You've had a bad week," he said. "Don't do this again." Then he lowered me into the passenger seat of the police car, with his palm on the top of my head, and drove me home, where I fell drunkenly asleep on top of the bedcovers, still wearing all my clothes.

In the morning I had to call Noriko to take me back to my car. She said she would come, but the person who showed up, his face steadfastly neutral, was my father. He was wearing a blue baseball cap and jeans and, for some reason, a sports jacket. I offered him some coffee and he shook his head. We drove out to the glove factory in silence and all he said, when we got to my car, was that he would see me at the hospital. I started to make some hostile comment—"miracle of miracles" is what I almost said—but then buttoned my mouth.

When we got to my sister's room, no one was there except her. The lights were bright and the machines hissed and beeped and the hallway intercom was a constant broadcast. When my father saw Nicole, his face crumpled and his bottom lip jutted like a little kid's. "Stop it," I said harshly, and pushed him toward her bed. Obediently, he sat down and placed his hand over hers, whispering something to her I couldn't hear. He sniffled and put both his palms over his eyes. It wasn't the first time I'd seen my father cry. He cried when our mother left, and when his own parents died, and he even cried at movies sometimes.

Nicole and I used to make fun of him for it. It was unusual for a man of his generation, and I don't know if it meant that he was more sensitive than those other men, or more damaged. Maybe it meant nothing at all.

My father stayed by Nicole's bedside for a few hours, and he came back the next day, and the day after that. We didn't talk about Sam Postelthwaite or my mother; we didn't talk much at all. My father read the local newspaper to Nicole, scores from high school baseball games, the weather. The doctors began to lower the dose of Nicole's sedatives in preparation for waking her. They removed the respirator and she made a terrible gagging noise as if she might choke to death, but she didn't, and the nurse—her name was Charlene, and I'd come to know her well—grabbed my hand and whispered, "It's okay, that's normal," and I'll always be grateful to her for that. Two weeks after the accident, Nicole opened her eyes, and her expression was confused and unhappy. It fell to me to describe to her where she was and what had happened, and I did my best. My best was not adequate to the task. Nicole's voice was raspy, from the ventilator, and she wanted to get out of bed right away, and she had to be restrained.

Her behavior in those early days was troubling. She couldn't seem to understand what had happened, and she was upset—with me, our father, everyone. Her short-term memory had been affected, so that every day I saw her, every new hour, we had to start all over again.

Nicole didn't want to go to physical therapy. She wanted a drink. She wanted us to go away. Many times I stalked out of the room, unable to take any more of her quarrelsome confusion, while our father stayed, dipping into the deep well of his patience.

The doctors said her confusion was normal. They said her anger was normal. They said she might never be the same person she was before.

I cried in stairwells. My father shook their hands.

Eventually Nicole was moved to an outpatient facility, which she didn't like any better than the hospital. She was walking and talking but her memory and her mood did not improve. I spent part of each day with her, and otherwise I went back to work at the Blue Dragon, fending off questions about her condition with a noncommittal smile. I was having trouble sleeping, and on a Tuesday night I found myself loitering outside the Lutheran church, smoking a cigarette and watching people filter into the parking lot. The last one out was Lord. If he was surprised to see me, he didn't show it.

"Hey," he said. "How is she?"

I frowned. "I was wondering what happened to you," I said. I wasn't sure which had annoyed me more, his constant presence at Nicole's side or his sudden absence.

Lord looked over my shoulder. "Got busy, I guess."

"Seriously?"

He lit a cigarette, and so did I.

"I'm working at Bobby's now," he said. I knew Bobby's. It was a sad diner out on the highway where Nicole and I used to go when we were teenagers. We'd eat pie and flirt with middle-aged men and then leave suddenly, knowing they'd settle the bill. We thought we were so dangerous. We thought being girls was such a game.

"I don't understand you," I said tightly.

"Look," he said. "Your friend made it clear I shouldn't come around."

"My friend?" I said. "I don't have any friends." This was true.

I knew just about everyone in town, I saw everybody at the bar, and when I went home to my apartment I crawled into solitude. I dreamed about living somewhere I knew no one, dreams all the more powerful because I'd never tried to make them come true.

"Officer Hewey," he said.

"He's not my friend," I said immediately, before I understood this wasn't what Lord meant. He meant that Kevin was a police officer; that we were both white; that we were both from this town. I remembered Kevin saying "I don't recognize him" and making Lord sit down on the bench, and I remembered, though I'd tried hard not to think about it, how he'd run his hands up and down my body, owning it and then discarding it, because he could.

In the silence that followed we smoked. "I'm sorry," I said. "That guy is a dick."

He tilted his head, to say *whatever*. It didn't make a difference to him whether I was sorry or not. I rushed into the silence, wanting to ease my own discomfort—that's how I see it now. I told him about Nicole, how she'd woken up and was improving, but she wasn't herself. I told him how hard it was to see her so confused, how I had to keep explaining her life to her: the car accident, the brain injury, the rehab facility. I told him how I was about to start double shifts at the Blue Dragon, to help cover the costs. I even told him about our mother, how Nicole had wanted to find her, and how she would never be found, and how our father had blamed himself for keeping this secret and worried that Nicole would follow her same path. I presented my life to him in rambling summation, and he listened. We stood in the parking lot for a long time, the night mild and damp, smoking one cigarette after the next. At last I leaned myself against him and tried to press my lips against his, and to be honest it didn't humiliate me any less that he was very gentle when he put his hands on my shoulders and pushed me away.

NICOLE LIVES WITH ME NOW. SHE IS NOT HERSELF, BUT SHE is not not herself either. She is herself but more forgetful, herself but meaner. She laughs less than she used to but when she does it's loud and startling and violent. At Sam Postelthwaite's funeral—he died in his sleep, at home, and my father, who found him, said it was peaceful, but that's what he would have said regardless—she sat in the back and her shoulders shook with strange, dramatic grief. For some reason she hates to wash her hair and it hangs lank and tangled around her shoulders. There's something different about her face, not the features themselves but how they sit in repose, never quite settling, which doesn't mean that she isn't still beautiful. She is still beautiful. She has a job, answering the phones at a real estate office, which is good because she tires easily, and needs to sit down. She doesn't miss teaching kindergarten, she says. "I always hated kids," she says, and it's hard to know if she's just being honest or whether it's the brain injury talking. I always like to say "It's the brain injury talking," as if the injury were a force separate from my sister, an outside agent whose involvement one day can be curtailed.

This is a small town; people take care of her. If they see her lost in the grocery store they help her find her way home. The local news came to do a story on her recovery and she spat at them and sent them away. Our father shook the reporter's hand and apologized, and then he and Noriko made Nicole some tea. Nicole will tolerate both of them, but only for a limited time. She will tell them to get out, she's sick of them, and our father will say mildly, "That's not very nice," and my sister snorts with derision. I see in my father's face, at these times, a pained expression that is achingly familiar from my childhood, and I see how Noriko stands next to him; I see them drive home together.

Sometimes Lord comes over; he prays with Nicole and they talk about AA, and he is kind to me too, in a careful way that continues to embarrass me. I have understood that when he visits my role is to step aside. My sister listens to him pray, a frown on her face, and I'm not sure what she thinks about God now, if anything. She's hard to read. When I told her about our mother, her reaction was stony. Whatever need she had to find her seems to have folded itself away, inside the jumbled crevices of her brain, and I don't know if it will ever emerge again. I'm glad she lives with me. In the early mornings I wake and drink coffee, read the paper, watch the sky. I stand outside her room and listen for the ragged rise and fall of her breath.

Service Intelligence

I'VE BEEN MYSTERY SHOPPING FOR SIX MONTHS, EVER SINCE my epic flameout at school, and it already feels like forever. Sometimes while I'm driving to a store—well, Aunt Ava drives while I listen to music on my phone—I think about my philosophy class last spring, which I actually liked and kept attending after I'd quit the rest, and this thing we learned about called the trolley problem. It's a famous conundrum involving whether you'd kill one person to save a bunch of others. There are all these questions associated with it—would you pull a lever and divert a runaway trolley to save five people, knowing that the trolley would hit one person on another track? Or: Would you push a fat man over a ledge so that he'd land in front of the trolley and stop it, in order to save those five people?

I'm not even kidding, the fat man variant is a famous illustration of this problem and we were supposed to write a paper on it and everything. All these stories about the runaway trolley bring up questions about ethics and utilitarianism, but the fat man variant made my class explode.

"Why is it a *fat* man?" this one girl wanted to know. "Isn't that fatist?"

"He has to be fat enough to slow down the trolley," a boy in the back answered. He was one of those practical people who kept asking how philosophical ideas applied in the real world. "It's pure logistics."

"*Fatist* is so not a word," a girl in expensive jeans said. "The whole concept is made up by people who don't want to exercise and eat right."

"Oh you did *not* just say that," the first girl said.

"What I'm wondering is why the company didn't maintain the trolley properly in the first place," said the pre-law guy who wore button-down shirts to class.

Soon they were debating corporate liability and body image instead of where the trolley went and how you made your decision about it. People in that class had a lot of opinions and wanted to share them because participation counted as part of your grade. I didn't say anything; I was already failing, and I didn't want to draw any more attention to myself than necessary. I never turned in my paper, either; by the time it was due I'd stopped going to class and pretty much stayed in my room watching old episodes of *Boy Meets World*.

I don't know why I think about the trolley problem so much, other than that the scenarios are entertainingly gruesome. I don't hold anybody's life in my hands. But of all the things I learned or failed to learn at school, this is the one that sticks in my mind: the fat man standing by the ledge, not suspecting anything, taking in the view. How much pressure would it take to push a guy who weighed, like, three hundred pounds? Sometimes I can't stop thinking about it. How powerful you'd be to make that choice. How shocked he'd be to find himself falling through the air.

. . .

AUNT AVA DOESN'T LIKE THE TERM *MYSTERY SHOPPING*, EVEN though that's what everybody else calls it. She prefers the corporate language, which is *service intelligence*. When she first suggested I become her partner, I thought it sounded cool, like being a spy—*I work for the Service Intelligence Agency* is a little joke I made to myself—but it turns out to be mostly driving and paperwork.

Even *mystery shopping* sounds more intriguing than the reality. We go into stores and make purchases to test whether individual stores are adhering to laws and company policies, evaluate customer service, etc., etc., whatever. I found out pretty quickly that Aunt Ava wasn't being generous by finding me a job; she could make more money if we did it together, since the most lucrative shops have to do with adult media content, cigarettes, and alcohol. The good thing about me from Aunt Ava's perspective is that I look younger than my age, which is twenty-one. This usually bothers me, but for service intelligence it's ideal. If I can get somebody to sell me cigarettes or booze without being carded, then the store gets a reprimand once we file our report.

By the way, Aunt Ava isn't even really my aunt. She's lived next to my parents ever since I was little and she and my mom are super close. When I got home from college in the spring it was Aunt Ava and my mom who were sitting in the living room waiting for me. My dad is an airline pilot so he isn't home much, which my mom says suits his desire for emotional distance from the family perfectly. She's supposed to say these things to their therapist but he's always missing appointments so she emails them to me instead. In April, I came in quietly, put down my bag, and sat on the edge of the armchair across from them, holding my clasped hands over my knees as if my legs might fall off without a good grip to keep them there. I was waiting for my mom to either yell at me or hug me and didn't know which one I dreaded more. I'd messed up in so many ways that semester, and one of them was waiting until well past the point of tuition refunds before withdrawing from classes. Karen, the counselor at school, had told me not to worry about my parents' finances—well, "You have to take care of yourself first" was actually what she said—but I knew from my mom's emails that money was another one of my parents' *zones of negotiation*.

I also knew she'd ask me why I hadn't come home earlier, and why I hadn't mentioned that something was wrong during all the emails and texts and calls we'd had. "Mom, I wanted to," I said, and burst into tears. Or maybe I didn't. Maybe I sat stone-faced, looking at my shoes. Lately when I'm in an uncomfortable situation, I go away inside my head, thinking about the trolley problem or Cory and Topanga from *Boy Meets World* or whatever, and so I don't even know what she said about dropping out of school. When I zoned back in, Aunt Ava was talking about service intelligence and how I could work with her while I figured things out, and apparently I'd already agreed.

So most mornings we head out in her Camry and she tells me what the shops are and then turns on the radio. She's obsessed with traffic reports, because some of the shops are gas stations where she fills up then gets reimbursed, and she wants to maximize the efficiency of the route to use as little gas on work as possible. Aunt Ava is single and thrifty. She's in her fifties but looks younger, with shiny, straight hair and zero wrinkles. She's Chinese-American, and my mom is half-Chinese—this is one of the things they first bonded over—and I'm a quarter. Everybody says I look more like my dad, who is tall and German and fair, but I'm short and small boned like my mom. Cassie Kranz, pint-sized German. In high school I did gymnastics and diving and I used to think I packed a lot of power into a small package, but I don't think that anymore.

The morning is cool and I shiver a bit in my shorts and T-shirt. Aunt Ava always wants me to wear something youthful, so I've dug out my old camp T-shirts and my hair is in two long braids and the whole experience is pretty infantilizing, which isn't the worst thing for an experience to be, in case you're wondering. We hit some electronics stores, and I get carded for trying to buy some video games *with adult content* and the middle-aged lady cashier gives me an amused look, which I try not to be embarrassed by but still am. After she turns me down I go find Aunt Ava and we sit in her car and fill out the reports.

Next we go to lunch at a burger restaurant, the kind of fake-homey place with fake-old black-and-white pictures of the restaurant on the walls and fake-handwritten menus advertising things like "homemade extra-loaded double-stuffed potato skins." I don't know anybody who makes extra-loaded double-stuffed potato skins at home. We order them, because we have to order something. Aunt Ava orders an iced tea, and I smile at the waiter, who is a paunchy, overwhelmed guy in his forties trying to keep track of too many tables at the same time, and ask for a beer. He glances at me for a second, then at Aunt Ava, then says he'll be right back. Once his back is turned, Aunt Ava looks at me and raises her eyebrows.

Procedure dictates that we finish our meal and pay before doing anything.

I don't want the beer, but it would look weird if I didn't drink any of it so I sip around half and even that makes me feel sleepy and dull. Aunt Ava spends most of lunch scrolling on her phone. At the beginning she used to try to make conversation with me, but when she didn't get anywhere she gave up and now she reads celebrity news and only talks if there's a story so salacious she can't contain herself.

After she pays, she asks to see the manager. This is also procedure, as specified by the company's own paperwork. The waiter says nervously, "Was everything all right with your meal?" and Aunt Ava smiles neutrally and asks again.

The manager is significantly younger than the waiter, probably not much older than I am, and he's wearing a spotty, unconvincing beard and a white shirt so thin it's see-through. I mean I can actually see two or three sparse tufts of his chest hair through the fabric. He comes at us with a scared, placating smile, and when Aunt Ava identifies us as *service intelligence* I can see from his expression that he has no idea what this means. Soon enough it becomes clear to him as she shows him the paperwork, and then there's a moment of awful surprise, for all of us, because, according to the paperwork, this company requires that he fire the waiter immediately, since he served me without asking for ID.

"Oh, but wait. Wait," the manager sputters. His name badge says LANCE, which somehow makes the whole thing more terrible. I don't want to know that his name is Lance and he has sparse chest hair. He probably went to my high school.

The waiter keeps glancing over at us, but he also has a bunch of other tables and a group of four ladies in the corner is bombarding him with questions about fat calories and gluten.

"You don't understand," Lance says. "We're understaffed today, because a girl called in sick—"

Aunt Ava tells him she doesn't make the rules, which is something I've never heard somebody say unironically before.

Lance lowers his voice to a whisper and hisses, "He's my *uncle*."

Aunt Ava says nothing.

"He's been out of work for months and my dad said to hire him here. He has three kids. I can't fire him. I mean I literally can't fire him."

Mentally I turn over whether this is the correct use of *literally* or not, and I can't decide. The crazy thing is that the guy hasn't even done anything illegal—I'm twenty-one. But company policy is to ask for ID for anyone who looks under thirty-five, and he's in violation.

Aunt Ava says, "If you don't fire him, somebody else will, and probably you, too."

Lance goes paler than his shirt. The waiter comes over then, and when Lance won't tell him what's going on, Aunt Ava does, in detail, showing him the paperwork. She's like a killer in a movie, the kind of icy but long-winded villain who has to explain everything to the victim before finishing him off, because it's important he understands why he's going to die. The waiter, who's older than I thought at first, lays a hand on Lance's shoulder and says, "It's all right, son, it'll be all right," and then I realize they're both crying, both of these men, and Aunt Ava shoves a stack of paperwork in Lance's hands, which he refuses to take, so it lands on the table in a puddle of condensation from her iced tea, and when we get back in the car she turns up the air-conditioning and the radio and I see her hands are shaking.

I say, "I don't think I want to do this anymore."

But Aunt Ava lives in a house she bought herself with money she made selling funeral plots to old people over the phone. She's never been married and got rid of her cat after it brought her a mouse as a gift, its little body wreathed in saliva but not quite dead, and she had to kill it herself because it was too far gone to save. My mom says there's a thing called a tiger mom which means women who are really hard-core and strict with their kids, but Aunt Ava doesn't have any so I guess she's just a tiger.

She says, "Too bad."

STILL, WE TAKE A FEW DAYS OFF. I DON'T DO MUCH WITH it—I don't sleep well at night anymore, and during the day I mostly lie on the couch and watch TV while my mom's at work. My dad comes home for twenty-eight hours and takes me to a baseball game, and that's the only time I relax because my dad is the one person in the world who wants to talk about stuff less than I do. The Phillies lose.

Then he takes off again. He's on a Singapore route these days and sometimes he sleeps in a hotel room in Newark instead of coming all the way back to the house. Before he leaves I make a joke about him having a second family somewhere and he gives me such a dark look I wonder if it's true. What *if* my dad had a second family? Do they know about us? Does he choose them over us, then us over them, over and over again, back and forth, switching from one track to the other, like some bigamist version of the trolley problem?

No, I decide, there's no way he could handle a second family. He can barely keep up with the problems in ours.

Karen from the counseling office sends me an email. *I just wanted to check in and see how you're doing. Drop me a line when you get a chance. When you're back to campus I hope we can continue our conversations.* I can't decide if Karen is being optimistic or dense, thinking I'm coming back to school. I delete it without answering.

Unlike Karen, my mom's given up checking in. At first she asked a lot of questions, and when she didn't get satisfactory answers she made me go to therapy with her. The therapist, Fern—who is their *marriage therapist*, by the way—was wearing a pale blue shawl cardigan and her office was decorated with pictures of flowers and windswept dunes that were meant to be soothing, I guess, and later I saw one of these prints at Target when I was picking up toilet paper and detergent for my mom, and it struck me as relaxing and I almost bought it before remembering where I'd seen it before, so she must be onto something. When she asked me to talk about what had happened at school my tongue lay thick and flat in my throat and I couldn't say anything.

In the car, my mom said, "Well, you proved your point. I just wish I knew what the point *is*."

Now she lets me do my own thing, but I know she's angry at me. I hear her on the phone with Aunt Ava, talking about how I used to be such a great student and what about my lost potential and all this over a boy, because she thinks I got my heart broken and couldn't concentrate on school. "She's always been so secretive," she tells Aunt Ava, and that's true. I'm like my dad; we both file the important things away for safekeeping. My mom puts them on display.

She's wrong about me, and if I could bring myself to talk about it I'd tell her so. But the thought of talking to her about G and the smell of chlorine from the pool and Red Bull and rum shuts my brain down. What makes it worse is I know G never stopped going to class and stayed in his room watching TV; he's probably walking around campus like everything is fine, which for him, I guess, it is. He can have that life, I've decided, that college life with quizzes and papers and dining hall food and the trolley problem. My life is service intelligence. Most of the time, it's not so bad.

. . .

ON TUESDAY WE GO BACK TO WORK. FOR THIS SHOP WE HAVE to buy something at Target and then try to return it without a receipt to another store, to see if they'll give us cash. They're not supposed to give cash no matter how much of a fuss we make. The instructions include a whole script to follow but they never change it and it sounds totally wooden and the people who work there are onto it by now, so I tend to take some creative license. Aunt Ava doesn't like it when I do this but I tell her it's better than us getting busted as mystery shoppers—the cashiers go all rigid and smiley and follow every rule to the letter, while secretly seething at us for wasting their time—and she knows I have a point.

"Cassie," she says as we park, "just don't go too far, all right? No tears. No dead people." This is a reference to a previous story I made up, about a toilet plunger I claimed, in the heat of the scene, had been bought as a gift for my late grandfather before he died—"and he never even got to use it!" (They gave me the cash, the triumph of my career to date in service intelligence.) I'm not great at real-life emotions but fake ones can be pretty enjoyable. "If they remember too much about it, they can contest the report and we don't get paid."

"Okay," I say. She takes a picture of the item—which is a phone—on her phone, and I make a joke about the meta-ness of taking a picture of a phone with a phone, which is humor that works better in an academic context, and she rolls her eyes at me and then we go in. She has to make notes while I'm doing it, about how many people are working, who talks to me and what they say, how long it takes for me to get service. All this goes in the report. And she can't get busted by the store workers while she's doing it, so she winds up just muttering into her Bluetooth while pretending she's super interested in lawn furniture or whatever.

As I walk up to the counter I'm rehearsing my script in my head, coming up with a plausible scenario, and I've got some adrenaline going and I sort of do feel like a spy for at least a couple of nerve-jangling moments, and I'm so engrossed in my task that I don't notice Monica until she's right in front of me and I can't escape.

"Cassie," she says. "Cassie Kranz! *There* you are!" She says this in a high-pitched, singsong voice, as if I'm a kitten that's been hiding under her couch. I know her from school; we're friends, I guess, in a glancing way. Once Karen asked me about my friends, and I said I had lots but not many I liked, and she asked how I could have friends I didn't really like and I said, "I'm sorry, have you ever been around girls?" and she laughed in a tone that made us both feel sad. Anyway, Monica and I used to do Zumba together sometimes. She's a theater major and an air-kisser.

Sure enough she gives me a big loud *mwah* that pops next to my ear like a tiny firework. "Where have you *been* this semester?" she says, still looking for me under the couch. I glance over at Aunt Ava, nervously—this encounter is messing up all the timing information we're supposed to write down in our report—but we're also not supposed to communicate with each other, so she just glares at me and I don't know what to do with that. "The operation has been compromised," I would say if I were an actual spy. "Abort. Abort."

But unfortunately I'm not an actual spy. So I just say, "Hey, Monica. What's up?"

What's up is a greeting that doesn't require an answer but people like Monica never realize it. She launches into a whole thing about coming home to visit the dentist and soon she's opening her mouth to show me the bloody gaps where her wisdom teeth used to be and I'm saying that I'm in a hurry and I start to edge away.

Monica purses her lips in a pouty, little-girl frown. "Let's hang out this weekend since we're both here! I never see you lately."

"I'm not in school anymore," I say, which I mean to end the conversation but of course it's a mistake because her jaw drops open like a drawbridge.

"Why not? What happened?"

Behind her I see Aunt Ava pointing at her watch, although she doesn't wear a watch, she uses her phone like everybody else, so she's just fingering her wrist where a watch would be.

"I don't believe in it anymore," I tell Monica, and then I say I have to go, and she looks confused but I realize, as I approach the exchange counter, that it's the best reason I've given anybody so far.

I wind up following the script exactly and I don't get any cash.

On my way out, a receipt for store credit in my hand, I run into Monica again. She picks up as if we never stopped talking. "You know who was asking me about you"—and I'm so worried she's going to say G that I mutter, "Yeah, I know," before she can get the word out and I grab Aunt Ava's hand, something I don't think I've done since I was five years old, and Aunt Ava gives me a weird look but doesn't ask why, and she walks with me fast, holding my hand, all the way back to the car.

KAREN THE COUNSELOR WANTED TO KNOW WHY I DIDN'T RE-port what happened. She talked a lot about owning your experience. "I do own it," I'd say. "I just don't want to have to prove it."

"It's like the trolley problem," I told her one time. I explained the whole setup to her. "You pull one lever and somebody dies, and you pull another lever and other people die. Either way somebody dies." What I meant was, there are no good options.

"So for you," she said, "reporting is like pulling a lever that would kill either him or you?"

I shook my head. "You don't get it." I was trying to convey how the whole thing had made me feel like a bystander to my own life, to my own body, even when I was in the middle of it. A person watching an accident, a runaway trolley moving fast on the tracks. What happened was this. I was pregaming with my friend Lauren at her apartment, and a bunch of guys came over, including G. That's how I think of him, because I don't even like to have his whole name in my head, only a letter, and if you're wondering it's not the real first letter of his name; I like to pretend he was *George* or *Gerald*, both of which are terrible names, and that pleases me despite being what Karen would call an *inadequate coping mechanism*. He was in my Voices on the Margins lit class, though I'd never talked to him before. We all went to a party and we were dancing and it got really hot and then G suggested that we break into the pool and go swimming. So four of us headed over there but somehow by the time we got to the pool it was just him and me. I don't remember the walk over there too well so I don't know where Lauren went, or G's friend. When the pool water hit me I sort of woke up with a shock and G had my arms twisted behind me and he was laughing like it was a game and I was sputtering and trying to get out. "Okay," he said, "okay." I was so relieved. He picked me up like I was a princess in a movie and carried me over to the bleachers and laid me down. "I don't feel good," I said, or think I said, and he kept saying, "It's okay," as if it were reassuring, what was happening, and each time I turned my head away or put my arm up he'd just move someplace else. There wasn't enough of me to stop him.

I woke up in the women's locker room with my hair wet and my clothes in a pile. I never told Lauren what happened. I never told anybody, except Karen, and even she only got the sketchiest details, mostly because sketchy details were all I had myself.

"Help me understand," she said after I brought up the trolley problem. "What goes into your decision to pull the lever?"

I was exasperated. "I'm not the person pulling the lever," I said. "I'm the fat man."

She nodded in the way that meant she was confused but hoped if I kept talking we could clear it up. She was an expert at nodding: she had the understanding nod, the sad nod, the appreciative nod at some lame joke I made, the nod that said *Let's go deeper*, the nod that said *Our time is up*. I made fun of her nodding but she was really nice, Karen. I liked her. I only stopped going to her because she wasn't making me feel better, and besides some of our sessions conflicted with when *Boy Meets World* was on.

WE HAVE A DULL WEEK WHERE THE SCHEDULER SENDS US around to stores to photograph merchandise and make small purchases, like a dollar or less, and I don't even know what the point of it is. There's no script and no adult beverages and it's tedious but at least no one gets fired. A couple of times we have to drive past the burger place, and we both avert our eyes like it's the scene of a car accident or something. After a while Aunt Ava gets so bored that she starts telling me about the celebrity news she reads about, the divorces and babies and affairs. She gets mad when I don't know who all the minor celebrities are, so I act like I recognize everybody and am shocked that their marriages aren't turning out well. Aunt Ava likes to weigh in on their choice of spouses. "There's already one baby in that marriage," she'll say. Or: "Of course it didn't work out. They both need to be the center of attention."

She has a lot of opinions about marriage in general, for someone who's single. I wonder what she thinks about my parents', but probably it's better I don't know. She doesn't even really need me for these shops—she could do it all herself, and not split the money—and it saddens me to realize that she's probably lonely.

We're driving by the burger place again—funny how I'd hardly ever noticed it before and now it seems like every route in town takes us past it—when she says, very casually, "You know, I used to be married."

"You were?" I had no idea. Aunt Ava living next door by herself is a constant of my life. She has spent every Christmas with us, every New Year's Eve, every Fourth of July. Sometimes she goes on dates but it never seems to work out. My mom says she has high standards, and my dad says something different but under his breath.

"I knew you wouldn't remember him. You were so little when he left. You liked him though. Jack. He threw you up in the air and almost dropped you. Of course you didn't know he almost dropped you. You thought it was delightful."

I search back in my mind for this, but I don't come up with anything. I read somewhere that our memories aren't really our memories; they're actually composed of stories other people tell us about our lives. So everything I know of my past—the holidays and vacations, the trips to the zoo and family movie nights—is what my parents told me about our life, and there's no Jack in it. It's pretty creepy, as if childhood is just one big thought experiment performed on you by your parents.

"What happened?" I wonder if she got rid of him just like she got rid of her cat.

"We got divorced," she says in that abrupt way of hers. She acts like the question is stupid, but I don't know why she brought it up if she didn't want to talk about it.

After a while she seems to relent, and goes on. "He wasn't a trustworthy person. At all." We're parked in front of a strip mall now. I'm supposed to go in and try to buy cigarettes at a convenience store while Aunt Ava documents. But she's still sitting in the car, staring straight ahead at the store window, as if it's a puzzle she's trying to solve.

"He took a lot of my money," she said, "and he slept with another woman. It broke my heart."

It's weird to hear Aunt Ava say something like "It broke my heart." What's even weirder is that she's crying. Not a lot, not sobbing or anything, but tears are wobbling in the corners of her ears, tiny and fat. I don't know why she's telling me this, either, and why right now, in front of a convenience store.

"It happens to everybody," she says. "Even movie stars. Everybody gets their heart broken sometime."

I see what she's saying, what she's trying to do.

"I'm not heartbroken," I say. "I'm full of rage." Which is something I never said to Karen, but as I say it I know it's true. I am *at capacity,* from my toes to my heart to my eyeballs to my brain, so replete with rage there's no room in me for anything else.

She looks at me like she's seeing me for the first time. "Okay," she says.

We get out of the car and hit the store, ready to make our mystery purchases, and I go up to the cashier and ask for some Camel Lights. She's a tired-looking lady with frizzy brown hair, wearing a red smock over her T-shirt, and I bet she smokes herself so you'd think she'd be sympathetic. She looks me up and down says, "Are you a minor?"

I shake my head, and she asks me for ID.

"I'm old enough," I tell her.

Sometimes people say "The law's the law" or "I'd like to but I can't." But this woman's tone is like acid when she says, "Honey, you're just a kid. I can't help you."

"Thanks for nothing," I say bitterly, forgetting the script, and she laughs at me. Her teeth are yellow and mossy. I want to spit. I'm angry and I feel like I will always be angry, there is nothing outside of my anger and no place to put it, and Aunt Ava follows me silently out to the car.

She puts her seat belt on, but doesn't start the car. Then she says, "I am also full of rage."

The way she says it, so serious and stilted, makes me laugh. It's an angry laugh though, not a happy one, and Aunt Ava seems to get this, because she doesn't laugh back, only nods. We sit in the car together, an aunt who isn't an aunt and a kid who isn't a kid, a tiger and a fat man, shoppers and spies. I put my headphones on and Aunt Ava turns the key in the ignition and doesn't say where we're going next.

We drive.

Taxonomy

tax·on·o·my noun / tak-ˈsä-nə-mē / : the system or process of classifying the way in which different living things are related by putting them in groups

ring-tailed lemur (kingdom: Animalia; phylum: Chordata; class: Mammalia; order: Primates; family: Lemuridae; genus: *Lemur;* species: *Lemur catta*)

ON THE WAY TO LANCASTER, HE STOPS TO BUY HIS DAUGHTER a gift.

It's a residual habit from long-ago business trips, though Meredith is both far away and past such things. But this trip is for her, or at least undertaken on her behalf, so it feels right to get her something, a talisman from the journey, as he would have when she was young. WELCOME TO AMISH COUNTRY says the sign in the little country store attached to the gas station— though surely the Amish themselves would never erect a sign like that—and inside are displayed butter churns, quilts, dolls, and pies. Picking up a wooden spatula, he notes that it's made in

China. The man behind the cash register smiles vaguely out the window, his mouth hung open to reveal small colorless teeth.

At the back of the store, he spots a basket of stuffed animals. At twenty-four, Meredith hasn't cuddled a teddy bear in years, but the selection here is startlingly varied: gorillas, monkeys, snakes, and something that, if he squints and holds it at an angle, might be a lemur. What these animals might have to do with the Amish, he doesn't know, but a lemur is a perfect gift, since that's the animal Meredith is studying, in Madagascar. Studying and saving, or trying to save. As a budding conservation biologist, she's researching the many species and subspecies of lemurs, along with their vanishing habitat. So she has explained to Ed—in frankly a bit too much detail—in passionate, jargon-heavy emails.

A lemur it is, a long-limbed tube of fur with wide plastic eyes.

After paying for the toy and the gas, he gets back in the car. The GPS sends him north on one road, south the next, a route so erratic he can't help but wonder if the calm robotic female voice is messing with him. But the landscape quiets his irritation: eastern Pennsylvania in July, green hills dotted with small farms, is a place of tidy safety. Not like Madagascar, which has seen a sharp rise in attacks and robberies, particularly crimes against tourists. When he copied the US government warning link to Meredith, she sent back a message that began: *I'm not a tourist. I'm a scientist.*

Always very self-serious, his girl, very conscious of categories. He's glad she has a sense of purpose, if one he struggles to understand at times, and that he wishes hadn't sent her halfway around the world.

Meredith loves animals, her work, her friends. She loved

Christine, with a complicated intensity that belied the fact
that they weren't biologically related—they fought almost
daily until Meredith was seventeen, and then the skies cleared
and they grew so close he sometimes felt like an outsider. She
loves the lemurs. She loves him, at least he hopes she does.
About the errand that has brought him here from Philadelphia,
and the woman who was her biological mother, she seems to
care nothing at all.

cow (kingdom: Animalia; phylum: Chordata; class: Mammalia;
order: Artiodactyla; family: Bovidae; genus: *Bos;* species: *Bos
taurus*)

FOLLOWING THE GPS DIRECTIONS, HE PASSES THROUGH A
small, well-kept town (diner, consignment shop, fruit stand)
and then it's back to farms. The cows are curled up in the fields,
legs beneath them, dozing, placid hulks. This is Phoebe's world,
the place she couldn't wait to leave and then returned to, the
trip equally frenzied in both directions, which was how Phoebe
lived her life. Their time in Philly was short: first romantic
and dramatic, then terrible and dramatic. It was like living in a
tabloid, every conversation a shouted headline, every scene a
sensation. They met in a bar, got married in a hurry, had Meredith, then commenced hating each other as if this had been
their goal all along. Ed had grown up in Quakertown, the son of
an accountant and a school librarian; he'd always been a quiet
person. Sure, he liked to go out drinking with his friends, but
who didn't, at that age? He had a college education and was
saving for a house. Then suddenly with Phoebe he was drinking
whiskey in the afternoon and calling his wife a *bitch* and a *cunt*
while his sweet little baby slept in the next room. He used those

words; he did those things, and worse. The fact that Phoebe goaded him to it, that she turned out to be as purely, irredeemably crazy as a person can be, did not excuse him.

The night she left, "to get away from his bullshit" she said, he got down on his knees—though he'd never been religious—and prayed to God to be returned to the person he used to be. Then he prayed that Phoebe would never come back, never try to take the baby from him, that life in their apartment had been so hellish she wouldn't want a single reminder of it, even one composed of her own flesh and blood.

To his endless surprise and gratitude, these prayers had been answered.

As Meredith grew up, Ed monitored her for signs of her mother's illness, but she was levelheaded and literal-minded, like him. She and Ed were calm together, placid creatures, rooted to the earth. He tried to talk about Phoebe sometimes—not out of allegiance to his ex-wife but because he thought Meredith might need to know later, might require answers to the questions of her own past. But she showed no interest in the subject. He married Christine when she was three and she didn't remember any other mother. The past was an abstraction. Even as a toddler, she'd most wanted to be down on her knees with her hands in the dirt, looking at frogs and ants and worms. Whatever she needed to know about her existence, she seemed to find it there.

It was Ed who waited each year for Phoebe to write or call, to demand contact, to sue for custody. Despite their arguments she'd shown affection for the baby, cradled her in her arms, sung her lullabies. She must have had regrets. He loved his daughter so intensely that when he had to leave on business trips he always wept, and he took to departing before dawn so that he wouldn't upset her. He couldn't fathom that anyone related to Meredith *wouldn't* feel the same bond. He knew that one day Phoebe would show up at the front door, demanding her rights as mother.

But she never did. Instead, last month, a letter came to the house, and how it found him Ed didn't know, seeing as they'd moved several times in the intervening years, from a son Ed wasn't aware she'd had. Mordecai. Phoebe was dead, he wrote, without further explanation, and she'd left something for Meredith. Maybe Meredith wanted to come pick it up. Maybe she'd want to meet her brother.

A brother. Ed hesitated over this letter for days before deciding to go himself, without telling his daughter about it. Though she's never shown interest in Phoebe, Meredith has a scientist's mind; she likes to figure out where and how things fit together. Will she not one day want to know about her own kind?

dog (kingdom: Animalia; phylum: Chordata; class: Mammalia; order: Carnivora; family: Canidae; genus: *Canis;* species: *Canis lupus;* subspecies: *Canis lupus familiaris*)

THE PROPERTY LOOKS MORE OR LESS AS ED REMEMBERS IT from a few bitter weekend visits back in the day: still dilapidated, but with newer cars rusting in the front yard. Phoebe's grandparents built a neat, just-profitable dairy farm, with a vegetable plot that fed the family during the summers, food they canned to see them through the winters. She spoke of these thrifty, hardworking people with nothing but contempt for their labor; it was a hard life, she said without admiration, implying that they should have found an easier one. The property passed to her parents without the work ethic to sustain it; they let the place go to seed, but would never relinquish it. Injured in a car accident, her father went on disability and drank; her mother operated an informal daycare in her living room, four or five kids who always seemed, Phoebe said, sick and snot-nosed and screaming. Wanting to get away from a place like that, Ed could understand. Less clear—in fact completely opaque—was why she'd ever moved back. Phoebe never went to college; she was working as a bartender when they met. He supposed she thought it was temporary, and probably she didn't have other options.

As he pulls up, tires crunching on the dirt, dread waves across him. The house, once white, now peeling and grey, looks lopsided, as if subsiding into the earth. On the porch a skinny brown dog lifts its head wearily at his approach. A black dog comes around from the back, panting in the heat, wagging its tail. Neither one barks at least, and in fact when Ed gets out of the car, the black one noses its head into his palm, wanting only attention. Then it follows him up on the porch, where he steps over its compatriot and knocks on the door. As he waits, he surveys the land around him—the two poplars beside the house, the silo in the distance, as lonely a place as he's ever seen.

The door opens and Mordecai, presumably, sticks out a hand. Ed is relieved to see he looks normal: just a guy in jeans and a navy T-shirt, buzz cut tinged with grey. He looks at least forty years old. Ed's confused—didn't he say he was Phoebe's son?

"Ed," he says, with a strong grip. "Good to meet you. Meredith with you?"

Ed shakes his head. "She's in Madagascar, as I mentioned."

"Oh, right. I saw that movie," the other man says. His tone is ambiguous. It's possible he thinks that Meredith is *at the movie* right now. "Whelp, come on in."

Expecting the worst, Ed's glad to find the place clean and

neat. The only noticeable smell is the faint funk of dog, and indeed a couple of other ones trot up in greeting, these ones little, and white.

"I foster," Mordecai explains, leading him into a sunroom at the back, where plants line a shelving unit, their tendrils reaching to the window. Against the wall is a small tube television with rabbit ears. The two men sit down on opposite sides of the room, and Mordecai offers him a beer.

Ed shakes his head. He wants to get this over with. "I was sorry to hear about Phoebe," he launches in.

From the way Mordecai lifts an eyebrow, Ed understands that Phoebe has told him the truth about their marriage.

"Well, she didn't suffer too bad," he says. "Pancreatic cancer. Gone in weeks. Barely enough time to settle any of her affairs."

Reaching over to a side table, he picks up a framed photo and passes it to Ed. It shows an elderly woman with her arm around a younger Mordecai. It takes him several confused seconds to understand this woman is—was—Phoebe. A jolt strikes his chest, though he couldn't even say what emotion causes it. Picture Phoebe weighs easily three hundred pounds, and her lank brown-grey hair lies flat against her ears in a stringy bob. She wears a shapeless housecoat-dress. And she's smiling.

At twenty, Phoebe wore tight black metal-band T-shirts and acid-washed jeans and feather earrings that dangled almost to her shoulders. She had a leather choker jutting with spikes. Hers was the kind of figure that silenced men in the bar, so they could concentrate on looking at it. Then, when she was pregnant, her body grew ample, her skin taut and glowing, and she was even sexier than before.

Ed knows he looks old, too, but come on.

"She only put on the weight after magic was born."

"What magic?" Ed says automatically.

"Magick. With a *c* and a *k*. Meredith's brother." Mordecai passes him another picture, this one showing a little kid in a baseball uniform. "This is old. We haven't been much organized to take pictures since my dad died."

"Oh," Ed says, understanding. "So your dad—"

"Married Phoebe when I was twenty-five. Magick's my half brother. Meredith's half brother, too. We're all related by halves."

Ed, absorbing the news, can't decide if it's good or bad.

"He's around here someplace," the other man goes on. "He's a bit shy. Bit shook up with his mom gone, of course."

A couple of the dogs make their way into the sunroom, leading with their noses, as if they've been on Ed's trail this whole time. The black one stands next to him, leaning suggestively against his knee, though he can't figure out what the suggestion is. A small white one curls up on an armchair and goes to sleep.

"And his name is Magick?" Ed says, unable to shave the judgment from his voice.

Mordecai looks at him steadily, his hands on his knees. He has replaced the two photographs on the side table. "You know Phoebe. She put a big premium on *unique.*"

And Ed laughs, the sound rolling out of him before he can stop it, remembering one of their first big fights, over Phoebe wanting to name the baby Ocean. He thought it would condemn the child to a lifetime of ridicule. So they compromised, and Phoebe would say, every time she introduced their daughter, "her name is *Mer*, which is French for ocean," and Ed would grit his teeth.

Mordecai sighs. "She was kind of nuts."

Ed is surprised. "She was when I knew her. I thought maybe—"

"Nope," Mordecai says steadily. "Nope."

goat (kingdom: Animalia; phylum: Chordata; class: Mammalia; order: Artiodactylia; family: Bovidae; genus: *Capra*; species: *Capra aegagrus;* subspecies: *Capra aegagrus hircus*)

MORDECAI OFFERS TO SHOW HIM AROUND. BACK ON THE porch, the animal he thought was a dog stands up and reveals itself as a goat. He'd been so intent on getting to the front door that he hadn't even noticed. It's mangy and scruffy, with hard little eyes.

"Magick's lactose-intolerant. Seems to do okay with goat's milk, though."

The goat looks at him quietly, either tired or trusting.

"Good idea," Ed says inanely.

"Phoebe didn't much care for animals. She always had a lot of business plans. Came up with a lot of internet-based stuff. But in the end, this property—" He sweeps his arm out widely instead of ending the sentence.

Ed swallows. "Do you know why she never got in touch with Meredith?"

Mordecai looks at him. They're around the same height, not far from the same weight. He seems on the verge of saying any number of things. The goat bleats as if disturbed by the silence. From the highway comes a distant rumble of truck traffic, or maybe it's just the wind. The quiet here is not tranquil. It used to be that Phoebe couldn't stand to be in a room without music playing, couldn't drive a car without a soundtrack to her life. If she hadn't been crazy before living here, this place would have guaranteed it.

The goat nudges him and Mordecai signals their way off the porch. "She never talked about Meredith much," he says as they tramp around the property. "I didn't even know she existed until just recently, to be honest with you. Phoebe kept some things close. They didn't tell me she was pregnant until they brought Magick home from the hospital."

IN THE BACKYARD, WHICH IS NOT A YARD BUT A WEEDY EX-panse of agricultural land no longer cultivated, they come upon him. True to his name, he's wearing a black cloak and huddling over a tree stump as if performing incantations. He doesn't notice their approach. Ed thinks of a video he saw online once, of a kid fighting with a light saber, leaping and jumping, lost inside his kinetic reenactment. There was a pure joy in it people had to make fun of. Ed felt sorry for him. What was childhood if not the time before you understood how stupid were your pleasures, how necessary to keep them secret?

Though in retrospect he'd probably laughed at the *Star Wars* kid and Christine had been the one to talk him out of it, to show him a kinder point of view. That was what she did for him. In the year and a half since she'd died he felt himself getting sharper-tongued at work, more sarcastic and impatient, less interested in other people, even in Meredith's monologues about her work. He was getting meaner again, as he'd been when he was young.

"Magick," Mordecai says. Then louder: "Magick."

At the sound of his voice the boy turns around, the cape swirling cinematically as he does. Ed feels sharply sick, bile rising into his mouth. Because the face is Phoebe's: sensual, instantly recognizable, like a rock star's. Thick lips and high cheekbones. A violent confrontation in the eyes. Phoebe's beauty was androgynous; she was a challenge, a woman without coy glances or feminine gestures, a hard place you'd have to scramble to get to, and oh how men wanted to get there. Here in this awkward teenage face—he's maybe thirteen, fourteen— you could see not the sex but the defiance, a *fuck-off-world* stare written too large on his slender face.

The kid hates him, Ed's sure. "He knows who I am?"

"I'm not sure what he knows," Mordecai says, and his tone holds a warning, though maybe not the warning Ed was expecting.

The boy comes over, a sword dangling from his hand.

"Say hi, Mag."

"Hi Mag," the boy says mechanically.

Ed puts his hand out, and the kid ignores it. Up close, the resemblance to Phoebe is even starker. Under the cloak, the kid is wearing an Eagles jersey and black cords—clothes far too warm for the weather—and his body is all angles and bones.

"I'm just giving Ed the tour," Mordecai says. "Come with."

The boy neither agrees to this nor disagrees. His large green eyes are so wide-set he almost looks like an alien. They head around the opposite side of the house, where Mordecai points out a storage shed full of Phoebe's things, "business materials," and then back inside via a side door. Ed is shown a dining room, the hutch with Phoebe's china in it, and a living room with family photos on the walls, Phoebe's husband a Santa Claus type with a belly and beard. There's an oil painting of the house itself, done by Phoebe, whom he never knew to paint or draw or anything. Throughout the tour Mordecai offers up a steady stream of information, most of it financial: the tax assessment on the house, the rising cost of heating oil, the price of a much-needed new furnace and roof. He seems to think Ed cares about this minutiae, like he's in the market for a broken-down house in the middle of nowhere.

In the living room, Ed finally asks—he has to interrupt a sentence about the cost of weatherproofing the windows—what it was that Phoebe left for Meredith. When the other man goes to fetch it, Ed puts his hands in his pockets, then takes them out again, then plunges them back in.

This is the only message Meredith will ever get from her mother.

The interval stretches, unbearable. Ed and Magick are left alone. They sit down on a green couch draped with a yellow-and-black afghan, the boy humming tunelessly and making small swishes with his cape. Between the humming he murmurs to himself, a bass line of words that Ed can't decipher but knows aren't meant for him anyway. He tries to connect this behavior to Phoebe, but for all her faults she wasn't remote from other people. If anything, she was too connected to them. She loved her coworkers at the bar, and also fought with them, sometimes physically. She was always yelling at Ed, but it was because she wanted more from him, more love, more sex, more heat, more anger. She cheated on him twice, both times with guys from the bar, because, she said she needed to feel beautiful and he didn't give that to her. She was a thrumming machine that never turned off, her need for attention a constant engine, revving.

The boy mutters and hums. Maybe he takes after his dad.

Finally Mordecai comes back into the room holding a pink stuffed rabbit, which he passes to Ed. He cups it in his palm;

it's cute but nothing special, its fur made of cheap polyester. It probably cost the same as the lemur that's baking outside in his Sentra.

Ed is perplexed. "Did she, was there, any explanation or anything?"

Mordecai shakes his head. "She just said to give it to her daughter. I assumed it was something she kept from when Meredith was young."

"If it is, I don't remember it."

Mordecai shrugs, abdicating.

"Did she say anything else?"

"Not really. My dad said there was a lot of unresolved issues there."

Ed raises his eyebrows.

"He was a pastor," adds Mordecai.

A pastor with sons named Mordecai and Magick. None of it makes sense to Ed. And there's no way the rabbit dates back twenty years; it's stiff and unhandled, pink fur bright from the factory. He wonders if Phoebe was hallucinating at the end, imagining some other life, some other daughter. He's heard such things can happen, when there is pain and medicine for the pain.

Just as he's about to leave, Magick stands up and faces him. Mordecai puts on a falsely jovial voice and says loudly, "You want to put on a show?"

The boy nods.

And he commences a set of tricks that are so good as to be professional. Not that Ed's any judge, but it *is* magic. What's missing is any kind of patter, the river of words that magicians use to distract you from the sleight of hand. The only sound in the room is the swish of polyester as the cape moves through the air. And yet, despite the silence, Ed can't see how the tricks are done; he can't find the seam that stitches one gesture to the next.

The kid swallows his sword and regurgitates a rainbow-colored cloth. He pulls a bird out from behind Ed's ear. The bird settles itself on a coffee table, pecking at something it finds there. He makes coins rain down from the ceiling, a clatter of dimes and nickels that land on the couch and in Ed's lap. From a deck of cards, he gets Mordecai to pick the eight of hearts and hold it in his hands, then finds the eight of hearts in Ed's pocket. Each trick is a silent impossibility, a wonder.

The boy claps his hands, and the bird disappears!

One minute it's next to Ed, pecking and seeming slightly unsanitary, and the next it's gone.

The two older men clap enthusiastically, and the boy nods, stooping slightly in acknowledgment, then leaves the room.

Ed doesn't know what to say. When he glances at Mordecai, his eyes are watery with tears. Ed's surprised, then not surprised. He thinks he knows the feeling. When Meredith was a child, less than six, he took her to a circus. In the parking lot a man was forming balloon animals, and they stopped to watch. The man squeaked and twisted a bumblebee, a snake, a dog. When he asked Meredith what she wanted, she said a spider. The balloon artist seemed taken aback, but eventually he twisted a black balloon around itself until he had made some semblance of one, a circle with legs sticking out of it. He handed it to Meredith, who studied it gravely, then gave it back. "There's no thorax," she said.

What astonished Ed was not her intelligence or her vocabulary—though he was bursting with pride over those—but the indefinable *personhood* of her. He had made her and cared for her and she had become, so quickly, something separate from him, something well and truly her own. She was herself, a girl who knew what a spider should look like, a girl who could name its parts.

mourning dove (kingdom: Animalia; phylum: Chordata; class: Aves; order: Columbiformes; family: Columbidae; genus: *Zenaida;* species: *Zenaida macroura*)

THE MAGIC SHOW OVER, MORDECAI SPREADS HIS PALMS OUT, as if to say, *Can you believe that?* Ed can't. He's never seen anything like it.

"That was impressive. Please thank him for me later."

"I'll try," Mordecai says.

"I should be going." Ed lifts the rabbit in a kind of salute. "Thanks for this, too."

The other man nods and then, as Ed is rising from the couch, he reaches out and grabs Ed's wrist with a forceful grip. "Tell Meredith," he says, and his voice is low but urgent. "Tell her he's here."

And Ed understands that *this* was the reason for the visit, not the plush toy, which may or may not have been earmarked for his daughter in the first place. Maybe Phoebe never wanted her to have anything. It's Mordecai who wants something, wants it desperately, judging from the pressure of his hand.

There's a rustle in the corner of the room and the bird from Magick's trick—a dove, he thinks, though he doesn't know anything about birds—is pecking around the base of a potted plant, trying to reach the soil. It doesn't look good, one wing hanging lower than the other, its walk a drunken stagger. He can't remember if it looked like that before, or if the trick damaged it somehow.

He turns back to Mordecai. "Meredith's off working on her studies," he says. "She's going to get her PhD and be a scientist. I don't see her coming back home much. Just so you know."

Whatever you want from her, he's thinking, you can't have her. I will protect her from your sad broken-down house and this unfathomable caped boy.

"He's her brother, too," Mordecai says, but the urgency in his tone is already fading into defeat. "It can't be all on me."

"I hear you," Ed says noncommittally, and the grip on his wrist lessens, then releases.

When Phoebe first left, she flung a beer bottle at him and it shattered on the wall behind his head. He vacuumed up all the glass, petrified that Meredith would get into the shards somehow, but still he kept finding them, days later, some tiny sliver that could have cut his daughter, could have gone down her throat. It was picking up that glass that solidified his hatred for his wife. When she calls to get the baby back, he thought, he'll say that Meredith cut herself, and that will be his proof that she can't be a mother.

But Phoebe never called. It was her mother who did—a tired, pallid woman with some sweetness at her core. She didn't make any threats; she was too timid for that. She only wanted to see Meredith, to visit occasionally. Ed said no. "It's too confusing for her," he said, though Meredith was barely a year old. Nothing and everything was confusing to her; she wasn't even walking yet. He knew the door had to be shut completely, or else the crazy would find its way back in. And he will keep it shut now.

He shakes Mordecai's hand and leaves the house, picking his way past the goat, the friendly black dog, and the weeds in the front yard. Midday sun has broiled the car and he rolls the windows down, turns the AC up, cool air dissipating into hot. An upstairs window opens and he sees Magick in the bedroom, maybe looking at him, but probably not; he's too far away to tell. The house is otherwise motionless, the whole animal kingdom settling in for a drowsy afternoon. The plush rabbit joins the lemur on the passenger seat. He's already decided not to tell Meredith where they came from. He'll give them to her, and she can do what she wants: name them, cherish them, or throw them away.

Nights Back Then

NIGHTS BACK THEN, I LIKED TO GO TO A COFFEE SHOP ON Eighth Street and sketch. I sat in a corner with my blue notebook, fixing an unseeing stare on the grainy wood of the table. This was during the first Gulf War, which—it was commonly agreed by everyone I knew—was motivated by oil, so images of oil snaked through all my drawings, viscous and shadowy, the secret bloodstream of the world. I also drew soldiers, those young men and women who were being asked to risk their lives for oil, sacrificing for a cause that didn't deserve them. That I did not personally know any soldiers, that my friends were all grad students and aspiring artists, didn't prevent me from drawing them. Around me in the coffee shop, couples—gay, straight, young, old, they were all couples—held hands, flirted, argued, broke up, and I sketched none of this, though looking back it's what I most remember. How the coffee shop seemed full of couples, each positioned at a different point along the spectrum from meeting to parting, as if the coffee shop were a laboratory for romance, an incubator of it.

I always went to the coffee shop alone, but when I was done drawing I'd head back up to Second Avenue, and to Robert. Home was a third-floor walk-up I'd originally shared with a roommate, Sasha, who left the city after a year, complaining it was too noisy and crowded. It's possible she meant the apartment specifically was too noisy and crowded, given that Robert spent so much time there. Sasha moved to Chicago and almost immediately reported that she was dating a friend of ours from college; that they were probably going to get married; that they were saving for a condo. I rolled my eyes at all these choices. I saw her move as a failure of will. She was giving up on life in New York for being too hard, I thought, and taking refuge in some normal suburban life. As if there were refuge anywhere.

Robert was an artist. He made large, brash paintings plastered with encaustic, abstractions that included found materials like magazine pages, CD liner notes, grocery store circulars. Stenciled on top of all this were repeated shapes: circles upon circles, squares upon squares, the letter *e* in a thousand different fonts spaced at intervals across a canvas. The impression was not of neatness but of a person ferociously—and not entirely successfully—exerting control, trying to tamp down chaos with a pattern. Which is exactly how Robert was. To me he was the kind of person who only made sense in New York, who perfectly belonged there. He made use of everything he found in the city. One day, at the Astor Place station, he took a liking to a movie poster covered in graffiti tags and spent over an hour carefully cutting the whole thing out as I watched. When he finished, turned to go, and saw me on the platform, he seemed surprised that I was there; not that I was still waiting, but that I existed at all. Far from being offended by this, I admired the intensity of his concentration. When I came home from the coffee shop, he was often about to head out to his studio in Gowanus. He'd stay up all night then crawl into bed with me, waking me to have sex in the lightening dawn. That we rarely spent a whole night together didn't bother us. We had an unspoken agreement to be different from other people.

I'd met Robert at the restaurant where we both waitered part-time. It was a crowded, overpriced Mediterranean place in the West Village where we made excellent tips, enough to live on by working three dinner shifts a week and the occasional brunch. The food was standard upscale yuppie, and Robert and I used to make fun of it during our breaks. All the dishes, we noticed, were made with babies: baby arugula, baby artichokes, baby eggplant. Spring lamb. Veal. New Yorkers love to eat babies, we used to joke. Every shift we came up with new reasons why. Because we're monsters. Because babies are succulent. Because babies are soft, and life here is hard.

The owner, Dmitri, was heavy-lidded and good-looking and before deciding to be a restaurateur—as he referred to himself—had aspired to be a painter himself. As a lingering artifact of these youthful ambitions, he employed a lot of artists. He hired Robert and me at around the same time and seemed pleased when we fell in love, as if matchmaking were yet another profitable business venture. A few years older than I was, Robert was thin and blond, with eyes such a light hazel that they looked gold. His wrists were delicate and bony, his fingers long. His slight frame looked even slighter when he was dressed, as he usually was, like a construction worker, in Dickies work clothes and thick-soled boots. During our breaks we smoked cigarettes he rolled and discussed the war, our scorn for the president uniting us, though it was hardly a unique point of view for artsy people in their early twenties. Despite talking easily with me, he was painfully shy with others and seemed to have no friends in the city. Sasha called him the Ghost, or Little Mr. Rauschenberg. She could be pretty snide, and I wasn't sorry when she moved away.

The first time I saw Robert seize, I was visiting his studio. He was in the middle of a sentence—"I'm still working on this," he was saying—when his whole body clenched, his eyelids screwed shut, and he fell to the floor, narrowly missing hitting his head on a metal file cabinet where he kept clippings and sketches. For all its terror, the seizure was the most mechanical-looking thing I'd ever seen: the body like a robot on the fritz, all rigid angles and jerky spasms.

"Robert!" I said. I had no idea what to do. There was no phone in the studio. I cradled his head, saying his name melo-dramatically, like a woman in a movie. He was making strange guttural sounds at the back of his throat. I tried to hold his hand but he swatted me away with his robot strength. I ran to the door and opened it, looking down the long, empty hall-way. "Hello?" I said. There was no one around. When I turned around, Robert's honey-colored eyes were open, staring at me.

"What happened?" I said.

He shook his head. He seemed angry with me, as if I'd in-truded on a private moment.

"Does this happen a lot?"

He didn't answer, simply lay there looking at the ceiling. After a minute I said, "What is this?"

He sat up gingerly, ignoring me. I was annoyed and so, it seemed, was he. Slowly he got to his feet, turned his back to me, and busied himself rearranging canvases. The one he'd been about to show me, an enormous, lurid red-and-orange painting that looked like an explosion, he returned to the stack without comment.

I lit a cigarette. "I should call somebody," I said.

He shook his head. He was willful, Robert; he rented his own studio and though he spent most of his time at my apartment he still kept his own. He didn't like to share, and he worked at the restaurant as much and as well as he did only so that he could afford not to. I knew that if I called someone, if I tried to take him to a doctor, he'd walk away—from the situation and from me.

Later that night, or the following morning, he showed up at the apartment, laid his head on my chest, and started talking, assuming I was awake to listen, which soon enough I was.

"The meds stop me from seizing but they also flatten everything out," he was saying. Either I'd dreamed it or he'd said it while I was still sleeping: epilepsy. "It's not that I can't execute while I'm taking them. It's that I don't see the point. I get lazy and dull."

I lay there with his body tangled up in mine, his blond head just below my collarbone. I put my fingers in his thin dirty hair. He smelled like sweat and turpentine. "What's it like?" I said.

"I told you," he said irritably. "It's a flatline. I don't think clearly. I don't see clearly."

"No," I said. "The seizure."

He rolled off me and turned his back. My bed was small and we were pressed up against each other just as tightly as before. I put my arms around his waist and rested my head next to his, my nose against his neck.

"It's like being struck by lightning," he said.

MY OWN WORK WAS SMALL. I DREW ON A PAPER TABLET THAT I balanced on my knees, in bed or on the tiny tables at the coffee shop. I was experimenting with faintness: I'd make a drawing and then rub it away, leaving only faded lines behind littered with the pink dust of my eraser. A soldier peered out from the page, ghostly and lost. An oil tanker shimmered on a vanished horizon. That my work was self-effacing while Robert's was large and drenched with color was not a fact lost on an educated young female artist such as myself. But what could I do? This was how I saw the world: powered by forces that were either forgotten or just out of sight.

I watched Robert the way a zoo animal watches its keeper: to see what it was like to live beyond the cage. He was what I thought an artist should be—lonely, volatile, ill at ease in the world—and I took my cues from him. He didn't do drugs or even drink coffee but he somehow worked a dinner shift at the restaurant then headed straight to the studio after, fueled by the ideas burning inside him. Sometimes, imitating him, I'd go home to my bedroom and try to sketch for a while, invariably waking, the next morning, to find a bold pencil line that shot across the drawing at an erratic angle and the creased indent of my head where it hit the paper. I'd wonder what it was like to be him, to have lightning inside you, instead of coaxing out shadows bit by bit, line by line.

The next seizure was at the restaurant, and it was worse. Robert was in the middle of setting down a large metal tray on which several hot dishes were balanced. When he seized, the food flew into the air in a high, steaming arc, landing on the table next to him—people yelling "Hey!" as if the food were a stranger who'd bumped into them on the subway—before clattering in a riot to the floor. Robert hit his head on a chair on the way down, and he was making terrible noises, much worse than I'd seen before, angry moans, half-words of protest. It sounded as if he were not just dying but being killed. I ran to him and cleared the furniture and said his name over and over, as if it would calm him, which it didn't.

It took a moment for me to realize that Dmitri was there, too. Usually he watched everything from a distance with his heavy-lidded eyes, whispering directions into the ear of the hostess or the chef, never seeming anything other than mildly amused. But now he took charge, ordering another waiter to call 911, then sitting on the floor and holding Robert's head in his lap, cushioning it from the blows it was trying to inflict upon itself.

"Where are his meds?" he asked me.

"He won't take them," I said.

"Idiot," he said, and there was no fond indulgence in his tone. He let the seizure play itself out, staying just close enough to Robert to make sure he didn't hit his head and that he wasn't choking. He told the hostess to comp every meal, every drink, and to stop serving. The paramedics arrived, and the restaurant emptied. I spent the night with Robert at St. Vincent's, and the following afternoon called Dmitri to let him know everything was okay, and to thank him.

"Don't mention it," he said. The next time Robert reported to work, Dmitri gave him two weeks' severance and told him he was fired.

I QUIT IN SOLIDARITY. I WAS LIVID. I THOUGHT OF DMITRI'S large hands on either side of Robert's head, the relief I'd experienced when he took charge, and felt as if I were the one betrayed. I was still seething when he called me two days later.

"I understand you're angry," he said calmly. I could picture him talking on the phone by the front desk, wearing his designer jeans and collared shirts. He was rich and good-looking and I'd never seen him upset. "But I can't have scenes like that at the restaurant. If he won't take his medication, he has only himself to blame. Not me, and not you. Come back to work."

"No," I said, and hung up.

I like to think I would have held to it. But Robert was ignoring me; he was sleeping back at his own apartment, and rarely returned my calls. When I did reach him his voice was thick tongued, sullen, and he didn't want to see me. I had no idea if this was due to his mood or the medications. I had no idea about anything.

"He's probably embarrassed," my friends said pragmatically when I complained to them. "Give it time."

I refused to believe that Robert would be given to an emotion as pedestrian as embarrassment. But whatever he was feeling, by Friday night, a week later, he still wasn't talking, and I went to the restaurant to work my shift. I needed the money. Dmitri welcomed me back with little more than a nod. When I signed out for the night I saw I'd been scheduled for extra hours that week, to make up for what I hadn't worked the past few days.

He came over when he saw me studying the schedule. "It's okay?" he said. He wasn't Greek from Greece—he'd been born and raised in Brooklyn—but every once in a while he used this old-world intonation that I found pretentious. I told him it was fine. I stood still, waiting for him to ask me about Robert, but he didn't.

"How is your painting?"

"Drawing," I said.

He looked at a spot over my shoulder, and it took me a second to realize he was blushing. "I'm sorry," he said. "I thought it was painting. You don't talk about it very often."

"It's not going well," I said. He was the first person I'd admitted this to, and I'm not sure why I did, except that he was virtually a stranger and I didn't care what he thought. "I think I'm about to give up on it and go to law school or something."

He reached out and clasped my hand tightly in both of his, which surprised me. I'd seen him dating a variety of tall beautiful women he brought to the restaurant, never sticking with any of them very long. He didn't strike me as a serious person. The fact that he had majored in studio art at Pratt had always seemed like a weird anomaly, a blip on an otherwise blank screen.

"Give it time," he said, echoing my friends, and let me go.

I DID. I GAVE IT TWO MONTHS AND DURING THAT PERIOD started working in charcoal—still small-scale, but more confident, I thought. I drew aggressive, angular shadows that skulked, partial but huge, across the page: a dome that you might not realize, until you looked at it for a while, was a soldier's helmet. The rain of smart bombs on a fractured city. A mother's arm extended across her child's body in useless protection.

Every once in a while, as we cleaned up at the end of a shift, Dmitri would ask me how it was going, and I'd linger for a while, telling him. He knew enough about drawing to ask good questions but not so much that it was intimidating to answer. Sometimes a couple of other waiters would be around, sometimes not. Dmitri would open a bottle of wine and we'd drink it; afterward, I'd walk across town at three a.m. kind of buzzed, smoking a cigarette, feeling armor-plated.

On a Saturday night in June we stayed at the restaurant talking until late. It was the longest day of the year and all evening I'd felt buoyed by the light, carried along by it. I stood chattering to Dmitri about something—I don't remember what—as he closed up the restaurant. He was crouching down to lock the grate, smiling up at me, a particular smile he sometimes gave me that meant I was being a little foolish and also funny. Some movement or sound alerted me and I turned and saw Robert. He was standing in the street, gazing at us, not moving. He was wearing a brown suede jacket I'd never seen before, too warm for the weather and too big for him, and he looked pale and wan.

"I didn't know you two were together," he said.

Dmitri stood beside me and snaked his arm around my waist, and I realized only then it was true: we were together. Robert's eyes were so forlorn that I almost forgot he was the one who'd stopped seeing me. But Dmitri was steering me gently away, and I allowed myself to be led. I wasn't angry at Robert, or in love with him anymore. He seemed very sad to me, and very lost. I held Dmitri's hand and I thought, with a pang of guilt and excitement, *We are the lucky ones.*

I LEFT MY LITTLE APARTMENT AND MOVED IN WITH DMITRI IN the West Village. For a while I kept working at the restaurant, but Dmitri urged me to quit. "I'm not trying to make you a kept woman," he said. "I'm just saying you can afford to take some time to focus on your art, if you want it. Two months. Six months. If you want."

I resisted and resisted and finally gave in. The deal was too good to pass up. And it was an offer extended without conditions or manipulations. Dmitri wasn't using me to fulfill his own lost artistic inclinations—he was perfectly happy in business; it suited him—and he didn't want to control me. He was just offering because he could. So I grabbed the chance. I shared a studio in Red Hook with a couple other artists and if I stayed there late, drinking beers with them, he didn't mind. Other evenings we hung out with his friends, who ran nightclubs and limousine services and wore linen suits and fancy watches. They were as foreign to me as I was to them and we found each other entertaining, dipping in and out of each other's worlds like tourists for a night.

After six months I felt like I'd made some progress, but not enough, and I applied to grad school. I took out loans and Dmitri helped me with the rent. He said it wasn't a big deal—"I'd be paying the rent on this place with or without you"—and I believed him. Things were always easy with him. After I graduated, I put together the ingredients of a career in art: nothing spectacular, but enough for me to feel that it was real. Group gallery shows, the occasional solo one in New Haven or Boston. Small grants. Adjunct teaching in different schools in the city. I paid rent and helped Dmitri out with hostessing when he needed it—he opened another restaurant uptown, then one in Brooklyn, not far from his parents' place, in a neighborhood that had once been unfashionable and was now getting discovered. He came to all my shows. On the night of my thirty-first birthday, we had dinner at home—Dmitri never enjoyed going out to dinner at other restaurants; he couldn't stop comparing and critiquing—and I took a tiny sip of wine and told him I was pregnant.

"Wait, what?" he said. He tried to pretend he was shocked but a smile was already overtaking his mouth. We hadn't been trying but we'd been sloppy, both of us knowing what was happening without discussing it. He put his elbow on the table and covered his mouth with his hands, his broad white smile showing through the gaps in his fingers. We gave up on eating and went to bed, and when I woke up in the morning he was smiling in his sleep.

. . .

OVER THE OBJECTIONS OF HIS FAMILY, WE DID NOT GET MAR-
ried. I wasn't opposed to it so much as I simply didn't see the
point. Putting on a fancy white dress, walking down the aisle
of a church I didn't belong to—it felt like something a stranger
might do. It was like Sasha buying the condo; a choice that felt
too regular for the kind of life I had. So we just focused on
getting ready for the baby. I took vitamins and had doctor's
appointments. Dmitri's mother began showing up at the apartment bearing gifts of food and advice. We looked at other apart-
ments, bigger places with room for a nursery. I was five months
along when I woke up in the middle of the night with a stabbing
pain in my abdomen. In the bathroom, I saw my underwear
bright with blood. I closed my eyes, wanting to unsee it. Dmitri
found me sitting on the toilet, eyes closed, my forehead slick
with sweat.

"It's over," I said. I already knew, as if I'd dreamed it in
advance, what the next few hours would contain: the trip to
the hospital, the ultrasound, the drugs that made me contract,
the tiny white dead baby they put in my arms for a few minutes
before they took her away. And then I was home again, at the
apartment. They gave me a card with the baby's footprints on
it. We didn't give her a name.

I THINK I HAD BEEN TOO LUCKY IN MY LIFE. I DIDN'T HAVE
enough practice with grief. Or maybe I was simply wired wrong
for this particular experience, which proved to be my undoing.
It unknit me like a thread loose from a sweater. Six months
later, everyone had said how sorry they were—our friends and
family had said it, Dmitri and I had said it to each other—but I
could not stop grieving. I couldn't explain why. My sorrow took
strange and specific form. I carried the card with the footprints

around with me, in my bag, and touched it before and after I did anything—when I woke up and went to sleep, when I went to the bank, when I got on or off the subway. I stopped being able to ride in cabs, because I kept imagining that we were going to run over a baby. I would hear the crunch of a stroller or bassinet beneath the tires. The whimper of infant flesh giving way. After a while I couldn't ride the subway either, always seeing a baby crushed beneath the train, electrified on the third rail. I had to walk everywhere, and if it was too far to walk, I stayed home.

Dmitri was very patient. He encouraged me to take time off—"Give it time," he said, just as he had before—and then, after a while, to go back to work. Ever the obedient one, I listened to him. I went to the studio, and did some teaching, and I chose not to admit to him or anyone else how little engaged I was by any of it. I papered over the hole in myself but it was still hollow beneath. He could tell, of course, and he did his best to comfort me. He wanted to try again; he still felt optimistic about the future. It was easier for him. I understood this, but I couldn't forgive it. The straightforwardness of his recovery from loss felt like a betrayal.

A year went by in which we didn't have sex. We went out with friends, we went to couples counseling, we went to work, and we came home to an apartment that was increasingly divided into his space and mine. At last he did a final, generous thing: he paid the rent for six months in advance and then moved out, letting me have the place. I was relieved to see him go.

I DIDN'T LEAVE NEW YORK. MY HISTORY WITH THE PLACE stabilized me, the sense of my own past extending across neighborhoods and years. I stayed, and one day I stood on the platform of the C train at West Fourth, steadying my breath, and

I felt something unlatch inside me, like a door opening into a hallway. I knew I was letting go not just of the baby, but of that phantom life all three of us were going to live together. And now, no longer. I got on the train; I kept teaching; I began working in collages, layers of images that I slapped with paste and then liquid paper and then drew on top of so that only I knew what lay beneath. I found comfort in this burial, the secrecy of the hidden pictures, the delicate bulk of paper laid on top of paper. Dmitri, I heard, moved to Brooklyn, married a Greek girl he met through his mother, and had twins. Eventually I started dating a sculptor named Luca I met at CUNY, where I was teaching drawing three days a week. Luca was older, with a twenty-year-old son back in Rome. He'd come to New York several years before under vague circumstances—I assumed there was a woman involved—and fallen in love with it.

"I am anonymous here," he told me. We were talking in the hallway; his office was next to mine.

"Were you a movie star in Rome?" I said, teasing him.

He frowned. He was in his fifties, and losing his hair, but he dressed well and had bright green eyes. "Of course I was," he said. "Did you not see me in *Life Is Beautiful*?"

We didn't move in together. We were happy with a simpler arrangement: dinner a few nights a week, sometimes a film, the comfort of an arm slung over yours late at night. So I was surprised when, at the end of the semester, he invited me to go to Italy with him. Immediately he saw my doubt, and tried to allay it.

"You have never been to Italy," he said. "You will enjoy it. And me, I will have a companion, and this is fun for me."

I understood, then: his return to Italy would be triumphant with a younger woman on his arm. Both of us would benefit, another simple arrangement. So I went with him, and he took me by the arm through churches and museums, whispering to me about what we saw, like the teacher he was. I met his son and the rest of his family. We had dinner and drinks with his friends, artists and journalists and academics, and the talk was once again of a war in the Middle East and a president that I did not support, though I felt less confident in my judgments than I had when I was younger. I was more aware of everything I didn't know; this much, at least, had come to me with age.

We were at a cocktail reception at a gallery when I wandered around a corner in search of a restroom and saw a small gold painting by itself on a wall. I recognized it right away, just as you recognize a friend who has aged yet remains eternally, doggedly, the same. Back at the gallery desk, I located an information sheet on the artist and saw I was correct. *Robert Jorgensen, American, 1968–*. The painting was untitled, and there were two others like it in the gallery. He lived in California now, the biography said. He'd moved from large works to small ones and the found objects—the grocery store flyers and magazine pages that Sasha had decried as imitation Rauschenberg—had disappeared. In their place was simply paint, loosely laid, like a sloppily iced cake. It seemed to be layered and also glazed, as pottery is glazed, so that it shone with metallic sparkle, green-gold, blue-gold. Instead of repetitive circles or letters there were pinpricks: tiny holes marring the paint that you almost felt you could see into. Gazing at them, I felt that he'd found a way to harness the electricity in his brain. They were pictures of being struck by lightning, arrested in a moment that was painful and porous and gilded. And they were beautiful—beauty pricked with hurt.

I looked around the gallery. On the other side of the room

Luca, talking to friends, caught my eye, making sure I was all right. I nodded. The person I was really looking for, of course, was Dmitri—because who else would share my memory, who else would understand? If he'd been in the room I would have rushed into his arms and begged him to forgive me for having driven him away. But he wasn't. I had to keep to myself the strangeness of seeing those paintings, so thick and dense with luster, reminding me how little and how much can last.

Acknowledgments

Short stories are my first and greatest love as a writer and I'm forever grateful to everyone who reads, writes, and publishes them. My thanks to all the editors of the magazines in which these stories originally appeared, especially Deborah Treisman, Adam Ross, Evelyn Somers, Meakin Armstrong, and Ladette Randolph. Boundless thanks as well to Jenny Jackson and Maris Dyer at Knopf; Janie Yoon and Sarah MacLachlan at House of Anansi; and my agent, Amy Williams. I'm lucky, this year more than any other, to have the support of my friends and family, near and far.

"The Universal Particular" is an homage that owes a debt to "Hester Lilly" by the English writer Elizabeth Taylor. "Service Intelligence" was loosely inspired, in ways probably recognizable only to me, by the story "Sleet" by Stig Dagerman. The epigraph to this book is from "Dead Doe" by the poet Brigit Pegeen Kelly, gone too soon.

© Emily Cooper

ALIX OHLIN is the author of six books, including the novels *Inside* and *Dual Citizens*, which were both finalists for the Scotiabank Giller Prize and the Rogers Writers' Trust Fiction Prize. Her work has appeared in *The New Yorker*, *Tin House*, *Best American Short Stories*, and many other publications. Born and raised in Montreal, she lives in Vancouver, where she chairs the creative writing program at the University of British Columbia.

alixohlinauthor.com
Twitter, Facebook, and Instagram: @AlixOhlin

A NOTE ON THE TYPE

Pierre Simon Fournier le jeune (1712–1768), who designed
the type used in this book, was both an originator and a
collector of types. His services to the art of printing were
his design of letters, his creation of ornaments and initials,
and his standardization of type sizes. His types are old
style in character and sharply cut. In 1764 and 1766 he
published his *Manuel typographique*, a treatise on the history of French types and printing, on typefounding in all
its details, and on what many consider his most important
contribution to typography—the measurement of type
by the point system.

Typeset by Scribe, Philadelphia, Pennsylvania

Designed by Betty Lew